T0067584

Cobwebs in the Sky

Cobwebs in the Sky

MALATI JAIKUMAR

PARTRIDGE

A Penguin Random House Company

Copyright © 2014 by Malati Jaikumar.

ISBN:	Hardcover	978-1-4828-3739-1
	Softcover	978-1-4828-3740-7
	eBook	978-1-4828-3738-4

All rights reserved. No part of this book may be used or reproduced by any means, graphic, electronic, or mechanical, including photocopying, recording, taping or by any information storage retrieval system without the written permission of the publisher except in the case of brief quotations embodied in critical articles and reviews.

Because of the dynamic nature of the Internet, any web addresses or links contained in this book may have changed since publication and may no longer be valid. The views expressed in this work are solely those of the author and do not necessarily reflect the views of the publisher, and the publisher hereby disclaims any responsibility for them.

To order additional copies of this book, contact
Partridge India
000 800 10062 62
orders.india@partridgepublishing.com

www.partridgepublishing.com/india

Contents

Disclaimer

All the characters in this book are entirely fictional and any similarity to personalities, living or dead; or events past or present are purely coincidental.

To my father whom I lost early and
To my mother who filled the void.

Acknowledgements

In the long and lonely path of writing a novel I drew my sustenance largely from the wonderful people within my circle of family and friends. At the risk of sounding like the Oscars I wish to thank my family first – my husband whose faith in me saw me through difficult times; my daughter, Priya, whose very professional review forced me to look at the manuscript more closely and objectively; my son, Prashanth, whose cut and dry, no nonsense attitude combined with total loyalty put everything in the right perspective. My son-in-law, Tom, kept me smiling with his ready humour and encouraging words while my daughter-in-law, Deepali, with her innate warmth and affection lifted me out of my low moments. If my grandchildren, Meha and Mihir were my greatest stress busters, my centenarian mother-in-law's unflagging interest and curiosity about my work kept me going.

I am grateful also to some of my nieces and nephews— Kalpana, Ian, Arundhathi, Niranjan, Rebecca, Nitya and Lekha –who have all helped me at various times in various ways -- spurring me on with their unstinting support and words of comfort when the future looked bleak.

This book would not have seen the light of day if not for the brilliant team of Partridge Publications – right from Franco who encouraged me to take the first step; Ann who tirelessly helped me understand the complexities of editing and the dedicated team who provided invaluable insight into the maze of designing, printing and publishing.

A certain amount of research was necessary –from books and other sources but mostly by picking the brains of a variety of people, some of whom were not even aware that they had contributed to this book. My very dear and crazy friend, Kadambari, gave me an insight into the interiors of the real India; while Prabha and Arvind unwittingly added pieces of history and colour. Large parts of the book are my own memories of Coimbatore where I was born – the house on Raja Street did exist but has now been razed to the ground; the intoxicating puja time in Calcutta where I grew up and the grandeur of Delhi where I spent my whole career, with London and Chandigarh being my favourite much visited haunts.

But most of all I want to acknowledge the courage of women the world over. Women who have hit the headlines in newspapers as well as those nameless, faceless ones who have toiled silently and steadily, fighting for their rights every inch of the way. I have been inspired by innumerable women in various walks of life in villages and cities, all bound together in one long tireless fight for justice. I have been amazed at the way they have eked out a life for themselves and their children in spite of the torture meted out by their husbands and a heartless society. This book is a tribute to them.

Foreword

I am often asked if parts of my stories are true. The answer usually is yes because it is inevitable that some of my experiences or convictions get reflected in my work but then that is true of most writers. The core of a story or a bit of the beginning, end or middle may be something heard from a friend or a friend of a friend. It may be triggered by a news item or a feature in the newspaper or heard on television. While a large part of a story is a figment of the imagination there is a grain of verity somewhere which is why it touches a chord in the reader.

I have lived in 13 houses so far, yet the one that haunts my dreams is the very first one – the one where I was born. So much so that when I sat down to write this book the very first thoughts that came to mind and flowed spontaneously and smoothly through my fingertips on to the key board was about No. 47 Raja Street in Coimbatore. Although now it has been razed to the ground I wanted to bring it alive again in the very first chapter.

I have very strong convictions on some subjects and on top of the list is one aspect of life that I come across almost daily – the overwhelming importance of love, sex and marriage. In *Cobwebs in the Sky*, while recounting the saga of four girls who are trapped in the most horrific situations and who yet manage to pull themselves out by sheer courage and grit, aided by the unstinting support of their steadfast friends, I wish to send out a message to both the young and the old. The underlying theme is that love, sex and marriage have a great impact on one's destiny and can either drive people to acts of great courage and compassion or degrade them to commit the most heinous of crimes. This is one thing that has not changed over time.

Going way back in history Emma Goldman (1869-1940), an anarchist known for her writing and speeches on prisons, atheism, militarism, marriage, free love and homosexuality wrote "Marriage and love have nothing in common; they are as far apart as the poles; are in fact, antagonistic to each other"........ "Marriage is primarily an economic arrangement, an insurance pact. It differs from the ordinary life insurance agreement only in that it is more binding, more exacting. Its returns are significantly small compared with investments.

In taking out an insurance policy one pays for it in dollars and cents, always at liberty to discontinue payments. If, however, woman's premium is a man, she pays for it with her name, her privacy, her self respect, her very life, "until death doth part".

She even equated Dante's motto over Inferno with marriage: "Ye who enter here leave all hope behind."

Fast forward to 2014, with the high rate of divorces and more people opting for live in relationships and one can see that there are some who would still agree with Goldman. Fortunately for human kind, marriage has not gone out of fashion (yet) although one has to admit that both partners have to work very hard to make a marriage successful. Good marriages are the building blocks of a strong and productive society. And the rewards of an even "fairly successful" marriage are worth all the effort.

In India, love, sex and marriage are further complicated by issues of caste and religion; demands of dowry that reduce families to near poverty level and honour killing for daring to marry for love outside one's own caste. In the 1930s marriages were mostly arranged and that too at an inordinately young age, very often before puberty. Once the marriage was officially and ceremoniously performed, the bride went back to playing hopscotch and the groom went back to school. The day the girl attained puberty it was mandatory to pack her off to her husband's house. Inevitably the first child was born by the time the girl was 15. Sometimes more children followed at frequent intervals and the woman often died by the time she was in her early 30s.

In the present day and age, the urban, educated girl or boy is wary of the commitment to marriage and opt for "relationships" while the more conservative kind have arranged marriages either after meeting each other with the approval of their parents or at times after seeing photographs but not having met each other at all. A vast majority find their own mates after browsing through the matrimonial websites. But irrespective of the how and the where of relationships it is irrefutable that love, sex and marriage are of the greatest significance in the lives of both men and women and shape the destinies and the course of their lives – perhaps more so for women than men.

Some women from restrictive families blossom after marriage to a man who encourages her latent talents while some very talented women get suffocated and stifled in a family of domineering persons. Sexual and physical abuse, mental cruelty, humiliation and even death are oft heard stories in many marriages. Complete happiness in matrimony is very rare for there is always some compromise or adjustment to be made - in most cases by the woman.

Why is it that we teach our children to stay ahead in life's rat race; why do we inculcate social graces, politeness, and survival skills; why do we stoke their ambition for material gain but we never talk to them about the pitfalls of sex or the sanctity of love? We groom them for jobs but neglect to tell them the truth about sexual violence or sexual harassment. We teach them to discern right from wrong but avoid all mention of seduction and lust. Many people learn the most important lesson in life that relates to sex either through lurid stories related by friends or more often on a trial and error basis in which they get hurt or scarred for life. Sex can and does make or mar a life. And yet we hardly talk about it.

On the contrary, men and women are exposed to sex and erotica through the medium of literature, videos, magazines and the all powerful internet, most of which is titillating rather than educative. The core of the problems and pitfalls of each succeeding generation continues to be the same - love and sex. These spawn emotions and actions that are universally similar - lust, revenge, deceit, rape and abuse. Right from the dawn of history the honey trap has been the downfall of men in all strata of society and at all levels. Sex has been and will continue to be the most powerful weapon, the most lethal but also the least understood.

In its [2009/10] Gender Violence in India report, Chennai non-profit Prajnya drew attention to the National Crime Records Bureau's data on violence against women, highlighting some very startling statistics. NCRB had reported 6000 dowry deaths every year. Eighty-five per cent of the women who have experienced sexual violence have never told anyone about it. Rape is the fastest growing crime in India with 733% increase in *reported* cases since 1971. A rape occurs every 22 minutes and 75% of rapists are known to their victims.

The horrific incident of a 23 year old woman gang raped and brutally beaten by six men in a moving bus in Delhi and the more recent heinous crime in Mumbai (where one of the rapists confessed unabashedly to have carried out similar gang rapes many times earlier) has spawned a massive protest by thousands of young men and women all over India. In a single voice they are screaming for quick justice and capital punishment for rapists. This may seem excessive but there is no denying that there must be some very stringent punishment that would act as a deterrent if we are to ensure the safety of women all over India.

Statistics speak louder than words. It becomes even more terrifying if we remember that behind every digit there is an actual woman who has been brutalized and maybe some from our own family or our circle of friends. Those statistics are not mere numbers but women who have been traumatized.

The only silver lining is that in spite of the generation gap, in spite of all the evil around us, in spite of the most degrading and depressing incidents, our basic sense of values has not changed. It is only the strong bonds and unstinting trust and faith of family and friends that gives one the support and strength to cope with and rise above traumatic experiences in life. This is the one and only life line we have to hold on to and must never let go.

To the young I say enjoy life in pursuit of all your wonderful and challenging dreams and desires because these precious years will never come again. Nature dictates that there will be sexual urges but these have to be handled with care. Complete denial of sex leads to frustration and perversion. Safe sex with the chosen one is something that should happen with some maturity. This is where friends and family can play a large part and help to mould a character with a healthy respect for women. A man who is brought up to respect women will never stoop to harassment or rape. This education and molding of the mind has to begin at home and in all the schools.

To parents and guardians I say take time off to talk to and understand your children. Adolescence can be a time of great confusion and is the right time to put love and sex in the right perspective. A frank and open discussion will clear misconceptions whereas total denial of the issue will propel youth into subterfuge, lies and secretive behaviour leading to some sordid experiments with sex. Love and sex are the two most beautiful experiences on earth. We need to preserve and cherish it. It is up to parents, guardians, teachers, older friends and siblings to nurture it and help build a cleaner, stronger family that in turn will lead to a better society and a better world, where our children can grow up safe, free of pedophiles and other sex perverts. A Utopia? Maybe, but well worth striving for and not impossible to achieve in the long run.

Mandakini

COIMBATORE: 1968

Mandakini had not visited the house for nearly a decade and yet its aura flowed in her veins like a dormant virus waiting to strike when her immunity was low. They were all carriers of this virus. All those who had lived in the house and all those who visited periodically got infected too. There were very few who were untouched by the chilling nimbus of mystery, pain and death as well as the echoes of laughter, celebrations and birth that clung to every stone, mortar or panel of wood in the house built two centuries ago.

Mandakini took down an old, cloth covered album and settled herself on the couch. Her long fingers traced the paisley pattern on the mehndi green fabric. She leaned back, lifted her thick hip length plait over her right shoulder and shrugged herself into a comfortable position against the cushions. Her honey coloured eyes scanned the photographs for familiar faces, a tiny smile tugging at the corners of her wide mouth as she flipped the pages pausing now and then to look intently at some of the pictures.

No. 47 Raja Street haunted their dreams and nightmares. Mandakini's eldest sister whom she met rarely; her second sister who had withdrawn into herself and retreated into her own world; her brother torn between Vedanta and materialism and battling with cancer and her nonagenarian mother, shrunk and withered by age, who was born and brought up in that house, were all under the spell. It nestled in the soft folds of the subconscious, like grit in an oyster. It would be there forever, not to be shaken off, not to be wiped out on psychotherapeutic couches, not to be forgotten and never to be denied. The spell had seeped into their bones, into the very marrow giving them their phobia, their idiosyncrasies and their strengths.

Mandakini, for one, knew that her inordinate fear of dwarfs was triggered off in the narrow corridor linking the outside verandah and the huge hall. There was no light in the corridor, but for the daylight filtering in from the verandah or the light flickering from the hall. When she was five years old she was half way down the corridor when a dwarf visitor entered from the other end. She stopped short, turned around and ran back screaming and was still running scared.

No.47 was deceptively simple and modest from the outside but really huge and quite extraordinary inside. Leading up from the street to the entrance door of the house, there were six wide stone steps with smooth, sloping, cement balustrades on either side, just the right size for a five- year-old bottom to slide upon. They ended in a neat circular coil where Mandakini and her siblings landed with a thump every time.

The door at the top of the steps opened on to a largish, rectangular, covered verandah that was actually two verandahs at different levels linked by four steps. The *"thinnai"* or cement platform on the extreme right bridged the two verandahs. It had a curved flank on one side and was level with the upper verandah on the other. The children could run shrieking up the steps from the lower to the upper verandah, turn right, run till the end, and hop on to the thinnai, run up to the flank and jump down on to the lower verandah, run panting to the steps and up again. They could keep this on for hours with many variations and imaginary chases of cops and robbers.

In the wall just above the middle of the thinnai was a small barred window. All windows in the house had vertical or horizontal rods, usually painted a dull shade of green. As a five year old, Mandakini would stand on tiptoe to peep through the window into the verandah of the house next door. Her sisters, brother and cousins would look out and run screaming and giggling but she saw no reason to scream. The only thing she could see was a boy with a drooping head and a vacant stare with his hand wrapped around something sticking out of his shorts. But she screamed too and ran wiggling her arms.

It was on this thinnai that the four friends were huddled together one afternoon in the summer of 1968. They were all between the ages of 11 and 13 and had been fast friends for the past six years. They had met and played here innumerable times but this afternoon was very special. This was their last meeting before the parting of ways.

Padmaja was the colour of lightly roasted coffee beans and at 13 was beginning to acquire attractive curves on her way to maturity. Julie, 12, was the life and soul of the group. Her bright, snub nosed face, framed by short and curly brown hair, was always smiling with dimples playing hide and seek. She was the one who could patch up a quarrel, make them laugh or stay calm in a crisis. She was the glue that held them together. Babli, 11, fair and petite was already beginning to develop physically. But she was still very much a child in her attitude, quite the baby of the group in her behavior. She liked to dress up and gaze at herself in the mirror.

Mandakini, 12, was the tallest of the lot. She kept looking at her chest every day, disappointed to find herself almost as flat as a board. She felt she was a plain Jane with her irregular features and perhaps to make up for the lack of a figure she made the most of her height and the thick luxuriant head of hair that her mother insisted on plaiting although she wanted to let it hang loose. Her broad single plait (her mother measured it to be full six inches wide) fell well below her knees. A tomboy, she was the one who climbed the tallest tree, jumped from the highest step, scraped her knees and could wield the top or shoot marbles as good as any boy. She was the natural leader of the group with all the other three turning to her for decisions. She took the first step in everything be it mischief or work. It was a natural, unspoken hierarchy. At times she would let the others decide but if they looked to her, she would take charge. As she did now.

"Have you got the pins Padma?"
"Please yaar. Can't we do it any other way? I hate blood and it *will* hurt." Babli made a last attempt to escape.

"Of course not, silly. It is just a pin prick" giggled Julie. "Just wait till you start your periods and you will spurt blood - bubbling out like a spring". Never waste a chance to tease was Julie's motto. "Am I right Padma? Do you think my periods will start soon?"

Padma was the envy of them all being the only one to have sprouted breasts and had her periods. Her clear skin glowed with a charming radiance and her large kohl rimmed eyes fringed by very long lashes made her stand out in a crowd. When they went out together men looked at her in a strange way.

"Stop frightening Babli" grimaced Padma handing out pins to the other three. "I don't know why you want the curse. You just get a nasty backache and horrible cramps. You cannot go out, or touch anyone. You have to spend three boring days in a little room and wait for someone to serve you something to eat."

Babli held out her pin to Padma. "I cannot do it myself Padma. You do it for me. I will just shut my eyes real tight."

Padma tossed her hair back. "When my aunts have the curse they are untouchables and have to stay away from the rest of the family. They call it casual leave because they do not have to do any work but read magazines, play cards and eat. We cannot touch them because they are considered unclean but small children up till the age of four can touch them - after taking off all their clothes. The children I mean".

Babli let out a startled "Ouch" as Padma pricked Babli's thumb without any warning. "I wonder who laid down all these rules. Amma says periods are part of growing up and it is bad if you do not have them. I guess the elders just need the rest and periods are a good excuse."

"That was not too bad – just like an insect bite" said Bubli staring fascinated at the large drop of blood on her finger. The rest of them had pricked their thumbs and squeezed hard till the drop of blood stood out. They placed their thumbs together, closed their eyes and chanted:

"Blood red, blood red, friends we are and friends will be, Mingle blood and lick it clean, sisters forever we will be".

"Now we are all blood sisters as well as friends. Nothing and no one can change this. Ever" said Mandakini solemnly. The ritual had formalized the pact that made them honour bound to help one another at any time, at any cost.

No one wanted to acknowledge that this was their last day together. Padmaja was moving to Calcutta, Babli to Chandigarh and Mandakini to Delhi leaving Julie in Coimbatore. It felt strange that after having spent so many years together they were all scattering in different directions just as they were growing up and getting more and more emotionally intertwined.

The bond between the four was uncanny. They just knew that theirs was a lifelong friendship and even if they were scattered around the world they would always stay "connected". They had fought, made up, played, shared secrets and spent hours together. Even if they were miles apart they would be linked by this precious relationship, an invisible yet robust bond that was firmly anchored in their hearts and minds. For the past six years they had met almost every day, learning about the world around them, discovering their own bodies, talking about it and their burgeoning emotions and helping each other adjust to their families.

Padmaja's rich parents had no time for her except to ply her with gifts or anything she wanted. Her mother Sharada was happy that the servants did a very good job of looking after the house and her daughter, leaving her free to play cards at the club almost every day. Ponnamma, the oldest retainer, had started work as a little girl for Sharada's parents and had been Sharada's playmate. She came with Sharada almost as part of her dower and continued to look after everything. Under Ponnamma's supervision the servants ran the house most efficiently. Padmaja though fond of Ponnamma, yearned for the warmth of a family. She was gradually drawn more and more to Mandakini's house, which was always teeming with cousins, aunts and uncles.

Julie at the age of three had lost her mother to tuberculosis. Her father married again very soon after and her step mother, Sophie, viewed Julie as more of a burden. By the time Julie was six, she had become accustomed to eating whatever was given which was little and doing what she was told to do which was a lot. Cheerful and loving by nature Julie found her joy and solace in school. Her very first school friend was Mandakini and very soon 47 Raja Street was her home away from home.

Babli's family was from Punjab, living in Coimbatore running a business in textiles. Although they had been in the south for some years their house was a miniature Punjab-replete with Punjabi food, music, traditions and culture. Babli, seemingly timid most of the time, felt claustrophobic and hemmed in by all the traditions of a conservative joint family. She was thrilled by the freedom of Mandakini's large family. She too gravitated to the unique house and its boisterous crowd of inhabitants.

Licking the blood off their thumbs they decided to do one last journey around the house together. They trooped through the dark narrow corridor that linked the verandah to the main hall. The doors were so aligned that if the girls stood at the entrance of the corridor they could look straight across the hall right up to the kitchen wall at the far end and anyone in the kitchen could see straight out to the main front door of the house.

They stood for a moment at the threshold looking down at the "doormat" which was actually a mosaic of variegated shells, multicoloured glass and dappled beads embedded in the floor – a built-in welcome mat. They had heard that under the mosaic doormat an exorcist had buried some coins, talismans and parchment to drive away the spirit that had haunted the house. It was said that someone had cast a curse on Mandakini's great grand aunt and her mother said she had actually seen the aunt's sari suddenly catch fire and burn on the clothes line leaving the garments right next to it untouched. When the aunt ate she could not look away from the food in front of her for fear of it being suddenly covered by hair and dirt. But after the exorcist cast his spell it had all stopped. And this was just one of the many supernatural nuances of the house.

All four carefully stepped over it one by one – they always avoided stepping on the voodoo antidote mat. In the huge hall there were four pale yellow pillars, plastered smooth and shiny with crushed shell and lime. There was a time when all four of them had to join hands to encircle one pillar and now two of them could stretch out and touch their fingertips together. It was a square room, the four pillars forming the inner square and the equally broad space around the pillars forming the outer square.

There was a large skylight in the middle of the ceiling. It was open to the sky and had horizontal bars running from one end to the other. At night one of the men went up to the terrace and pulled a large tin sheet to cover the skylight. If there was a sudden shower in the day one of the children had to run up and pull the sheet and get wet in the process. There was always more than one volunteer for that job and inevitably they would all rush up and get wet.

No child, or for that matter, no woman, no matter how brave, dared to go up to the terrace alone. It was ghost territory even at high noon. It was there that Mandakini's mother had been dozing one afternoon when she woke up and saw two dhoti clad men sitting on the charpoy nearby, their backs towards her. She was just about to call out when they got up and glided off – off the terrace and into the sky. They had no feet.

There was very little furniture in the whole house. One was the wooden table with six chairs to the right of the two pillars, used exclusively by the men and children. Women never sat on the chairs. A colourful mat would be unfurled on the floor for women visitors. The other furniture was a heavy, dark chocolate brown cot that was actually a thick slab of highly polished teak wood resting on four carved legs. The cot was pushed against the wall, below the window opening into the dining area. At one end of the cot there was a natural whorl in the wood that Mandakini liked to poke a finger into whenever she sat on the cot. During the day women, children and visitors used the cot but once her grandfather came home it was his. He slept on it at night and during the day he received his visitors, the solitaire "kadukan" on his ears flashing as he moved his head animatedly.

There were two rooms, one on either side of the main entrance door. The room on the left was the granary and childbirth room and the one on the right was the safe, vaults and locker room. Mandakini's favorite was a standalone locker, four feet tall, painted light green. It had eight locks and a closed brass fist for a handle.

The four girls swung around the four pillars and went into the childbirth and granary room – the room where most of the children in the family had been born, including Mandakini and her mother. The wooden paneling on one whole side of the wall, stretching from the floor to the ceiling concealed a spacious granary. Rice still covered by the husk would be brought in sacks from the fields and emptied in the hall, forming a huge mountain. The children were asked to climb up the brown mountain and play, scattering it all over the place, as an auspicious act of plenitude. They did not need to be told twice. Then the rice would be filled in sacks again and carried into the room and poured down the opening at the top of the wooden paneling. A little trap door could be opened to siphon off the rice to be sent for dehusking when needed.

This room was always very dimly lit. There was something about the place that made them hesitate to stay there alone. Mandakini's grandmother and a few other women had died there in childbirth and some babies had been still born. The moans and screams of women in labour seem to cling to the walls making it more like a torture chamber. Her mother said she had sensed a presence when she was in labour for her second child and she had felt someone give her a resounding slap on the back. When she screamed and turned around, no one was in the room.

Women were not allowed to come out of the room for the first 11 days after childbirth so there was a small drain and a pot in one corner, to be used as a toilet. Mandakini decided very early on that she would never marry and have children.

There was a hushed silence when they were in the room and it was a relief to come out and run to the heavy door on the opposite wall that led to the dining area cum shrine. The weighty wooden door had three thick beams across it with four brass lotuses on each beam. The long rectangular dining area could easily seat ten on either side and five each at the shorter ends. The whole family used to sit on the floor and eat off banana leaves. Two older children had the task of collecting all the leaves and taking it to the backyard where it was flung over the wall for cows to eat. The aunts took turns to clean the floor after the leaves had been removed. First, water was sprinkled all over the place where the leaves had been spread. Then they would bend down from the waist, legs spread wide apart and with practiced ease they would clasp a small piece of dried cow dung in their hand and wipe the floor in arcs like a windshield wiper, their bare palm flat on the ground pushing grains of rice or small pieces of food into one small heap as they moved along. Finally, when it was all done it would be sopped off with a cloth and left to dry.

At the shorter end of the room was an enclosed rectangular space on a raised platform covered by a steel mesh with a door at either end. It was redolent with the fragrance of incense sticks, sandalwood paste, and camphor and oil wicks. The men climbed in from one end to perform the daily religious rituals. Among pictures of many gods and goddesses was an intricately carved wooden shrine with beautiful bronze statues. The most special item was a large conch that had ornate bands of gold around it with small round gold beads decorating the spiral grooves. On rare occasions and after much pleading the children were allowed to hold it and fondle it and keep it back before the mesh doors were locked after the morning ritual.

Their favorite room, however, was the large kitchen with a deep well dug right in the centre of a sunken area in the middle. There was a skylight above the well that made the water a canvas for the ever changing reflections of the sky, wisps of clouds and waving fronds of a few tree tops. Mandakini loved to watch ripples scatter the image and waited for the picture to form again like a kaleidoscope. The girls would let the "kodum" or pot hurtle down, with the coir rope unwinding so fast that it almost burned their fingers and palms. The pot had to be bobbed up and down till it was full of water and then came the fun of pulling it up hand over hand. The tricky part was reaching out to hold the pot and setting it on the ledge. They took turns at it supervised by the older women till they were sure the children could handle it on their own. The aunts always spoke of a time when the well was so full of water that they could just stoop down to scoop out the water in vessels whenever they wanted.

On one side of the well, the narrower side, were all the grinding stones – the flat 'ammikal' with its elongated stone and the larger 'aattukal' with its heavy pear shaped grinding stone that fitted neatly into the circular well in the middle of the base. The floor was made of square shaped stone slabs of different hues ranging from gray or yellow to pink and pale green. On the other side was the large triple mud oven. Three openings at the bottom were filled with logs and live red coals on top. The aunts would blow air through hollow iron tubes to get the fire going. Smoke would swirl around them, making their eyes water till the logs caught fire and blazed merrily. At the end of the day jackfruit and tamarind seeds were placed in the smouldering embers and left there till the next morning when the charred skin would be peeled off to expose the tasty, fragrant and softened white seed inside that made a tasty snack.

From the kitchen, a door opened on to a small corridor that had eight steps going down at one end leading on to another 100 feet long corridor stretching all the way to a heavy wooden door to the back yard. Standing on the first of the eight steps one could look through a window on the left at a huge circular well in the middle of the large courtyard next door. Mandakini's great grandfather had donated the whole area to the public and there were always people bathing or drawing water from the well that had eight rollers and pulleys all around. Mandakini, however, always associated the well with the bloated body of a boy in a pink shirt, being fished out of the water. He had failed in his final school exams and committed suicide.

At the end of the long corridor was the spacious backyard. On the left end of the back yard was another well and a sloping, grey pitted stone where clothes were washed, beaten clean, thwacked repeatedly against the slab. Behind the well was the bathing room with a tin door. A log fire inside the shed heated a cauldron of water, making the bath water fragrant with the smell of wood and smoke.

Another very heavy wooden door with three thick beams led to the magical two acre garden that looked more like a forest. A narrow cemented path wound its way almost till the end of the garden near the rear compound wall. There were several coconut trees, many palm trees and betel nut trees jostling for space with mango, bel and almond trees on both sides of the path. Fragrant jasmine, marigold, hibiscus and orange sembarathi flowers bloomed in between the guava and lemon trees. The garden, resplendent with trees and bushes almost blocked the light of the sun, the green canopy transforming everything to an emerald cavern. Large blobs of amber resin oozed out of the trees, drying out and trapping little insects inside. Mandakini loved collecting some pieces, especially the large tear drop ones. One particular tree in a small clearing grew naturally sideways, sloping gently upwards, affording a comfortable perch for reading and snacking on *murrukus* and *seedai* served in "katoris" or bowls made of dark brown coconut shells scraped clean of their kernels.

Irrigation for the shrubs and trees flowed in through narrow canals that carried the used water from the neighboring public well. The largest tree in the garden was a very old peepul tree. Legend had it that at midnight, a hefty, long haired creature sat under the tree, running its talons through a pile of gold coins. A treasure of ill gotten gain was said to be buried under the tree. The skinny, nut brown gardener never tired of telling the tale of when his father had found a single gold coin on the ground, the morning after he saw the creature under the tree.

The four girls on their farewell tour of the house ran back from the "forest" through the corridor to the hall with the pillars and thundered up the wooden steps to the first floor. They climbed the first flight and took the turn to the right, on to the short second flight to the landing. On the right of the landing was a large storeroom, always dark, conjuring up many imaginary horrors. Large vats held elongated cubes of jaggery, pickles, tamarind and dried red chillies. There were stories of spirits haunting the room, lurking in dark corners. Anyone who came up the steps scrupulously avoided looking to the right for fear of making eye contact with the creatures waiting to pounce on them. As long as one did not look the devil in the eye, one was safe. Even so, one could sense a presence watching and waiting to drag in the unwary and everyone instinctively ran past the room.

They were just scurrying across the landing when one of Mandakini's uncles came out of the room lifting one end of his dhoti and folding it above his knees revealing his stocky, black, hairy legs. Right behind him was a maid servant, her sari tucked in at the waist, both her hands raised up to tie her loose, unkempt hair into a knot, making her blouse ride up revealing half her breasts. Not in the least bit self conscious or guilty the man smiled at them and winked at Mandakini.

She winced as she turned her head away. Mandakini alone knew that the evil predator lurking in the room was more flesh and blood than supernatural. She tried to push the memory of that dreadful moment when she was forced into the room by a man whose hands and mouth and grunts made her want to scream for help, were it not for the horribly perfumed handkerchief stuffed into her mouth. This nightmare that haunted her day and night was a combination of fear of the supernatural and the revulsion of the abuse at the hands of an adult. This was one shameful secret she could never tell a soul, not even her dear friends. The memory surged back afresh, vivid and stomach churning. A wave of cold fear swept over her. Mandakini gagged as she felt the bile rise up in her throat and fainted.

Babli

CHANDIGARH: 1979

B abli died on the 26th of January 1979.

That morning when she woke up she felt so vibrantly alive and happy that she thought it was actually the beginning of a new life. There was general merriment all around her, with the rustle of silk saris, the fragrance of jasmine, roses, lilies and incense sticks pervading her dream world. There was constant music - a mix of old and new film melodies, the plaintive shenai with the intermittent bursting of crackers. Men and women in silks, brocades and georgettes shimmering with crystals and sequins, chattered excitedly as they trailed clouds of exotic perfumes.

Children ran up and down paying scant attention to the half - hearted admonishings of their parents. The heavily embroidered *chunni* over Babli's head seemed to weigh a ton and the *Ghaghra* was even heavier. The jewellery weighed her down even more. Everyone said she looked beautiful and she felt it too. Flushed with excitement, nervous and happy she unwittingly celebrated her own death. On her wedding day she happily said goodbye to everyone and everything that mattered to her or brought joy in her life.

Hers was an arranged marriage. After two years of hunting for a groom, her mother, Sarita Saxena, happened to run into her old school friend, Uma Mehta. The first half an hour of their meeting was full of shrieks, squeals, laughter and tears. Both of them had not finished school. Sarita dropped out of school because she had to stay at home after her mother's death and help look after her younger sisters. Uma left school because her family decided that a girl need not study beyond Class IV. Both married at the age of 15 and had started a family by the time they were 17.

They both started their lives in joint families. When they married their husbands they married the husband's family. Life revolved around obeying the senior members in the family whose word was law. Husbands did not interfere or even bother to find out if their wives were happy. Their loyalty was first to the parents, then to the elder brothers and last of all to their wives.

Sarita and Uma who had seen their mothers go through the same plight took it for granted and accepted the hierarchy fully aware that their time would come. When they would become senior they would wield authority over the next generation of youngsters. This was really the basic principle very similar to ragging at school. If you suffered you waited till it was your turn to make others suffer. And true enough in course of time the senior members died, the brothers moved away, the husbands had become more prosperous and they were on their own. Both Sarita and Uma revelled in their new found freedom and settled down to a routine of watching movies, enjoying kitty parties, shopping and gossiping.

Lives that had run on two parallel tracks now suddenly converged together. After the initial excitement of meeting each other and catching up with all the news Sarita and Uma discovered that both had eligible children. What could be more natural than bringing them together? Uma's son, Kunal, had finished his studies and had been in the UK for quite some time and was now visiting his parents. A meeting was quickly arranged with a reluctant Kunal and a rather apprehensive Babli.

Babli remembered wearing a mehndi green sari that day and Kunal, coincidentally was in a mehndi green kurta.

Her shining wavy black hair was gathered into a loose coif with a few strands hanging around her slender neck. The delicate gold and emerald necklace with the tear drop shaped earrings made her look innocent and very young. The chiffon sari accentuated her rounded curves. Kunal came with his parents and sister and they all sat around making polite conversation.

After a while her parents urged her to show him the garden and they both walked out rather awkwardly. He was 10 years older than her and she felt a bit overwhelmed by his maturity.

"What was your subject for graduation?" He had a nice voice with just the hint of a nasal twang.
"I did …a diploma. In fashion … designing". The words came out hesitatingly. Why should she feel inferior?

"What! No college? I thought a B.A.degree was essential for everything." Was that shock, surprise or contempt? Babli stifled her irritation but could not help defending herself. What right had he to judge her?
"I actually do not have any intellectual leanings. I did not want a university education. I prefer drawing and painting to books. I want to start my own business."

Why did she have to justify herself? She may have had a protected and sheltered life but her parents had always let her speak her mind. Her words came out clearly and decisively. She spoke about her ambition "I want to run a ready-made garment business or a boutique of exclusive salwar kameezes."

"I want to practice medicine and definitely wish to settle in the UK. You better be prepared to stay alone at home most of the time. I will be very busy. Will you miss India?"

Had he even listened to her? Or is he is trying to make amends she thought. She gave a shy tentative smile. "Not if you are with me." *I have given him an open invitation to say something nice. Wonder if he will rise to the bait she wondered.*

He seemed a bit embarrassed and quickly changed the topic altogether – to films and music. *Oh well. Obviously not romantic, she sighed inside.* She began to speak more comfortably and more animatedly about some offbeat Hindi films she had liked.

"Have you seen *Chetna* and *Dastak*? They were so different. Though I like Amol Palekar in *Gol Maal* and *Baton Baton Mein*. He was sooo sweet".

"No. It is a long time since I watched any Hindi films. Have you seen *Legend of the Werewolves*? It kept me on the edge of the seat. And *Jaws*? I think Steven Spielberg is one of the best ever. And Jack Starrett too – his *Race with the Devil* was chilling."

"I hate horror movies. And violence. And wars." Her voice trailed off uncertainly. No meeting ground she decided with a slight feeling of relief.

Their enthusiasm waned very quickly. As they walked back indoors she felt a bit uneasy and rather gauche. They were most incompatible and the whole meeting was a disaster.

Strangely enough the next day her mother excitedly told her that Kunal had agreed to marry her. And that too without any further meetings or conversations. He had to leave at once and could come back only for the wedding. Babli was shocked by the decision. She had no objection to an arranged marriage but there had to be a meeting of minds.

She did try to say a firm no that was swept aside. Babli tried to stand up for herself but her parents were deaf to her entreaties. Grounded in tradition she could not think of a way out without alienating her parents. She tried to cajole her mother and argue with her father but to no avail.

After Kunal left he wrote no letters or cards but did call once in a while. Mostly the trunk call connection proved bad and they spoke of general, practical arrangements for the wedding and travel without any personal details whatsoever. She thought he was very reserved and besides he seemed so much older that they seemed to belong to different generations. She spoke excitedly of the gorgeous dresses and jewellery and the songs for the sangeet and was met with silence from the other end broken by some flat comment. He took no interest in any of the arrangements for the wedding.

"Don't worry beti. Love happens after marriage not before. So what if he is older than you? He will take care of you and treasure you more than any younger man. And he is a doctor – in London at that. He is a prize catch. What more do you want?"

"Mummy. If you like him so much you can marry him yourself."

"What are you saying? I am telling you Babli. If you reject him now you will be a spinster for a life time. And get that nonsense about romance-shomance out of your head. You see so many films that you think life is like a film". Her mother's irritation gave way to nostalgia. "Why your papa and I did not even see each other till the wedding was almost over. We looked at each other's photo and agreed to marry." Her mother had a slight smile on her face and a faraway look in her eyes. "I saw your father only on the wedding day and even then his face was hidden behind the "sehra". And I had my face covered by the ghunghat. But once I saw his face – oof. He was so handsome. And when he lifted the ghunghat, one look at me and he was 'lattoo' over me. And you know Babli **that** was love. We have been happy. You will see the same thing will happen to you."

Little by little over the next six months Babli convinced herself that Kunal was the right person. She became used to the idea of being married to him and then became gradually excited about a trip abroad and settling in London. She had a wonderful time choosing her trousseau as well as some good clothes for the London weather. Her rather conservative parents now gave her a free hand and smiled indulgently when she chose some tight fitting jeans and short tops. So far she had been permitted to wear only salwar kameez and saris. Jeans had been taboo.

The big day dawned. Mandakini and Padmaja wore their gorgeous Conjeevaram silk sarees, looking stunning in the shimmering vibrant colours. Julie looked like a Bollywood actress in her stylish salwar kameez and her western dresses.

They were all with her during the weeklong festivity. They danced with great zest and abandon during the sangeet and teased her mercilessly with their jokes and songs.

"Has the doctor prescribed anything for you yet?" giggled Julie.

"How can he? He needs a prescription himself" Manda was the wise one.

"He won't get his medicine now. He will have to wait till after the wedding."

"Unless Babli takes pity on him earlier. That should cure them both".

The resounding laughter was interrupted by Julie. "Hey. Look. Babli is actually blushing!" This set off more jokes.

All three hovered around Babli all the time, rearranging her Ghaghra every time she sat down or got up, brushing off a petal from her arm or straightening the garland that was slightly askew. She could feel their love and fondness in every glance and gesture and at times she felt so overwhelmed she struggled to hold back her tears of joy.

All four girls, who had sworn undying love, had gradually moved into different orbits in life until Babli's wedding brought them all together in Chandigarh for a whole week. Years of separation made no difference. All the intervening years vanished and it was as if they had never been separated. They may well be meeting after a long holiday.

Kunal was comparatively silent and bore the jokes with a rather embarrassed smile. He found their girlish giggles and interminable chatter rather tiresome.

The actual ritual of marriage was witnessed only by a few close members of the family. Most of the guests had become exhausted waiting for the bharaat to arrive and no bharaat worth its name ever arrived before 10pm even if the time on the card said 8pm. The guests concentrated on eating and drinking. For them the wedding was as good as over.

"They are all a bunch of KPKs" mumbled Julie, "Khao, Peeo, and Khisko."

For Kunal the ritual seemed interminable. By the time the sindoor was applied and the seven "pheras" were completed almost all the guests were on their way out. The family and friends continued to celebrate until well past midnight and then the painful "vidaii" began. Each and every one of Babli's family hugged her and bid her farewell, most of them weeping copiously.

Kunal wondered how much of all the crying was for real. Did people cry because they were expected to or because they really felt sad? Whatever the reason it was in bad taste thought Kunal as if the bride was being dragged to the slaughter house and the sole purpose seemed to be to make the bridegroom feel the utter villain of the day. He wondered if he really was a villain.

Kunal and Babli finally set out for the five-star hotel for their first night together but not before another bout of tears and a lot of hugging and kissing by the bride's family. Babli could see her mother trying to control her emotions and her father looking grave and stoical, wiping his face with a large handkerchief as if he was sweating but actually furtively dabbing at his eyes. She hugged them and felt very close to tears herself.

The drive to the hotel was rather quiet and she desperately tried to think of something clever or interesting to say but her mind was completely blank. This wasn't the time for words but for loving gestures, looks and caresses. She kept hoping he would touch her hand or murmur a compliment or some words of love. The silence settled down heavily around them, a silence that was almost tangible like thick velvet drapes that could be pushed if she put out a hand to touch them.

He probably felt it too because he made a weak attempt to say something complimentary about her family and the wedding before lapsing into silence again. She wondered why he made no attempt to even accidentally brush against her when the car swayed while taking a turn. Perhaps he is very shy she thought - after all the driver did keep glancing at the rear view mirror.

The staff welcomed them at the hotel with garlands and before they knew it they were alone in a huge, beautifully decorated room with a large flower bedecked bed. The very sight of it seemed to trigger Kunal's irritation. He became tense, his face looked flushed and his mouth set in a stern line.

"What the hell is this? A film set? I don't think I can sleep on that" he barked.

He went to the bed and pulled down some of the garlands and swept off some flowers strewn over the bed with his hand. She stood shell shocked, too scared to move or even look him in the eye. How could she say that she rather liked the décor and had expected him to whisper romantic sweet nothings in her ear?

"Well. We cannot be standing here all night like this. I need to talk to you and if you have been brought up on a diet of Hindi films you better forget all the song and dance. Sit down and listen to me."

He began to pace up and down the room and after some time when he found her still standing by the bed not knowing what to do, he held his head in his hands and said through clenched teeth "Oh God. For heaven's sake woman, do sit down and take that stupid thing off your head. I cannot even see your face properly when I am talking to you."

His voice and his attitude had changed completely. There was not even a trace of concern on his face. In fact, there was only sheer anger and impatience.

She sat on the edge of the bed, all her preconceived fantasies of the first night totally shattered. He was supposed to lift her veil gently and gaze speechless at her beauty instead of which he had rudely asked her to remove it all herself. Unthinkingly, she automatically started obeying him. She took off the ghunghat and let it drop by her side. The sight of her pretty face, with all the little touches of a bridal makeup agitated him even more.

"Oh lord, forgive me. What have I done" he muttered and then dragged a chair up to the bed and sat facing her, looking quite wretched and apprehensive.

"Listen carefully Babli. You are way too young. You will realize my predicament better when you are a bit older. You have to try and understand me now and forgive me. I did <u>not</u> want this marriage. I have been living with a British woman for the past few years in London. I am not married to her because she does not believe in marriage. But I cannot be a husband to you. It is too complicated and you will not understand it all now. Just give me some time and listen to what I say."

She sat stupefied. Her heart plummeted down and she felt as if she had taken a body blow that had knocked her out of breath. She looked at him aghast, her eyes reflecting the horror of the situation. Her throat felt constricted and she was at a loss for words. The beauty of her bridal grandeur by contrast accentuated her terrified expression. A face that should have been radiantly smiling was a picture of anguish and alarm.

He got up swearing and sat down again. "Look. I know this must be a shock. And I did not want to get into this. But I had to do this for my parent's sake. My father has a heart problem and he kept insisting. I will provide you with all the comforts you wish and take care of everything. You can have full freedom to do what you like. When you find someone you like we can work out a divorce. I have thought about it all and I am sure we can be good friends."

Sheer panic followed the initial shock. What would she tell her parents? They would be devastated. Her father had spent so much money on her wedding, had even taken a loan that would take a few years to pay back. And she had a younger teen-aged sister whose future would be affected by this scandal. A slow anger began building up within her as his words sank in.

She looked up at him with hatred in her eyes. "How dare you do this to me? You have ruined my life just because you were afraid to tell your parents the truth. I am going out right now to tell my parents. We can get a divorce as early as possible and you better pay me for all the agony you are causing me and my family."

"Did you even listen to what I said?" he hissed between clenched teeth. His anger flared, fuelled by the awkwardness of the situation. "My parents do not know anything about this. My father's health is not good. This marriage is for my parents, not for us. Please I beg of you. Just tolerate this for a few months. Once we get away I will arrange the divorce for you. Till then you can live like a queen. I will sleep on that side of the bed. I will not even touch you. Just think it over. I promise you I will make it up to you."

Her surge of anger was once again replaced by panic and fear. The enormity of the situation sank in as she carefully but mindlessly removed all her jewels. She had watched such scenes in Hindi films so many times but reality was so different. In the films the woman would either weep and wail and throw herself on the man or wrench off all the ornaments and hurl them at him. But here she was quietly taking off her ornaments and putting them away in a very orderly manner. She needed time to think and by doing this she felt calmer. What would she gain by running out now? If she had to divorce him anyway she could wait a while and maybe he would change his mind. At least her parents would be spared the shock of it all immediately after the wedding.

She looked at him coldly, amazed at herself for being able to talk to him sensibly instead of weeping and wailing. "I need time to think. But I will not tolerate this for very long" she said. "And we will set some ground rules. And never ever will you take advantage of this situation".

Kunal felt a huge wave of relief sweep over him. At least she was not ranting and raving. Of course it was unfair on the woman but if it were not for circumstances pressurizing him to get married, all this may not have happened at all.

Babli hardly slept that night. She would doze off out of sheer exhaustion for some minutes of total oblivion – it had been a very tiring day- only to wake up with a start and remember the shocking revelation. Each time she thought about it her heart sank; she had a hollow feeling in the pit of her stomach. The cold fear would fill her mind and travel down her legs making her weak all over. That night would always be etched in her memory as her dying day, not her wedding day.

By the morning, the Babli who died was replaced by a new Babli who was determined to live through what destiny had ordained and live with hope and as much dignity as she could muster. She had decided to carry on the charade for a while for her parents' sake but she would make him pay and pay dearly.

She was happy that only in India could a newly wedded couple pretend to be normal and happy. They did not have to hold hands or hug each other in public to prove they were happy, unlike foreigners who were always touching each other. When she stayed out of his way it was put down to shyness and as long as she could put up with a bit of teasing it was fine. The one person she could not fool was her mother who seemed to sense something was wrong. But no amount of coaxing or veiled questions would make Babli talk about it.

Sarita caught hold of Babli and took her into her bedroom. "Why are you avoiding me? Every time I want to talk to you there is always something urgent you have to finish."

"It is nothing Ma. I am fine."

"I did not ask you if you are fine. There is something wrong".

"Nothing is wrong. I am just going through a new experience. It can be unsettling."

"Is he being rough with you? As a wife you must do what pleases him. You will learn to enjoy it after some time".

If only she knew. He will not touch me at all!

"Ma. Just leave me alone. I will handle it myself" said Babli giving her mother a big hug. Suddenly Sarita burst into tears. The thought of her daughter going so far away hit her afresh. Stroking Babli's head she murmured "My darling. You are such an innocent. Not like all these modern girls."

I have to become a very modern girl now. I have to be brave to face an alien world, survive a loveless marriage day in and day out; reinvent myself and learn to stand on my own feet. I must do it and I will! But oh God I am so afraid. Please give me the strength I need. Babli who had wanted to cry on her mother's shoulders and had restrained herself so far now cried her heart out. Mother and daughter had a good cry, each for a different reason and ended up consoling each other.

Babli found the days tolerable as they were surrounded by relatives and other guests. The nights were more difficult. At first he tried to talk to her.

"You will like London. It is so easy to get around and the tube is an excellent network. You will get to know all about it in no time." There was no response.

"Wembley is just like a little India. You can get all the vegetable and spices you want and the house itself is small but very comfortable."

She continued to comb her hair in silence, and did not look in his direction.

"Once you get the hang of it you can even start designing salwar kameezes and I can help you set up a business. I have some money tucked away and you can start in a small way at first."

"No thank you. I do not want your money".

"May be not now but later. Isn't this what you have always wanted to do?"

"Will you stop talking to me? It is bad enough that I have to share this room with you and breathe the same air." Her voice was tinged with anger and hatred when she began, and ended in a half sob. The helplessness of her situation, the futility of the relationship smote her afresh. Gradually he too fell silent and they spoke only when it was necessary.

Babli marveled at how soon the mind could adjust itself to the environment. She had always wondered how some women put up with drunken husbands, abusive mothers-in-law and physical cruelty all through their lives without rebelling or protesting. Now she knew. One just switched off and let routine take over. Routine can eat up hours, days, months and years. Routine eats up most people's lives. She remembered her great aunt, a child widow who was now 65. She lived in the same house, went through the same drudgery, the same routine from the age of 15. She would continue to go through the same routine till her death. A whole life span gobbled up by routine. She shuddered.

By the end of the week Babli was amazed at herself. Where did she find the strength to survive this indignity and injustice? She, who would cringe from any argument, any pain; she, who was always so used to being loved and looked after; she, who had lived with blinkers on for so many years was now dealing with a terrible truth and had still retained her sanity.

She knew that some of this strength had come from her friends. A few days after the wedding, she had got them together one afternoon. She had thought a lot about what to say and how to say it but when she was with them it was like a dam bursting. She poured out her agonizing tale and all three fell silent, too shocked to speak. It was bad enough that Babli, the girl who had always been scared of pain, who had been unable to prick her own finger to draw a drop of blood, who cringed from harsh words and was afraid of being alone, had been rejected on her wedding night. To expect her to withstand the agony and trauma of living a loveless life miles away from home in a foreign land among strangers was impossible. It would kill her.

Mandakini reached out to hold her hands, kneeling at her feet. Julie and Padma sat on either side and put their hands across her shoulder. Babli for the first time broke down and cried as she had never cried before leaning her head against Padma. Her friends were used to seeing Babli's tears for she was highly emotional and they knew that her eyes welled up when she was happy or touched. She always cried at the movies much to the amusement of her friends, especially Julie who giggled at the wrong moments. But this was the first time they saw her totally shattered and they could not bear it. They sat huddled together till her sobs subsided.

"Walk out of it Babli", Mandakini's voice was firm and clear. "Your parents will be hurt and angry but once they get over the shock they will be glad you told them. They will stand by you and we can make him pay for this. The marriage has not even been consummated. You will find someone later I am sure of that, someone much better too. We are all with you."

"I think you should wait," said Padma, her voice full of anger and hatred. "Get to know Kunal better and find out what he is up to. Keep a watch on him and note his weaknesses. Do not let him off very lightly. Strike when he least expects you to strike. And demand a huge alimony and take him to the cleaners. Any punishment will be too little for the bastard after all the suffering he has caused you".

Julie gave Babli a hug and kissed her on her cheek. "Be practical Babli. What do you gain by walking out of the marriage now? Your parents are going to be devastated; they would have to face their relatives and friends and every time they look at you they will feel guilty for arranging this alliance. Someone should have checked on him and even now it is not too late. As Padma says we need to find out all we can about him. I say go to London. You have always wanted to travel abroad and this is your chance. Give him some time and see what happens. He may even ditch the other woman and love you. If not, kick him out when the time is ripe and as Padma says take him to the cleaners."

"It is very easy to say Julie. But think of Babli in London carrying the burden of her suffering alone. We will all be so far away." Mandakini's face was full of concern.

Babli took her yellow dupatta and wiped her face, sniffing loudly. "I feel so much better already having told you girls. I do not know what I would do without you all. I had already decided to some extent what I should do but hearing all of you has made me more determined." Her voice was strong and confident. "I will go along with this charade and beat him at his own game. I am scared and I know it will be very difficult but I **can** do it. Promise me you will all keep in touch." The new found courage cheered her friends.

"I am not surprised Babli" said Mandakini with an admiring smile. "Quite often the most timid person, when provoked, can be a very fierce adversary. And I know you are far from timid. Remember girls. When we got tickets with great difficulty for the posh concert at India Gate and the organizers tried to make us give up our seats to some swanky folk? It was Babli who fought them and refused to budge. We were too embarrassed to create a scene but Bubli was just great. And she got her way in the end." They all laughed at the memory, lifting the aura of gloom.

Julie kissed Babli on her cheek. "Little does Kunal know that he has to deal with a wild cat".

Babli's decision was also shaped by her love and concern for her parents. Bound by conservative and traditional beliefs, she knew they would be devastated if they heard the truth. She had to break it to them gently over time. Her love and anxiety for them moved her enough to keep her grief well hidden. Her friends were right. She did not know anything about him. She decided she would keep a close watch on Kunal, get to know his habits, his work, his weaknesses, his likes and dislikes. She would make sure that she had the upper hand when she divorced him and would make him pay for all the anguish and torture he had caused.

While she cleared the room she folded his clothes, much against her will. She did it only to search for letters, photos or any evidence of the double life that he led. She found absolutely nothing. That itself made her suspicious. It was natural for normal people to have little scraps of paper, bills, memos and lists in their pockets. But Kunal had nothing except a wallet that contained some money. She soon noticed that there was a dark blue book that could be either a small diary or a phone book which he always carried around with him. He kept it in his pocket and even took it to the bathroom with him which seemed very strange indeed. He made quite a few calls and received some too, mostly at night but he always had the diary on his person. She must be patient and wait for an opportunity she decided.

The day before Kunal and Babli left for London, was fraught with emotion. Her mother could barely contain her tears at the thought of sending her daughter so far away.

"Mamma. I thought I just took this out." Babli lifted a big stack of "Mattri" and a bottle of "aam ka aachar". "I really cannot eat all this and neither will he". She even avoided saying his name out loud. "And I do not want any spices either."

Fifteen minutes later when she came in to the room and opened her suitcase she found packets of spice and a box of kaju katli had been sneaked in. They seemed to come in as fast as she kept weeding them out.

"London is not in the middle of a desert Mamma. There are many Indians and Indian shops there." But her mother was not convinced.

Babli tried to be brave in her mother's presence but she could not help breaking down once in a while. The thought of going to a strange land where she would be surrounded by people of an alien culture was terrifying. She wished she had at least a friend or two or even a distant relative. There were some people remotely connected to her father who lived in Scotland and some in Bristol which was no use at all.

Babli had always dreamed of traveling abroad. It was a yearning that had grown deeper over time. One of the reasons she had agreed to marry Kunal, was to fulfill her dream of traveling abroad. It had not been love at first sight but a well considered marriage of convenience and now even that had been shattered. Julie's practical words came back to her. In keeping with the businesslike relationship with her husband she decided she would make the most of her stay in London. She would see as much of the city and the surrounding areas as she could before breaking away.

Babli's parents drove down to Delhi to see her off at the airport. Her mother broke down when she saw Babli enter the cordoned area. Babli looked back, her eyes brimming with tears and a hard lump in her throat. It broke her heart to see them standing outside waving goodbye, her father's hand resting on her mother's shoulder. Suddenly they both looked frailer and more lost. When would she see them next and how shattered they would be when they heard about the divorce? Fresh doubts assailed her. Should she just have made a clean breast of it all and stayed with them? Now it was too late. She just had to soldier on. She waved to her three friends who had all postponed their departure to be with her till the last minute, encouraging her, supporting her and giving her lots of advice.

Her spirits lifted as the plane soared up into the sky. She had asked for a window seat and gazed down fascinated at the Earth as it receded. This was her very first flight and everything about the plane was a novelty. It was a long cherished dream come true – but at what cost?

Kunal who sat by her side with a rather bored expression now looked amused at her perpetual wonder about everything. He showed her how the table unfolded and how to work the headphones for the music. In spite of her resolution to keep aloof she found it impossible not to share her excitement with him. The flight had taken off at 6am and it was still dark.

The unbelievable joy of actually flying over the sands of the Thar Desert, the cluster of civilization at Karachi, the gas flames from the oil wells that looked like flickering lamps had to be shared. The stunning colours of the sunrise were heart stopping and unwittingly her hand went out to clutch his. It was a moment before she realized what she had done and hurriedly snatched her hand away, a slow blush reddening her cheeks.

The short halt in Dubai, all glitter and gloss, then cutting across Saudi Arabia, the Red Sea and the startling blue sweep of the Mediterranean, were all a scintillating experience. She almost forgot her woes and the child in her was diverted by the spectacle and the thrill of the journey. Alexandria,

Crete, the West coast of Italy, the middle of France, across Paris, the Channel, swathes of yellow rape seed fields and then finally the touch down in London. Kunal too forgot the chasm between them and took delight in her pleasure and eager curiosity. Accustomed to sophisticated and blasé women, he found Babli a refreshing change. The gleam in her eyes, the irrepressible smile and the spontaneous exclamations of delight amused him.

The long hours of her flight had been a strange mixture of emotions. Excited to be winging her way to new experiences; pain at leaving her family behind, the wrench of leaving her loved ones for the bleak unknown; anxiety that all should be well; a growing apprehension about the people she would have to deal with and in between these tangled thoughts a queer sense of flat incredulity - that it was all happening to someone else and not to her.

When one has wanted something very much – so much so that the wanting is almost a constant physical pain- the sudden cessation of that pain, the actual fulfillment left her feeling empty inside.

Now she was back on terra firma, back on earth, back to reality, to the bleak future ahead. The grey skies of London, heavy with unshed rain reminded her to hold back her tears.

She had a strange, numb and flat feeling. She had yearned to set foot in a foreign land but not trapped in a loveless marriage.

This was her life now and she had to find a ray of sunshine somewhere, anywhere, wherever she could find it. She drew the shawl closer and turned her head away from Kunal to stare blindly out of the window of the car. A light drizzle had set in forming droplets on the glass panes before streaking its way down in squiggly lanes. Babli looked down as a drop splashed on her hand and then realized that it was not the rain but her tears.

Padmaja

CALCUTTA: 1980

Durga puja in Calcutta can be exhilarating and exhausting. Right now the sound of the drums kept rhythm with the pounding in Padmaja's head. She could foresee two painful days of migraine and total starvation. She closed all the doors and windows and tied a soft white cloth tightly over her head and ears. But that did not muffle the sound much. She swallowed a couple of painkillers and settled down to weather it out.

Padma remembered the summer of 1968 when she first moved to Calcutta. It was a wrench to leave her friends and they wrote to each other on light blue inland letters coaxed out of their parents. As they grew up they had so much to say to each other. It was like writing a diary, a confession of their innermost thoughts and doubts, their hearts laid bare, confident of not being misunderstood. They could say anything off the top of their heads, without a second thought, secure that no offence would be taken. They never had to weigh their words or censor their confessions.

Little blue letters fluttered their way between Coimbatore, Chandigarh, Calcutta and Delhi, some tearful, some cheerful, at times whimsical or philosophical. News was swapped, messages conveyed, highs and lows recorded and confidences exchanged. The pages were crowded with dark blue ink sentences that crawled like centipedes in the margins and corners with arrows and asterisks pointing to or emphasizing paragraphs. The recipient had to be very careful when opening the letter for fear of tearing it somewhere in mid sentence. Babli, who was always in a hurry to tear open her friends' letters, would keep a cello tape handy to piece the letter together most carefully. Very rarely, a page would be torn off a notebook (which meant there had been a crisis, disaster or a major romance) and posted in a stamped envelope.

They never spoke on the phone. Long distance calls were very expensive and only adults had that privilege of using them. Early morning or late night calls were dreaded, triggering off great anxiety. Such calls inevitably spelt bad news. Padma's mother would have an alarmed look on her face while her father took the call. She would stand by, looking at him anxiously till he smiled or laughed. If it was bad news of death or illness her mother would hear him responding with "oh", "when", "where" and "hm" and it was a torture to stand by and wait for him to finish. At times he would cover the mouthpiece with his hand and whisper something like "Ambi is in hospital – accident" which was more of a torture because she had to wait for all the details – was it critical? Would Ambi survive?

As long as she could remember Padma's ambition was to marry a handsome man, have four children and keep a pretty house, bake and sew and host parties. When Padma was a child and people asked her "what do you want to be when you grow up?" she would say "I want to be a wife and mother". She wondered now if she said it because it evoked so much laughter and they thought it very cute. But she knew that as she grew up, she stopped saying it out loud, more out of embarrassment rather than lack of conviction. For in her heart she knew that domestic bliss with prince charming was all she dreamed about. Not a career, not excitement, not even adventures. All she ever desired was just marriage and babies.

While Mandakini was striving towards her Masters and Julie was working to realize her childhood ambition of becoming a doctor, Padma opted to drop out of college. Her father gave in to her wishes after some protest and strong words. The full support of her mother tilted the balance. Padma happily enrolled for and excelled in classes for embroidery, fabric painting and learning exotic cuisine. Her comrade in arms was Babli who took to tailoring and fashion designing straight after school in keeping with the tradition in the Punjabi family that women need not go out to work and should learn skills that can be put to good use at home.

Babli the youngest of the four friends had got married first and Padma the oldest, was still waiting for her knight in shining armour resisting all attempts at an arranged marriage, very confident that her true love would sweep her off her feet. She had decided long ago to settle for nothing short of a "love" marriage.

It was during the sixth day of Durga Puja. Padma, at 25 was a luscious beauty. She had a natural swing to her walk that fascinated men, young or old. That she was innocently unaware of her sex appeal made her even more attractive. She was wearing a red sari with a red blouse, the colour of *kumkum*. She had washed her long, thick hair that morning. It was still slightly damp when she set out so she let it flow free, swirling around her like a dark monsoon cloud.

Durga Puja in Calcutta was always unique. For the very elderly men and women it was a spiritual high. If they were able to step out they made a beeline for the "pandal" nearest home, to sit through the arati that mingled with the heady fragrance of incense and camphor, the throbbing of the dholak and clanging of gongs. They salivated for the sweets which for some would be taboo at home on health grounds but on the festival day, away from the prying eyes of the family and care givers they could indulge themselves. Like children without a baby sitter they were heady with the very sense of freedom rather than the freedom itself. They would gossip with their friends and bless all the young folk who came to touch their feet, the old men letting their hands linger on the young girls. After all what more could an old man do but touch?

The middle aged folk were the organizers, the movers and the shakers. They allotted duties to the younger generation right from collection of the "chanda" for each locality to participating in the evening cultural programmes. They felt important making announcements and welcoming and talking to the VIPs.

The young girls and boys had the time of their lives. Everyone had new clothes to wear for every single day. Puja meant the relaxation of many rules. Young girls in groups of four or five could roam freely away from home. Pandal hopping was essential for Puja time was courtship time. Like animals and birds that preened and pirouetted, the youth paraded in vibrant colours and sent subtle or not so subtle messages to one another. Their main aim was to see and to be seen by other young people of the opposite sex.

New romances burgeoned while older ones flourished and grew deeper. Some rifts were healed and some just tested the waters. Friends of friends would arrange rendezvous with one another, introductions sought, so called serendipity playing a large part in repeated meetings at various pandals. The bolder girls would meet up with their boyfriends and go out for the day asking her girl friends to cover should her family come looking for her. Women unhappy in their marriages found soul mates for solace, being able to sneak an hour or two away from home with impunity for their peccadilloes under the umbrella of piety.

There was magic in the air, colour all around, gaiety and festivity in every road or lane and a wealth of creative talent displayed in the performances staged every evening. This was not restricted to the Bengalis alone for the joy and elation spilled over to touch people of all religions and cultures settled in or visiting Calcutta. Romantic liaisons between Bengalis and youths from other regions were all too common. The ten days of fun, frolic, fervour and fecundity was the highlight of that year. All the days before the festival were full of anticipation and the days after were filled with either regret or gratification.

It was late afternoon when Padma peeled off from her friends. The pandal was nearly empty. She was just going back home when she stepped on something very sharp. She sat down on a chair and hitching up her flaming red sari, she placed her left foot on her right knee, unwittingly revealing a large portion of a very shapely, long and smooth right leg. She peered at the small sliver of wood embedded in her heel. Her friends often teased her about south Indian women carrying safety pins on the chains around their necks. Pins sure come in handy she thought as she started fishing for the chain that had slipped inside her blouse.

A shadow crossed over her and she looked up to see a man in a black kurta pyjama with the most snapping black eyes she had ever seen. His lips broke into a teasing smile revealing very even white teeth as he said "I could freeze frame you now – red sari, half the leg and most of your neckline exposed. Why, you are inviting trouble my dear".

Padma suddenly felt short of breath and the retort she intended to give choked in her throat. She hurriedly withdrew her hand from inside her blouse in the act of pulling out the chain and was horrified to realize that the top hook had become undone in the process. Before she knew it he was kneeling in front of her cradling her foot in his large warm hands.

"Tsk. tsk. Let me help you. Do you have a pin? Of course you would. My aunt has about four or five on her chain all the time... Hands it out to everyone in need and then stocks up again I guess." His deep, sexy voice made her heart beat faster. He gently detached the pin off her chain. His hand brushed her skin most delicately, lingering just a mite longer than necessary and she felt her body grow warm with desire. His nearness and the smell of his after shave were disconcerting. He carefully prodded around the little splinter and in no time at all he had taken the offending piece out of her foot. He then put the pin back on the chain, fastened the top hook, gazing down at her all the while. His hand very deliberately pressed gently at the hollow of her neck setting her pulse racing wildly. Very bold of him she thought as she drew back after a moment's hesitation. She pulled down her sari and stood up and found her eyes level with the top buttons of his kurta that was open. His tanned neck and chest screamed for attention and her mouth went dry.

"The name is Madhav in case you need my help again. And do you have a name other than Kali or Durga? You look like her anyway," he said his voice playing tricks on her again. Her vocal cords were giving her a hard time. "Padma" the response came out slightly squeaky although she normally had a husky voice.

Just then a familiar voice called out. "So there you are Madhav. Why do you keep straying away and making me search for you? I should put you on a leash." It was Kanti from the neighborhood. "Oh hello Padma. Was my nephew bothering you? He is a Casanova so don't get taken in by what he says. He flirts with every girl he comes across and with older women as well. Just put a sari or skirt around a pole and he will be chasing it."

She came up to him and took his arm. Kanti was a plump, dark woman in her mid forties. Her sari was always slipping off her shoulder and she would keep pushing it up and pulling it around only to let it slip again. Every time it slipped, one could glimpse a bit of her very large breasts that were squashed tightly into always ill fitting blouses. She looked up at him, her eyes large and her thick moist lips set in a mock angry pout.

"Come on Madhav" she said, "we are late already". He looked at Padma, made a face and shrugged helplessly. "See you soon" he mumbled at the same time as Kanti said "Bye Padma. See you later"

As she limped back home Padma could still feel his presence, in mind and body. The touch, the timbre of his voice, the twinkle in the eye and the tanned neck were all she could think about. He was the prince charming she had been waiting for all her life. It was love at first sight. She went to sleep hugging his memory and woke with the picture of him in his black kurta.

She did not see him for the next few days but he was always in her mind, every minute. Madhav was her last thought before she slept and the very first thought that drifted into her mind when she opened her eyes. His teasing banter and strong sexuality seemed to hover around her. She could not eat for the hunger in her belly was not for food. Her mind and body ached for him. If this was what one encounter did she wondered what the second and third meeting would bring.

And then, after a week of torment, she saw him most unexpectedly at the British Council Library. She was browsing through a rather heavy volume and had just decided to walk with it to the table. Still engrossed in the book, she turned around and nearly collided with him. He had come up behind her and was standing, very quietly, right behind her. She nearly dropped the book but he caught it and her hands with it. The contact was electric and neither of them made any move to disentangle their hands. Looking deeply into her eyes his fingers began to stroke her hand ever so lightly beneath the book and she felt more and more helpless. He was going far too fast for her but she liked it.

"I have been thinking of you every minute". The whisper made her go weak at the knees. "How about we go out for some coffee? I will not take no for an answer. I will just carry you away."

The words seem to come out of a cloud for she was surrounded by a haze of desire that muffled the sounds and sights around her. Like a zombie she went along with him, conscious only of his presence and the fire within her. They went into a restaurant that had a row of cabins with curtains meant for families or couples who wanted privacy. They went into one of them and as soon as they sat side by side, his arm came over to rest on her shoulder.

"Oh my God. You are so beautiful. I do not think I can control myself. Do you do this to everyone?" His voice was thick with passion.

A flush crept up her cheeks. The butterflies in her stomach fluttered wildly. With his other hand he turned her face towards him and kissed her softly and gently, full on the lips – her very first kiss. His tongue lightly brushed her lips as she just melted inside and found herself getting quite wet. With great difficulty she struggled free just before the waiter came in. Looking back she realized that their meetings were always dominated by a very strong physical attraction with hardly any time for talk of anything else.

She knew she was hurtling headlong into something beyond her control but she did not want to apply the brakes. They met almost every day for two weeks and she had to think of some excuse every time to get away from home. But that was not really difficult as both her father and mother were too busy – her father, busy making money and her mother, busy spending it. She had always been alone and her friends were her family.

He wooed her with romantic poetry and lyrics from popular ghazals. He brought a single long stemmed rose or jasmine for her hair. They sat by the Lake, holding hands, watching little fish dart between the weeds swaying languorously in the water. Their favourite spot was the lawn outside Victoria Memorial, where they walked in the early morning, cloaked in the soft grey fog, pausing to kiss now and gain. If it was afternoon, they sought the shade of a tree, his head resting on her lap, gazing at the gleaming, elegantly regal structure while her fingers combed through his thick hair. Most often they met at twilight when the Memorial formed a stunning silhouette against the red, setting sky and they could lean closer together.

They walked across the Maidan; strolled by the Strand and held hands in back rows of cinema theatres. At times he would hire a taxi to drive around Calcutta for an hour. They would sit in the back seat together, cuddling and kissing. None of the sights registered in her mind. The world around her was blanketed in a love mist and all she could feel was the blood rushing to her head, her stomach churning and the fire deep down below yearning to be quenched. She was very conscious of his body next to hers and even the slight "accidental" brush against him sent waves of longing surging through her. On every outing she waited for the moment when he would begin to kiss her and when he deliberately refrained from kissing her it only heightened her longing for him. They spoke very little of their families, their work, their ambitions and plans for the future.

It was enough to touch and look at each other.

She knew her parents would not agree to their marriage and she was not even sure that he would progress beyond a relationship but she did not want to even think about it. It was enough that they were together now. Nothing else mattered. Not even writing to her friends. She scrawled brief letters at longer intervals and did not rush to open their letters. Two letters lay unopened inside a book on the table.

One day they went for a long drive in a car he had borrowed from a friend.

"Where are we going?"

"I am abducting you my love. Then I can get a huge ransom from your dad."

He freed one hand from the wheel and let it rest on her thigh.

"What makes you so sure my dad will pay up? He may want to get rid of me."

His hand was gently stroking her thigh. "Then I will pay him to take you away".

"You may regret that. I am not highly educated. I do not have a degree. I am a drop out from college." She resisted the impulse to pull his hand right up.

"Who wants a degree? You have everything necessary to make a man happy."

"And what is that"?

"I will tell you when we reach home".

Her heart skipped a beat. He was actually taking her home, maybe to meet his family. Did that mean he was serious?

"Where is home?"

"Chandranagore."

"Why didn't you tell me before? I could have dressed better. First impressions matter you know."

"What makes you think you are going to meet my parents? I don't have any. I will have you to myself in an empty house." She shivered. Was it anticipated pleasure or nervousness?

Every once in a while he would release one hand to touch her. Once he glanced ahead and behind his car and seeing that the road was clear, he dragged her closer and kissed her roughly on the lips keeping the car in slow motion with the other hand on the wheel.

She struggled free. "You will kill both of us."

"That would be very romantic...dying together."

Time passed very quickly in sweet banter and they reached Chandranagore. A small compact house furnished sparingly but well. He had given his servant the day off. They had picked up some food on the way.

He led her into the house. "Here you are. This is your house now and you are my queen. You can do whatever you like. I want you to behave as the lady of this house and serve me lunch. I will do whatever you ask me to do. Understand? And by "whatever" I mean anything and everything!!"

He followed her around touching her every few minutes. His hands lingered over her shoulders and neck. He languorously traced the curves of her body. This would lead to a kiss or a caress and lunch was very, very late. Lunch was just pretence for neither could eat much. They picked at the food, while his feet made love to her feet under the table. He put his hand on her thigh and then took her hand and guided it to his. When she thought she could not bear it any longer he got up, took her to the wash basin and washed her hands standing behind her. He washed them first with water and then fondled them with soapy lather. The sensuous feeling of his lathered hands and the hardness of his body against hers made her feel dizzy with longing. They could not wait to get into the bedroom.

She was ready to give herself completely for she had known that his passionate embraces would lead to much more intimacy sooner or later. They kissed passionately and long, their hands exploring each other. Suddenly he drew away, held her by her shoulders and looking directly at her he said hoarsely, his voice thick with desire, "I could take you right now but I will wait – till we are married. Will you be my children's mother?"

She was deliriously happy marvelling at his self restraint and gallantry. She wished he would take her then and there but Madhav was the gallant lover who respected the honor of his love. Marriage first he said and after that he would be so passionate he would make her wish he would stop.

The next major hurdle was to convince her parents. Padma decided to deal with one parent at a time. She knew that though her father, Srinivasan, was the main force behind all decisions, her mother, Sharada, when she set her heart on it usually got what she wanted in her own quiet, manipulative way. Sharada rarely opposed her husband and usually avoided confrontations. As long as her purse was full and she could go out with her friends and indulge in shopping for saris or jewellery she was happy. But once her mind was made up no one could change it.

Padma leant against a cupboard watching Sharada coiling her hair into a smooth bun. She was sitting in her maroon petticoat, her very fair and slightly plump arms and neck looking even fairer against the sleeveless burgundy blouse, the deep U cut neckline showing her cleavage to great advantage.

"You do not look 51 amma" she said. "More like 35."

"What do you want my dear? Why this flattery?" said Sharada, though quite pleased with the compliment. She was much admired by her friends for perfectly matching her saris and jewels and she had to admit she had a better figure than many women her age at the Ladies Club.

"Why would I want anything? I just said what I felt was true. How old were you when you got married Amma? And how old were you when I was born?"

"I was just 15 when I got married but I stayed behind with my parents for a year before I was sent to his house for our first night. We had our nuptials, only after I was 16 because the astrologer had predicted disasters to both the families if the marriage was consummated any earlier. After that you were so long in coming. I had almost given up hope when I conceived you after nearly ten years."

Sharada grimaced as she put on her earring. Did her ears hurt or was it the thought of those barren days wondered Padma. "You cannot imagine the torture I went through and what I had to put up with in those ten years. There were constant jibes from the dragon of a mother in law, questions from hundreds of relatives, endless visits to astrologers and temples, fasts and going around trees. And all the time your father was gallivanting around. He thinks I do not know it but he likes to stick himself into any woman willing to have him."

"Why amma.. How can you…"

"Well you are grown up now girl. What is wrong in saying it out loud? Well. Look. You have made me late with all your chatter."

As Sharada stood up to drape her sari Padma gave her a hug and quickly blurted out "Amma. I want to get married."

Sharada smiled. "You have been saying that ever since you were 10 years old."

"No. I want to get married <u>soon</u>. To Madhav. Kanti auntie's nephew"

Sharada pushed her away, her eyes widening in surprise and shock. "No way. Never. Not the nephew of that woman with half her breasts popping out of her blouse all the time? Have you gone mad? Their family has a bad reputation and we do not know anything about the boy. We will not have any connection with that family do you hear?"

"Please amma. He really loves me and I love him. He is a thorough gentleman. You do not know him. I will be marrying him not the family".

"Padma. Enough of this nonsense. If all you want to do is to get married soon we will find a good man for you. Now just get rid of this stupid idea. I will talk to your father this evening" said Sharada. "How long have you been seeing him? No more of it. Now behave yourself. I have to go but I will be back soon."

As she got into the car Sharada's mind was in a whirl. This relationship had to be nipped in the bud. On no account could Padma marry that boy. She wondered how far the relationship had gone. Were they intimate and had Padma been stupid enough to be led astray? That day even the Club activities could not keep her occupied for long. She went back home earlier than usual.

To her dismay she found that Padma was not at home. She agonized over where she could be and what she would be doing but there was nothing much to be done except wait for her husband and daughter.

Padma came home looking radiant. "Where have you been Padma? Don't tell me you have been with that scoundrel again. If you are not ashamed at least have some common sense. You are falling into a trap."

"Stop it amma" Padma cried out as she ran away to her room ignoring her mother's orders to "Come back here this instant". She locked her door and flung herself on her bed, confused and in tears.

Padma avoided going down to dinner till the last minute. Finally she went down feeling very apprehensive, guilty and angry. She found her parents already seated at the table. Her father, Srinivasan, looked up at her as soon as she entered.

He was a tall man, with broad shoulders that made him look even larger than he was. His booming voice sent a shiver down Padma's spine. "What is this I hear? You are going around with that rake Madhav? I thought my daughter would have more sense". Padma was her father's pet and she looked up hopefully. Maybe he would relent and make her mother accept it too.

"We love each other Appa. We want to get married. Once you meet him and speak to him you will understand."
"I understand right now child. He is a rogue and you are going to regret it for the rest of your life. He is just taking advantage of your innocence. I know you have not been interested in studying. You managed to get into college only to drop out. Your shorthand typing, sewing and embroidery and smattering of French will not get you a job. You are not qualified for anything. If this fellow leaves you in the lurch what do you have to fall back upon?"

Well. I am well qualified for marriage thought Padma restraining a smile "I will resume my classes after marriage Appa. I promise."

"Isn't he Kanti's nephew?" asked her father looking at Sharada. "Yes. And well you know that" came the quick response from Sharada. "Is there any man who does not know Kanti or does not ogle at her? She flaunts herself shamelessly. And don't act so innocent Cheenu."

"Stop it Sharada. I am not the topic of discussion now."

"He is not a rogue Appa and I got to know him well…." Padma tried to put some conviction into her voice but it sounded hollow even to her ears.

"Enough. You are not to go out with him anymore and I already have someone in mind for you, someone more suitable for you and for the status of our family".

Padma picked at her dinner dejectedly before escaping to her room. There was no arguing with her parents. She could try pleading, coaxing, threatening but she knew that it would be an uphill task. If they were adamant so could she. If there was no other option she knew what she would do.

When she met Madhav by the Lake the next day she sighed as she leaned against him. "I guess I would have to run away from home. There is no other solution."

Startled, Madhav straightened himself, dislodging her. "Hey. Hold on. I do not want to be responsible for breaking up your family. I am sure we can convince them".

"You do not know my father. Once he makes up his mind that is it. There is no other way. Unless, we stop seeing each other. It will be good bye then" she said very close to tears.

"Don't sound so tragic. Let us think about it. Better not be too hasty." His one arm drew her closer to him as she rested her head on his shoulder. "Give them time, my love. We have all the time in the world."

Over the next few weeks Padma's parents told her time and again that the match was totally unsuitable and praised the virtues of a boy from Delhi. Padma equally stubbornly refused to agree and the discussion usually ended in angry words or tears or both. Meanwhile, she continued to meet Madhav surreptitiously every weekend when he came from Chandranagore. Not being able to see him during the week was sheer agony.

Padma could never make out Madhav's mood. Some days he was charming and a passionate lover. At other times he kept aloof and would argue passionately against eloping and a registered wedding. He sounded like the most honorable man in the world who did not want to hurt the girl's parents. Then again he would become the despondent lover who could not live without his beloved and was willing to die for her. But irrespective of his mood Padma was besotted with him to such an extent that she could not think straight.

He gradually persuaded her that a registered wedding was not advisable. He spoke romantically of eloping and having a temple wedding. The thought of being united in the eyes of God in holy matrimony began to appeal to Padma. After all, he reasoned that when they were reconciled with her parents, they could have a proper wedding.

Running away was akin to facing certain death. It lent certain poignancy to every action that she did or word she spoke. She felt more affectionate towards her mother and father for she knew she would not meet them again for a long, long time. She caressed the little objects around the house that she had grown up with which she would not see again. She would be cutting herself off from her whole life and all the people that mattered to her. By stepping out of the house she was erasing the whole 25 years that was her life.

She wrote long letters to all her three friends telling them all about Madhav and their plans. Mandakini was the first to reply. She bluntly called Padma a besotted fool and warned her against taking any drastic step. She intuitively felt that Madhav was up to no good. Babli's joyous response was tinged with worry and doubt. Cast in the traditional mode she encouraged Padma to wait and get married with the consent of her parents. After all if he was such a great guy they would have to agree in course of time. Julie was neither elated nor critical. She did not want to judge Madhav without seeing or knowing him but practical common sense pointed towards waiting and watching. What was the hurry? Just enjoy yourself yaar she said. Why commit yourself to one person so soon? Meet more people and take your time she said. All this was of not much use to Padma. It only made her more confused and befuddled.

The moment she was with Madhav, however, everything seemed very clear. Life with him would be sheer joy and once the first baby would arrive she knew that her parents would take her back. They would not turn their back against the first grandchild.

She began to collect her clothes, surreptitiously selecting and keeping the ones she needed, small pieces of jewellery, her favourite silver bangles and some books. Sharada watched her daughter and put down her tense silence to being thwarted in love.

Padma carefully planned and waited for just the right day when the house would be deserted. She picked a day when both her parents would be out. Ponnamma, the maid was also on leave for a few days and Sharada had a meeting followed by lunch at the Club. Madhav was to pick up Padma at noon. She had butterflies in her stomach. She was plagued by a million doubts. Was she taking the right step?

She was very close to tears and the weather seemed to echo her feelings.

The humidity hung heavy in the air and the day had dawned grey and overcast. Swiftly a mantle of dark grey cloaked Calcutta, effectively blotting out the sun. The eerie stillness was punctuated by the nervous twitter of smaller birds loathe to get their feathers wet, seeking shelter before the storm broke out. Padma did not need weather forecasts or twittering birds to warn her of the Nor'wester so peculiar to Calcutta. If one had lived in Calcutta one came to respect the Nor'wester. You treated it like a Lord, welcomed it, and prepared for it not knowing what it may ask of you and just coped with it when it came.

The rain always had a knack of getting into Padma's soul, uplifting her heart and bringing a song to her lips. She had always been a rain person and she loved breathing in the heady perfume of damp earth – especially the first rain after a long dry spell. But today there was no magic in the rain song. Today her heart felt heavy.

She could smell the storm in the air long before the first gust of wind came in. Like the darkening of a concert hall before the curtains went up, the sky was a black canopy. There was a refreshing coolness, the opening notes of a breezy overture, a feather light minuet that strummed a tune from the tree tops. The teasing flirtatious breeze with its passion reined in and held in check, beguiled the unwary. It tugged at saris, billowing skirts, ruffling hair and tossing up dry leaves in the air.

Then it slowly gathered pace, whipping up loose debris on the road till suddenly without warning the wind blew fiercely, slamming windows and doors; plucking at tin roofs and muddying the air with dust. Anything that was not tied down to the ground was tossed into the air. Padma had already fastened most of the doors and windows. She wished it had been a clear day.

Large drops smacked flatly against the ground, vanishing instantly, almost magically, soaked up by the hot, thirsty earth. The staccato rhythmic drops, drumming on the ledges and against glass panes, sent slowly quivering patterns of water, meandering down in hypnotic streaks.

Then all of a sudden the rain began to pour down in sheets, dashing against the walls, and gushing noisily down into the drains in a rhapsody of tunes.

Padma placed the letter she had written the night before on the table and put a little bronze Ganesha on top to hold it down. She had spent a long time trying to write that letter and cried a lot too. She took her suitcase near the door. She paced up and down the room stopping every now and then to go out to look at the deserted street. No sign of Madhav. All she could see was the driving rain that was now slowing down into a steady drizzle.

She was just about to turn back when she saw a car in the distance. As it drew nearer she knew it was him. It slowed down and stopped three houses away. She ran in, picked up her suitcase and ran out again, slamming the door shut behind her. She almost turned back but the sight of Madhav sent a fresh thrill down her body. This was a major step into the unknown and she hoped she would not regret it. After all she might come back soon if her parents relented. As she ran out Madhav brought the car forward. She clambered in, already slightly wet by the rain.

After the first flurry of excitement, the enormity of her action began to sink in. Now there was no turning back. She moved in closer to Madhav and he smiled at her reassuringly.

"What? Frightened already? There is so much more ahead."

She rested her head on his shoulder for a moment. There was adventure and new experiences awaiting her. She was ecstatic and yet there was an undercurrent of guilt and fear.

She tried to be chirpy but was surprised that she did not feel the joy she had anticipated. The rain was now coming down again very heavily; visibility was poor so he had to concentrate on driving. As they drew out of the city the weather cleared a bit.

Almost an hour later as they moved towards Chandranagore it was almost as if it had never rained. The streets were dry and although it was overcast it did not look like it would rain any more.

They stopped at a Kali temple where Padma stepped out hesitantly. Suddenly everything seemed very wrong. She felt like turning around and running away but found her hand held firmly in Madhav's grasp. She looked up at him to see him smiling at her encouragingly. As the priest began the puja she looked at the Goddess Kali whose stone eyes were looking directly at her. Padma quickly lowered her gaze feeling stupid and guilty. It was only a statue but the deep rooted traditional beliefs made it impossible for her to look the Goddess in the eye.

Madhav gave the priest some money. The priest took some kumkum and gave it to Madhav who smeared it on her forehead just at the parting of her hair. The priest gave them two garlands and they garlanded each other. Padma closed her eyes. Her mother would have come home by now and seen the letter. It was all most surreal - like living on two levels of existence simultaneously. She was married – in the eyes of God.

She thought of her three friends. She had neither replied to their letters nor left any forwarding address. Cutting herself off from her friends was as bad if not worse than severing connections with her parents. She remembered vividly the last time the four of them had met. It was at Babli's wedding a year ago when they had all been in their early twenties, with stars in their eyes and full of plans for the future. She remembered all three of them sitting with Babli after the wedding, consoling her and advising her as she wept at the thought of her life ahead in a strange country among strangers. So much had happened since then. Padmaja's life and attitude had changed so radically after Madhav came into her life. She wondered if her friends were the still the same or had life changed them too.

Julie

MADRAS: 1983

The warm fragrant water came up to her ankles and Julie leaned back in the black chair with a deep sigh of contentment as the pedicurist began to scrub her feet. Rose petals floated in the water reminding her of the *gulkund* that they had relished as children in Mandakini's house. They would dip their fingers into the bottle of pink and red rose petals damp with sugar syrup. Even now when she had a rose in her hand she was tempted to eat the petals. Padma would place the petal carefully on her nail and press gently till it took the contour of the nail and became stuck to it, making it look as if she had nail polish on her finger. Rose polish they called it.

Julie had successfully completed the back breaking grind of training to be a doctor. She remembered night after night of sleeplessness, sitting at the table poring over books by the light of a slightly crooked table lamp; the unbearable Madras heat and humidity in the afternoons with the clothes sticking to her body and sweat dripping down her forehead and escaping to the beach when there was time. She preferred walking alone on Eliot's beach. The soft grainy sand would sink below her feet till it became more hard packed near the water line. The waves frothed up and moved back pushed by the return of the previous wave only to succumb to the next stronger wave that surged in again. The beach had been her energizer. It infused fresh life into her when she was at the end of her tether. And now she was ready to be let loose on the world at large.

She had known it would be hard work but she was not prepared for the mental stress that had been even more exhausting in the first few months as a medical student. The vision of cadavers, the intestines, liver, kidneys and the multitude of human organs inside the body loomed up before her eyes for the first two weeks. The smell of the chemicals lingered on in her fingers and hair. The very thought of food became nauseating. She needed all her strength to hang on and continue with her studies.

Gradually she began to view everything more clinically. The miracle of life was fascinating; the way in which the human body was put together, so complicated a piece of machinery, so wondrous in its working and so intricately and exquisitely intertwined and interdependent. Maybe if people could see their insides they would not abuse it so much she thought.

There was a party the next day for all the newly qualified doctors and their mentors and for once she would let down her hair. Literally. She had always tied up her hair but today she decided to let it hang loose. The short curly hair of her childhood was now much longer and people often asked her if her hair was permed. They would not believe it when she told them it was natural.

She giggled as her feet tickled with the scrubbing. She felt like a queen with the minions tending to her on all sides, one girl giving her a manicure and another pedicure. The present was so different to her future. She would be working in the villages soon where she would count herself lucky if she got water for a good bath. Water was a scarcity even in the city and getting clean water was next to impossible.

Her recent experiences during her visits to some villages in Tamil Nadu and Maharashtra had made her very angry. The villages around Coimbatore were appalling with very poor sanitation – whatever little there was of it. In the absence of bathrooms choosing a spot to hide and defecate was easier for men. Women had to look more carefully and menstruating woman had even more problems. They went further into the fields to ease themselves, tapping the ground with a stick to scare away snakes or scorpions.

The village girls were married off at a very young age to cousins and uncles within the family. That was the practice and no one could deny an aunt's son the right to wed the niece. A denial would be tantamount to a crime and slur on the family honor for which they could be hacked to death with impunity.

Childbirth was a torture and a risk. There was no doctor in sight anywhere and a so called government maternity clinic existed many kilometers away but without any equipment whatsoever and no regular staff. There was no reliable form of transport and women quite often gave birth on the way to the clinic. Women in the interior rural places were quick to gather around a woman in labour. Men were strictly kept away and for once women's word was law. The father of the baby would be kept a good distance away. The fear of death, however, was a constant companion and in many cases became a reality. Most opted for childbirth at home or in a makeshift "labour room" that was a space outside with saris as a screen and a mat for a bed. Mortality at childbirth for both infants and mothers was quite common. One had to be lucky to have a normal delivery and even luckier to have a baby boy. The moment the child was born the trouble began. If it was a baby girl the woman's life could be hell. Some girl babies died either due to lack of attention or deliberately killed. If it was a complicated childbirth there was nothing that could be done. The midwife would do her best but death was always a possibility.

Julie had sat with the head of the Panchayat and other members one evening and while everyone drank coffee from a steel tumbler, the chief was given a mud cup because he belonged to a lower caste. When she asked him if he did not mind it he said with conviction that it was only right and in keeping with the unwritten law of the land. After all he did belong to a lower caste and he was not ashamed of it. The hierarchy was in the scheme of things and had to be observed for the greater good. The caste system was rampant and it was flaunted blatantly with confidence and pride. They wore it like a medal and the lower castes accepted the indignity as though it was ordained by God.

Julie sighed. How could one change such mindsets? And in how many years? She would be working in a village near Nasik which was not as bad as the places in Tamil Nadu but it was a close second.

She looked at her hands, beautifully manicured with frosted pink nails that would transform itself in a week or two into plain workaday hands with the nails cut short. One evening of fun and then it would be work, work and more work- work that she had always dreamt of doing - helping the poor and the uneducated. It was a challenge and she loved challenges. This time it would also mean goodbye to many comforts and hello to many inconveniences and harassments. She was going into it with her eyes open. She had to survive amongst people who thought and acted differently. She had to win their confidence and trust, convince them and educate them about health and hygiene and in the process she hoped to bring some redeeming and enduring changes in the lives of women.

She stood up and looked at her hands and feet, scrubbed clean and glowing after the cream massage. The colour of her nail polish would match her dress perfectly and her hair was a lustrous cascade. She smiled at the thought of Rajat who liked to play with her hair. She wished he could see her now. She missed him sorely with an intensity that grew with every passing day.

By the time she arrived at the party the hall was full of people. It was not a big hall, just enough to hold about 75 people with a few tables and chairs to the left of the door and a square patch of space cleared for dancing. Taped music blared out from a boom box and there were a few couples waltzing on the floor. One had to shout to be heard and gestures worked better. The general mood of relief after accomplishing a doctor's degree made even the more sedate ones go wild that day.

She stood at the doorway; her pale pink satin dress set off her smooth olive complexion and accentuated her pert figure, hugging her waist before flaring out in a wide skirt. She had twirled in it in her room and watched it rise up like an umbrella. It would not do to reveal her pink panties underneath. She must remember not to twirl too much she thought wryly. Her curly hair, left open, made a beautiful frame for her heart shaped face. Her dimples flashed off and on as she smiled at her friends and she was soon swept up in the midst of the crowd. She dragged some of the senior staff onto the dance floor; the grey haired and balding men protested at first but gave in to her pleas and banter.

She kept her distance from a rowdy, raucous gang of four who were notorious for being wild at parties. There had been an incident involving them when two girls had been found in the boys' rooms but it had been hushed up and the boys had been merely reprimanded by the principal. At another time a couple of the boys had made objectionable remarks and harassed Julie but she had warded them off and filed a complaint after which they had kept their distance.

After a couple of farewell speeches the senior doctors departed and Julie decided she would go too. She missed Rajat. Her head was beginning to ache and she was not in the mood for more dancing. Hot and tired she wended her way to the table near the door with a tall glass of Thumbs Up to slake her thirst. She had hardly taken a sip when someone careened on to the table and sent the glass flying from her hand, spilling half the contents on the floor and the rest on her dress. Apologizing profusely one of the four boys insisted on getting her a fresh glass and in spite of all her protests he soon set one on her table and withdrew with renewed apologies. Relieved to be rid of him so easily and in a hurry to get back to her room and change Julie gulped down the cold drink very fast before she made her way out.

A light breeze tugged at her skirt and she took a deep breath of the fresh air. It had been suffocating inside, the air heavy with cigarette smoke. It was a nice walk to the hostel, down a path lined by trees and past a car park. Three lamps by the pathway cast circles of yellow light.

Ten minutes later she was halfway down the path when she suddenly felt a bit dizzy and realized she had not eaten anything for a long time. She would have to fix herself a good snack and wondered what she had in her room or if she should swing by the canteen store to pick up something. It was just past ten and the canteen was open for tea and snacks till 11pm. Just then she thought she heard a step behind her and turned around. It will be good to have some company she thought. But the place was deserted. She sighed and walked on again past the car park when she felt another spell of giddiness. She lurched forward to hold on to a car, stood leaning against it for a few minutes, the dizziness coming in waves. Then very slowly she sank to her knees as darkness enveloped her. Her last thought was how comfortable it was to be floating on air and wondering if this was how it felt like to be in space.

When she opened her eyes she felt a blinding headache, saw stars and closed her eyes again. She became conscious of the grass under her hand and a wave of nausea hit her as she sat up, her stomach heaving. Her head was clearing slowly and she felt a pain between her thighs. She looked up at the sky. There really were stars up there. It was not her imagination. She was under a tree and something was terribly wrong. Her body was sore and she felt something sticky and wet between her thighs. She found her bag right next to her. Whoever had done this horrible thing to her had not robbed her. She stood up. The burning pain between her legs confirmed her worst fears. Scared she looked around, tears threatening to course down her cheeks. She could see her hostel entrance. The gate was still open so it was not yet midnight. The guard must have gone around the other side. All she wanted to do was to run and hide.

She walked across the clearing, through the gate and up the stairs wincing at the pain and the terror clutching at her heart. She fumbled with the key, and managed to open the door and get inside, happy that she had not been seen by the guard.

She switched on the light and looked at herself. Her dress was stained with the cold drink that had been spilt at the party. The sticky substance on her thighs rubbed together as she walked and she nearly vomited again. She rushed to the bathroom and took off her underpants. The sight of the blood stains made her crumble. Safe within the four walls of her room she collapsed on the floor, sobs racking her body, sobs that came from the pit of her stomach. She cried as she had never cried before, cried in helplessness at the brutality of man, at the bleak future ahead and at her own foolishness in venturing out alone.

When she was done with weeping, she cleaned herself, scrubbing till she was sore all over, scrubbing hard as if she were cleaning not only her body but her soul as well. She huddled in her bed clutching the pillows. She had been raped but she dare not file a complaint. She had not been conscious and she did not even know who had raped her. She had seen no one. She had no proof. This had to be her secret, a secret that would have to die with her, and a secret that would gnaw at her mind forever. She could not vent her rage against the rapist because he had no identity. He had ravaged her and had loitered to put the underpants back on her and rearranged her dress around her legs before leaving. Shame and anger consumed her and she cried again. She had been raped but in her memory she would be raped again and again many times over. This was truly worse than death. Death happened once but this would continue for as long as she lived, a wound that would never heal.

And what would she tell Rajat? Would she ever tell him about it at all? Would he understand? A tremor went through her again as she realized that in just a few minutes her whole life had changed. Her past now seemed so many light years away. She thought of her friends. If they knew, they would make her go to the police immediately. The very thought filled her with dread. Writing out a statement giving all the details and answering innumerable embarrassing questions was something she could not do.

She hugged her knees and leant against the pillow. She thought of Rajat who had been a pillar of strength for her in Coimbatore after her friends moved away to Calcutta and Delhi. Julie had been miserable after her friends left. A very bubbly and cheerful person by nature she continued to be her vivacious self but somewhere deep down there was an emptiness and a sense of loss. She had no one with whom she could share her crazy thoughts and jokes. She missed Babli's thoughtfulness, Mandakini's wisdom and Padma's romantic stories that she made up with great ease. Once back from school, time seemed to hang heavy and she could not think of anyone whose company she could enjoy.

That was when she began to notice Rajat Varma who sat right at the end of the same row in class. He was dark with sharp clear cut features, slightly built and not very tall. She waited for him to make the first move and sure enough he caught up with her one day as she walked out of the Science class saying "Hi. That was interesting. I think I would like to be a scientist".

She was about to tell him she could not care less what he became but when she turned she looked straight into two large brown eyes that reminded her of a cocker spaniel. One can never be cruel or cold to a cocker spaniel especially one whose eyes were fringed by thick lashes. The eyes held a curiosity, almost as if he was studying her under a microscope she thought.

"I want to be a doctor" she said.

"In a large, fancy hospital?"

"No. Not really. Maybe in a village" she said surprised at herself. She had not even realized that was what she wanted till that moment. It had just been an intuitive answer to a spontaneous question.

She found him easy to talk to. He was four months older than her, rather quiet with a droll sense of humour. Although he was 13, she was slightly taller than him. He had a sharp mind and was a voracious reader. They began to exchange books and he opened doors to many new subjects and to a new world. He introduced her to astronomy, the exciting world of galaxies and black holes. He had the uncanny knack of figuring out exactly what she wanted – he would leave her alone when she sought solitude and be with her when she sought company. She would tease him and he would take it with a quiet smile. At times when she was out of sorts he would bring her out of the gloom and make her smile with his funny or interesting anecdotes.

The foundation of their friendship grew stronger slowly, layer upon layer of trust and faith, cemented by care and concern for each other. Just the sort of friendship that Jo and Laurie had in Little Women, she thought. He discovered that her life at home was a living hell. Having lost her mother so early Julie was starved of affection and her stepmother, Sophie, could not care less about what Julie did. Her father's auto part business was moderately successful, just about enough to keep them fed and clothed and provide an occasional bit of luxury. He got drunk every Saturday, came home very late and slept half of Sunday. During the week he was busy with his business and had no time for his family.

Rajat invited her home and Julie took an instant liking to Rajat's mother, Sunita.

"So you are Julie, the girl who has brought my son out of his shell".

Julie looked questioningly at Rajat and turned to smile at Sunita. "He still withdraws into his shell at times. He has told me so much about you auntie. He is always quoting you."

"Ouch. That is not too good. I guess I do spoil him. I will be glad if you can knock some sense into him."

"Hey. Do you women realize that I am here too? I am not invisible am I?"

"Come, you two. I have got some fresh dosa batter. Wash your hands and Rajat set the table."

The warmth and easy acceptance of her presence brought great solace to Julie and she happily became a part of the

Hindu household. She got the care and concern that was missing in her life after her friends went away. This was more like home. She had grown up her entire life, so far, surrounded by an uncaring and insensitive family. She had never known the loving touch of her own mother and whatever hazy memory she had of her was too elusive – more like a gossamer dream. Mandakini's house and family had filled a void in her life but with her departure there was a big hole again.

Once when Rajat's mother combed Julie's thick, curly hair Julie felt a sense of deep comfort and security. Sophie had never been as gentle with her, more so when Julie's curls refused to be tamed. Sophie would pull her hair and rap her on the head with the comb or jerk her straight saying between clenched teeth "Why can't you sit straight for a few minutes without wriggling"?

What was it about the hair combing ritual, mused Julie that made it so symbolic of a mother's love, embodying all the virtues of a harmonious, peaceful and loving family? Even older women on a visit to the maternal home would have their hair combed by their mother or aunts. It was as comforting and as loving a gesture as laying one's head on a mother's lap. It evoked deep contentment, a sense of tender loving care that spoke volumes about the relationship without uttering a single word. In a traditional Indian home, hair care was equated with nourishment and nurturing of the body and soul. A girl with well groomed hair would be assumed to have a kind hearted, loving and caring guardian while a person with dry, unkempt hair presumably came from a motherless or unloving family.

Julie became a regular visitor to the Varma household. At times she would visit even when Rajat was not at home and help his mother in some chore around the house. Little by little Sunita pieced together Julie's life, her sense of loss and insecurity. She admired the girl for her innate cheerfulness that helped her rise above the frustrations and callousness of her parents. Sunita had always yearned for a daughter and Julie filled that void perfectly. Julie never complained but her reactions to the warmth and affection in the Varma family spoke louder than words.

Sophie was not happy with Julie's frequent visits to Rajat's house but there was no way she could stop her. She scolded her and felt like hitting her but knew that was one thing her husband would not tolerate. Despite his addiction to liquor and the fear of his wife, Sophie knew he would not tolerate his daughter being physically abused. Sophie's only weapon was her razor sharp tongue which she could use with impunity.

Rajat had continued to be a very good friend - until her 18th birthday when he became more than just a friend. They were sitting by a pond. It was past five in the evening, bird song time. The warbling and chattering of nest bound birds blended beautifully into a chorus, some singing seconds to the lead with brief interludes of hushed silence when nature stopped to take breath before the next aria. Stray sounds floated around from the road, a gentle reminder of civilization near at hand. The temple bell sounded far away and the chorus of birds died down leaving the wind to sing through the trees. They dared not speak for fear of marring the magic.

He quietly handed her a gift. She took it excitedly and was fascinated by the little jewel box. She held it and ran her finger over it before opening it. Then she gasped. Nestling against the blue velvet was an exquisite pair of pearl earrings. As she put them on he took out another small box and gave her a silver ring that was made of three strands of intricately worked silver all twisted together. He took her hand and said ever so softly "I am sure about it now. I love you. I want to marry you. Not now but later when we have both achieved what we want."

She almost snatched her hand away and then realized that she was not Jo after all and neither was he Laurie. She could not reject him outright but neither could she reciprocate in such full measure. She looked earnestly into his face "I like you very much Rajat but let us not rush into this please. I need time to think".

"I do not need to think Julie. I know what I want right now. But I will not talk of this again till you are ready. But if you dare love anyone else I will... I will..."
"You will what?"
"I will kill him in a duel!"
"I will love someone else just to see you fight" she giggled. "I cannot imagine you fighting. Though I can see you reasoning with him to let me go" she laughed, her dimples deepening.

The next year flew by happily with both fully immersed in work. Rajat's affection was an unstated but constant backdrop in her life. They worked hard and played hard. His calm unruffled demeanor was a perfect foil to her mercurial temperament.

It was a balmy day in July, with a light breeze rustling the leaves. Julie and Rajat sat at the edge of the pond that had become their meeting place, dangling their feet in the water. Julie remembered the day the previous year when he had declared his love for her. She had not been sure then but she was sure now. She did love him very much and there was no doubt at all. She stole a sidelong glance at his pensive face, staring at the water below. Amazing how boys could grow all of a sudden, almost by leaps and bounds. He had shot up in the last few years and was now tall and sinewy. His jaw was stronger and he had grown a small moustache. He would be leaving for Delhi soon to join the IIT and she would be going to the Madras Medical College a few days later.

No matter how clever they were, some men were utter fools when it came to love thought Julie. In the past year he had wooed her in many ways – with occasional flowers, small acts of consideration and understanding but never once had he professed his love for her. Even now when he knew that they were about to be separated he was silent. There was a lump in her throat and she could not bear the thought of not having him around. She cleared her throat and tried to be flippant.

"Why are you so gloomy? You know I hate long faces"

"And you are never serious. Today is one of our last days together and we do not know when we will meet again. How can you be so happy?"
She reached out to touch his hand. "I am going to miss you."

Come on. Say something, Oh my God. Is he waiting for me to take the lead?

"Then again maybe I will meet some good, rich (do the two go together?) boy in Madras. If he is rich enough Sophie will approve." she laughed.

He gave her a doleful look. "You are a chump Julie, wasting precious minutes on mindless chatter. But I am going to miss you too."

Chump yourself. You cannot even see what is in front of your nose.
"Maybe you will find a beautiful Punjabi girl who will be as serious as you are and you will have three serious children."
"Stop it Julie" he said gruffly, his voice thick with emotion.
Oh well. Here goes. "I know what we need. Some fun" she said as she pushed him into the pond. As he came up spluttering for air he heard another splash and found Julie had jumped in too. He swam up to her, caught her and kissed her gently, lovingly, and was surprised when she kissed him back, more than eagerly. They swam back to the bank. No words were spoken, no promises made or any loud declarations of love. It was enough to be together, like two halves welding into one complete whole.

Afterwards, they sat leaning against each other, chatting softly, losing all track of time. As the light began to fade they began to walk home. Sunita fussed over them, fondly scolded them for getting wet, gave Julie a change of clothes to wear and left them together, nursing cups of hot chocolate milk.

Much later they parted reluctantly but confident that their love would continue to be a source of joy and solace forever. It was as if they were ordained to be together. She had clung to him as they parted with a sudden fear that something would go horribly wrong. It was a moment of intense fear, the sort of fear that comes in the midst of intense happiness. As if to say this joy was too good to be true or too good to last without a bit of sorrow.

She had brushed it off then as a silly fear but now Julie thought how true it was. What could be worse that being raped before marrying your true love? Will the marriage ever take place now? No. Not for a long, long while if at all. Now she knew what a rape victim felt like and how society looked at the hapless victims. Even those who expressed sympathy, pity or concern would at times have a look in their eyes as if they were actually trying to think about how it had happened, every single detail. They tried to imagine, to visualize the whole incident and some she knew might even be turned on by it. She had once overheard a policeman say that when he took down the details of a rape case he found himself growing hard.

The worst part of it all was that she was not aware of what had happened. She had been drugged, of that she was sure. It must have been the glass of Thumbs Up but who had done it? And who had raped her? Was it just one person or more? She shuddered and closed her eyes. She heard the first bird call; one solitary chirp followed by another and another and yet another till in a few minutes the air was thick with winged rhetoric, questions being answered, mimicked and sung. She looked out of the window to see dawn breaking. Her night had just begun.

Julie had not slept at all and she had come a long way from the innocent girl happily setting off for a celebration. Now she was a soiled, frustrated, angry and helpless woman all because a brute of a man could not control his testosterone level.

There was a knock on the door. For a moment her heart beat faster in panic. Had someone followed her here to trouble her afresh?
"Who is it?" she shouted making her voice sound as normal as possible.
"It is a call from home. Come down to the reception desk" replied the voice.

The panic gave way to fear. A phone call at this unearthly hour meant something was very wrong. Her stepmother never called out of love. It had to be news and maybe bad news.

She slipped into her housecoat and ran down the steps, two at a time and into the reception downstairs. Breathless, she gasped a tentative hello.

It was her stepmother, Sophie. "Your father is dead. It was his heart. You better come soon and help out with the arrangements. The funeral will be three days later after his brother arrives from the US."

There was a click and the phone was disconnected even before she could utter a word. This was the second thunderbolt but this time Julie had no tears left. She had cried so much and suffered so much so soon that all she could do was walk back in a daze to her room and crawl into bed. Her last shred of support was gone - an alcoholic, ineffective but very fond parent.

She had to go to see his face one last time and bid him goodbye. She would then collect whatever personal effects she had at home. She suddenly felt as if a huge axe had cut off all her childhood years. She had no family, no roots. Already her mind was thinking of booking tickets, making arrangements for the funeral and dealing with her stepmother.

She had not thought of the rape for the past 15 minutes.

Mandakini

DELHI: 1984

The insistent ringing of the phone woke Mandakini. At first the ringing seemed to be a part of her dream but gradually she realized that it was coming from the bedside table. Reluctantly she picked it up with an irritated and sleepy "hello". She had been filing a report till late at night and it had not been an easy one.

The next moment she sat up straight in bed with a shocked "What?" while reaching for her pad and pen with her other hand.

"Indira Gandhi has been shot. She is dead and Delhi is burning".

It was the News Editor, Sharma. He was a man of few words, took snap decisions and kept his cool – the ideal news editor. The only problem with him was he expected his orders to be followed to the letter. Woe betide the reporter who exceeded his brief. Mandakini had crossed swords with him on a few occasions and he had not forgotten that.

"We are arranging a transport for four of you. You will be picked up last. Be ready at three and don't go out alone. The driver will carry the Press passes for you all. Do not do anything foolhardy. Come straight to the office. Meeting will be at 4pm". She heard a click. He had not even waited for her response.

Questions plagued her. Who had shot the Prime Minister? Why was Delhi burning? She called her colleague Anand who was at the office and had access to the latest information. She listened horrified to the full account. It was almost unbelievable. To be shot by one's own security guards was most appalling, a total betrayal of trust.

She came out of her room on to the terrace of her house in Anand Lok and walked around looking out as far as she could see. There was an eerie, ominous silence in the city, like the hushed silence before a storm. There was no movement on the streets, no people at all. The sky looked orange with wisps of black and then she realized it was not clouds but smoke and the orange was not the sun but fire. The truth sank in. Delhi <u>was</u> truly burning. In the distance she saw black smoke spiraling upwards. Those must be shops and houses in South Extension. Sikhs had been targeted because the assassins were Sikhs. She immediately thought of her Sikh friends, a legion of them; warm hearted, jovial and fun loving.

She dressed hurriedly pulling on a turquoise blue kameez over her head, stepping into a matching salwar and grabbing a bite to eat. But she had no appetite. She switched on to BBC on the radio and turned on the television. Phone calls poured in from her colleagues either to give or seek information. News streamed in, getting from bad to worse. There was looting and arson. Sikhs were being killed; some were burnt, some were knifed to death. People were breaking into Sikh homes and walking away with television sets, carpets and anything that was not nailed down to the floor. Some Sikhs had cut their hair short and some had even shaved off their beards. Name plates on houses had been removed or changed and the name Singh obliterated.

Lumpen elements took advantage and were on the rampage. There was no sanity, no mercy, and no pity whatsoever. It was unbelievable that violence could be so widespread so soon. It was like a huge bush fire fanned by the wind of hatred. Mandakini wondered if there were shades of political and personal rage behind the violence.

Her mother called to plead with her not to go out and asked her to stay at home. She reassured her and promised to be careful. Exactly at 3pm the van trundled in. It was a ramshackle vehicle badly in need of repair - not dependable in an emergency.

She scrambled in to face the other three pale and wan looking colleagues — two were people who were to work at the desk and the third was a photographer who was to be dropped on the way. All four sat speaking in whispers. How crazy thought Mandakini. It was not as if they were conspiring. It was just that the ominous silence which enveloped the city, a silence that conjured up scenes of violence and hatred, somehow made them lower their voices too.

Twenty minutes later just as they were passing a lane Mandakini saw an orange glow. It was a fire and she could make out the shape of black tyres. A safe distance from the fire stood a small figure, all alone, the slight frame silhouetted against the fire. Before anyone could react Mandakini ordered the driver to stop. The authority in her voice made him apply the brake at the same moment as two of her colleagues protested. "Manda you are crazy. You will get us killed".

Mandakini had already jumped down and was racing towards the figure calling to the photographer who followed promptly. He clicked on the run. As they neared the fire Mandakini stared in utter dismay at the charred figure of a man among the tongues of leaping flames. She could see the arms and legs and a tyre around the figure. Even as the camera clicked she saw the boy of about five. Without a second thought, she swept him into her arms murmuring words of comfort, turning his head away from the horrifying sight.

The little boy was shivering and as Mandakini held him she saw a mob turning into the lane from the far end. At the sight of her in a salwar kameez a cry went up and they surged forward brandishing sticks, knives, cricket bats and hockey sticks. Some had burning torches held high. The photographer started running back down the lane towards the van urging her to hurry up. As Mandakini began to run she saw the photographer reach the van and scrambling up even as the van started moving away from the end of the lane. Cursing under her breath and frightened she ran as fast as she could.

As her legs started pumping she felt her duppatta slide off and fall by the way side. There was still a good three hundred yards to the end of the lane and hopefully the van was coming in for her. The weight of the child slowed her down and she knew that if she was caught they did not have much chance of survival.

Just then she heard the roar of a motorcycle and saw it turn into the lane. Her mind vaguely registered the picture of a tall man in black pants and a black jacket astride the motorbike. The helmet and visor made him look like a character straight out of the books or movies. In no time at all he was by her side, his bike screeching as he made a sharp U turn. "Come. Quick." he said in Hindi. His voice was deep and had a ring of authority to it.

She flung one leg over the seat and sat astraddle holding the child in between. As the bike roared into life again she thought she heard a chuckle. What was there so amusing about all this? "This is no laughing matter" she said rather severely and looked back, grateful to see the mob receding.

As he turned left at the end of the lane she yelled above the noise. "I have a van waiting. Let me off".
"No you don't. I have sent them on".
"How dare you? I could have been killed back there."
"I don't care if you were going to be killed. There were more people in the van and they would have all been torched if they waited for you. Are you always so ungrateful?"

"If you are expecting a medal I am sorry. Thank you for rescuing us but you <u>are</u> going the wrong way and I need to get to the Herald office."

"I know. I saw the van remember. Don't worry. I am not in the habit of abducting women. I will be very happy to drop you off right now but I cannot. This route is longer but we will not face any danger on this path. I am not in the mood for fighting off angry mobs." She detected a hint of scorn in his voice and that riled her. He was treating her like a helpless teenager.

While she fumed and was hunting for a retort he said "No need to think of something witty. Just relax and enjoy the ride."

"Are you always so domineering and condescending?" she asked. "Obviously you are not a gentleman".

"Touché". His laughter was whole hearted and quite infectious. After a moment she could not help joining in. "I am sorry. I know you risked your life to save us."
"That is all right. There may be worse times ahead."
They drove on in silence. Mandakini was still shaken by the event and she occasionally murmured words of comfort to the terrified child.

As they neared her office building he slowed down. "Here we are. Your van is already here and I think your friends are waiting."

She swung her leg over the seat, got down and lifted the boy after her. She looked up to say good bye and caught a fleeting glimpse of two light hazel brown eyes flecked with green, alight with laughter. He had pushed down the visor over his face again before she could even blink.

"All the best with the boy" he said and zoomed off. But not before Mandakini had a quick look at the number plate. She had to find out who he was.

Her colleagues surrounded her and the little boy. Many Herald staffers were gathered outside on both sides of the main door. They cheered and clapped as Mandakini and her friends walked in as they had cheered every person who came in for work that day. It took courage and dedication to come to work that day. Many opted to stay home, some because they were too scared to venture out and others because their loved ones had insisted on keeping them home.

The next day the picture in the newspaper of the small boy silhouetted against the burning "pyre" caught the imagination of the people. Its stark simplicity spoke loudly and poignantly of grief, brutality and the inhumanity of man. It came to represent the horrors of the 1984 riots. The child's family was traced and the boy restored. The story was picked up by agencies and ran for a while.

It was a long time before the viciousness subsided and even then the Sikhs known for their valour, loyalty and vibrancy continued to be uneasy and quiet. They felt vulnerable, and discriminated against. Mandakini remembered how on the day of the assassination, when they left for home in the same van at five in the morning they had an extra passenger, a short and tubby Sikh journalist who was always full of life. For the first time they saw him silent and pale, reading about the latest atrocities on the ticker tape. They had made him crouch at their feet in the back seat and the ride to his house was the most tense ride they had ever had. The van was stopped once by a group of marauders who were satisfied, fortunately, by the press passes that were shoved out of the window. If they had inspected the van the Sikh would not have survived.

It was much later one day when Mandakini was clearing her handbag that she came across a slip of crumpled paper nestling deep in the recesses of one of the zipper compartments of the bag. She was just about to throw it away when the sudden memory of two very brown green-flecked eyes brimming with laughter made her smoothen the wrinkles and stare down at the number. Worth investigating she thought as she reached for the phone.

Her enquires led her to Special Intelligence. Further discreet investigations uncovered more facts. His father was British and mother from Goa. The passport size photo revealed a rather longish face with straight brown hair that fell partly over his broad forehead, rather bushy eyebrows over startlingly bright eyes. He had a rugged look with a rather pronounced chin. Not good looking but somehow interesting in an unconventional way. There was something hard about him. Not a person to antagonize, thought Mandakini, but good to have as a friend.

He had done his BSc at St. Stephens College, Delhi. He had a Masters degree and was a doctorate in Forensics from the US. He was a black belt in Taekowando. He had returned to India and was recruited by Intelligence where he had undergone Commando training. After that it was a like chasing a shadow. She could get no clear idea of what he did. Over and over again she found oblique mention in various major cases – the uncovering of a Pakistani spy; a regional political satrap connected with drug trafficking; the expose of a money laundering circle and the breaking up of a counterfeiting gang.

Sanjay Coelho was a chimera, always mentioned in the margins of all these events - never in the fore front. If one studied the cases closely one suspected that although the credit was given to another official the mover and shaker was someone else. But that someone was so elusive that the public gaze never focused on him.

The remarks on his behaviour and character were not all very complimentary. He was abrasive in his dealings with his peers and verged on impudence when he spoke to his seniors. He had some very staunch friends but more enemies. He had even been suspended from work for a month as punishment for disobeying his orders and going over the head of his seniors. Pompous ass thought Mandakini. He deserves to be taken down a peg or two.

She stored away every bit of information in the back of her mind. He excited her curiosity and the memory of her rescue was etched in her mind. She abhorred men. They were tolerable and may be even desirable to some extent only as fathers, brothers or friends. And even so she had come across some despicable fathers and friends. Women were so foolish to fall in love with men, men who wanted only one thing from a woman – her body. Well. She was not going to be a fool. Ever.

A week later Mandakini was at one of the leading hospitals visiting a friend. As she was walking down towards the reception area she thought she saw Babli's husband, Kunal. Since Babli's wedding in '79 she had met them only twice on their visits to India. Babli had professed to be happy but Mandakini was sure it was an act put on for the family and friends. She knew there was no genuine affection between husband and wife in spite of all the external trappings of domesticity. In the few minutes that she managed to speak to Babli alone she learnt that their marriage was still a farce and had not been consummated. At least it was good to know that Babli had held her own ground and had not been tortured or abused. It spoke volumes for Kunal's sense of honour as well as Babli's inner strength. Any other man would have exploited the situation.

It was strange that Kunal should be visiting India now with none of the friends hearing about it. She tried to follow Kunal but he vanished into the room of a nephrologist. Mandakini waited for a while and then approached the desk.

"Hi, Could you help me? I need an appointment with Dr. Mazumdar. It is rather urgent."

"Sorry ma'am. You might have to wait a week or so. He is all booked up"

"It is extremely urgent. Even if I could talk to him for a few minutes right now... I can bring the patient later for a consultation".

"No chance ma'am. He has gone out for a meeting".

"But I did not see him go out. If I can catch him just for a minute..."

The secretary's lips set in a firm line. Her voice was tinged with irritation. She spoke slowly with an exaggerated show of clarity. "There is an exit from his room directly to the lobby on the other side. He usually calls me just before leaving the room and he called me a moment before you approached the desk. Now if you don't mind I am rather busy".

Mandakini turned away disappointed. That meant that Kunal had gone out with the doctor. She turned and tried to walk sedately away from the desk. The moment she turned into the corridor and was out of sight of the secretary she started running. May be she could still catch them outside. At the end of the corridor as she turned the corner to go towards the exit door she crashed into what seemed like a brick wall except that the brick wall had arms that came around her to steady her and had on a white shirt exuding a very male fragrance.

Having the wind knocked out of her left her a bit breathless and when she looked up at the brick wall's face she became even shorter of breath. She also realized that the arms were still around her and with all her senses returning at once she gave him a violent push and staggered back.

For the first time she saw his full face in person. His longish face was offset by a rather pugnacious square jaw with an imperceptible cleft in the chin. The mouth that had looked rather stern in the photo looked quite pleasant now with a smile hovering around the corners. His eyes were as she remembered – light hazel brown with little flecks of green. His straight brown hair had a hint of copper when it caught the light. He impatiently pushed back the strands of hair that fell forward on his broad forehead.

Her bag was on the floor but fortunately none of the contents had rolled out. He quickly stooped to pick it up, brushed it off and handed it to her. He has forgotten all about me she thought as she turned away with a flustered thank you when his arm stretched out to pull her back.

"Is that all you have to say to someone who saved your life?"

She bristled at his touch and shook off his hand with more force than was necessary. Why did he always make her feel she was in the wrong?

"Oh. Was that you? I could not recognize you without your helmet and visor," she said with a polite smile.

"Or maybe I should replace the photo on my file with another one of me in a helmet so that people who snoop around can identify me more easily" he said with a straight face that did not quite match the mischievousness in his eyes.

He had done it again. She could feel the colour rising in her cheeks. She thought she had been very careful to cover her tracks but he obviously had someone watching out for him. May be the facts she had ferreted out were ones that were supposed to be fed to people. What a fool she felt. At five feet ten she was tall for a woman but he towered over her physically and made her feel even smaller. On top of that he had made her lose track of Kunal.

"Or maybe you should introduce yourself instead of behaving like a mystery superman when you rescue damsels in distress" she said smoothly.

"You don't fit the description – a damsel in distress. As far as I remember there were sparks flying from your eyes."

"I would love to keep bantering with you but I do have some work that has already been delayed" she said curtly, side stepping ahead.

"I am sure we will meet again when we can continue the banter" he shouted after her.

An infuriating man thought Mandakini. Thank God. This would be one person who would not bother her with romantic intentions. She was sick of turning down and putting off the men who ran after her in spite of her frigid ice maiden image.

Damn him for making her lose track of Kunal. She could not shake off a vague sense of uneasiness. Her instinct told her that something was very wrong. She was to go to Chandigarh on work later that week. She impulsively decided to go the very next day. She had not seen Babli's mother for a very long time and she might be able to get some information about Kunal and Babli.

She was at the Saxena's the next evening. Sarita answered the door, looking quite haggard. She had aged a lot over the past few years, her shoulders sagged and the lines on her face were more marked. The eyes had a tinge of sadness in them. She looked surprised and a bit apprehensive at the sight of Mandakini who gave her a quick hug to set her at ease.

"Hello auntie. I had some work here and thought I would drop in".

Visibly relaxed that there was nothing wrong, Sarita welcomed her in. "Come in child. Do sit down and let me get you some tea. How are you?"

"I am fine auntie. I have not heard from Babli for a long time. How are they?"

"Must be fine I guess. You know they say no news is good news. Babli does call me once a week but these two months she has been very erratic. I have not had a letter for some time but then young people are always so busy. I only wish they would have a baby. They have been married for five years now."

So Sarita was not aware of Kunal's presence in Delhi. Something was very wrong if he came all the way from the UK to India and did not even contact the family. There was obviously some connection with the doctor at the hospital and Mandakini intended to find out. But first she would have to call Babli in London. It would be interesting to hear what Babli had to say.

Couple of days later she called Babli. After some general chatter Mandakini said "So how is Kunal now?"

"Very busy Manda. He leaves early in the morning and returns late".

"Guess that is good for you. You are free most of the time. Does he go on tours often? You were always so afraid of staying alone at night."

"Not any more. I have learnt it the hard way! I just keep a night light on." laughed Babli.

'Is he touring now?"

"No" the denial came much too quickly. She then tempered it down saying "Not at the moment, though he has some planned for the next week".

Why was Babli covering up for him? When she persisted in asking questions about Kunal Babli suddenly remembered an urgent chore and bid goodbye.

Mandakini could sense a touch of fear in Babli's voice. Her journalistic instincts told her there was a story brewing, a story that she would have found thrilling had it not been for the involvement of her friend which made her more apprehensive. She had nothing much to build upon except her own suspicion which meant the only option was to wait and see. The disquiet rankled in the back of her mind as she realized that she was not very good at the waiting game.

Padmaja

CHANDRANAGORE: 1984

Padma remembered the first day when she had stepped into the house or rather when Madhav had carried her over the threshold. Each and every detail was etched so vividly in her mind that she had to but close her eyes and think of the day to feel his right arm under her shoulders and his left under her knees. She could only see his right profile as he carried her in, breathe in the unique fragrance of his body, see the way his hair was swept behind his ear, his mouth slightly open, the lips parted in a faint smile. It was just before twilight, the mellow sun painting everything with a golden glow. She had reached out to put her arm around him, nuzzling against his strong neck. There were moments when memory brought back, very briefly, the exact flavor of the time till it suffused all the senses to make it seem not then but now.

He had carried her straight to the bedroom. He was gentle with her and very loving. Time was of no consequence. The whole world ceased to exist for their whole world was encompassed by their two bodies. There was no beginning and no end, no clear well defined boundary for his body or hers. The pain and the discomfort of losing her virginity were more than she expected but it soon passed and under his guidance she enjoyed herself.

When the haze of passion cleared and the world swam back into focus her mind swerved instantly to her parents. Her mother looking lost and worried would be filled with embarrassment when she was asked about her daughter. She knew that Sharada would put up a brave front but she would collapse the moment she was alone, her mouth would quiver and work, trying to contain her tears. Her plump hands would be twirling the corner of her sari or she would keep ironing out the pleats with the palm of her hand as she did when she was agitated.

Her father would be hiding behind a newspaper or a book. Whenever he was angry or sad he would not talk at all. He would grow more and more silent and his face would become flushed. He would be unable to say even a word of comfort to her mother. They were both so different and so bad at communicating with each other. Her mother would be waiting for him to say something and his silence usually made her seethe with anger. She wanted comfort or sympathy voluntarily not on demand and the more he held aloof the more she would be irritated. That would move her to be short with him, sarcastic and scathing, driving them further apart. Padma had been the bridge between them. Her presence usually brought them around. Now she herself would have become the cause of the chasm between them.

Padma kept waiting for the phone to ring or someone to call from home. Surely anger could not last long against one's own flesh and blood. Could all the years of happiness and laughter in a family be wiped out by one rash act? Was not love and forgiveness the core of a family? Maybe they were waiting for her to call or to come back of her own accord.

As days became weeks and then months she wondered if they were well. The doubt in her heart settled like stone. Her parents must be very angry, so angry that they had cut her off. She knew she had betrayed them by running away but surely that was not so unforgivable? They too had betrayed her trust and faith by not accepting her love. She had not expected such a strong reaction. She expected angry phone calls, threats and pleas that would end in some mutual agreement of peace and tolerance. The cold, hard silence was unbearable.

Madhav was insatiable and Padma felt very much loved and needed. Life was as she had dreamed it would be. All through the day when he was away at work she kept herself happy cooking, cleaning the house, making little changes here and there which went largely unnoticed. The nights were full of passion till they fell asleep exhausted. And yet the stone weighed down heavier on her heart.

Six months later there was still no news from her parents. There was no message in the papers asking her to come home and that all was forgiven. She longed to see them, to beg forgiveness and to tell them she loved them. She wondered if they were well and if they even thought of her at all. She called her friends in Calcutta hoping to get some news through them. Obviously her name was dirt and her friends' parents had forbidden them to associate with her. Most cut her off with a curt message that they could not talk to her. Some hastily whispered their concern and asked her not to call again as their parents had told them to sever all connections with her.

Madhav never spoke of his work or his friends. When she wanted to meet them or call people over he would change the topic or tell her he did not want to share her with anyone in the world. Short shopping sprees and walks broke the otherwise unredeemed sentence of imprisonment at home.

She was getting a bit tired of the love making routine and wished he would give her a break.

Another six months later Padma realized that she had made a huge mistake. She was just a sex object and her feelings or needs did not count at all. She was trapped in a torture chamber and could not escape. She had no one to turn to and very stupidly she had burnt all her bridges. She feigned headaches and stomach aches to avoid him but these excuses did not work for long. He had his way nonetheless.

It was not natural she thought. This could not be what all married couples did. There must be more to life than sex. Once during her menstruation, her body wracked by cramps, he took her by force and after finishing with her he went to the other room leaving her to clean up the mess and change the soiled sheets. She began to dread his nearness. It was difficult to conceal her revulsion and that only angered him more. He began to use crude language and dirty talk. She stopped dressing up for him. As she did not go out and was at home most of the time she was always lounging around in her home clothes. This again invited his sneers and curses.

She yearned for her family now and in desperation called home one afternoon. Her mother picked up the phone but cut her off as soon as Padma said "Hello". Another time the response was a curt "wrong number". It was no use calling home. The stone in her heart grew heavier. That was when she started writing to her three friends pouring her heart out but withheld her address and told them not to reply. She told them not to worry and that she would be in touch with them again once she was free.

On their second "wedding" anniversary Padma wondered if she could have a sane discussion with Madhav. She would make one last bid to sort it out amicably. She cooked a good meal, lingered over her dressing and took care to look good for him. The table was set with candles and flowers.

He did not come home till 2am. She had been sleeping fitfully still attired in her orange chiffon sari that set off her dusky complexion and her voluptuous figure. He lurched in, drunk, made his way to the bed and fell on it without even taking off his shoes. He did not even look at her. There was no use even talking to him and Padma went back to her room, changed and collapsed on the bed to have a good cry.

And so began his visits to the brothel or was the correct word "resumed"? In a way Padma was glad that he left her alone sometimes. While many women would try to stop their husbands from going to the brothel Padma was glad to have a break and prayed he would go more often.

Then he sacked a servant increasing her work load. His absences from home at night increased. One night he brought a woman home. Padma's protests and ranting and ravings had no effect.

She decided enough was enough and asked for a separation. He laughed. "Why Princess, what gave you the impression that we are married? God was our witness but He cannot come to court. The priest has been paid well enough to lose all memory of our visit. You, my child, are living in sin, and it is sinfully pleasurable".

That was when the thought of suicide first entered her head. Padma considered suicide as an option though not for long. She smiled cynically to herself as she thought of all the forms of suicide and discarded each one of them as too painful or unreliable. If she could smile at herself she could continue to live. She had always lived life with passionate intensity and even in the depths of despair her instinct was to fight. And fight she would. At the end of it all she shelved the suicide plan altogether. It was now three years since she ran away from home. She would first make an attempt to see her parents. If they still loved her, life would be worth living.

She found immense relief in writing to her friends at regular intervals. They were her invisible link to sanity.

She decided she would escape and with or without the help of her parents she would study again and make good. She regretted not having been a more dedicated scholar. But it was not too late. With motivation she knew that if she tried she could do anything.

She had to climb out of the pit she had fallen into, a pit she had cheerfully dug with her own hands. She had to redeem some self respect before she could look her friends in the eye. All that could not be achieved in a day. She had to bide her time. She had to lull him into complacency and have some money before she could escape.

She began saving bits and pieces from the housekeeping money he gave her. She stinted and saved on groceries. She just needed enough money for the bus ride back to Calcutta and some extra to survive for a few weeks before she started a part time job and night classes. It had been a long time, more than long enough to repent. And repent she did with all her heart.

Just when she thought her misery had touched rock bottom he would humiliate her even more. He tortured her with his scathing remarks, his taunts and whip like tongue lashing that reduced her to a piteous terrified state bereft of all self confidence or self respect.

She was traumatized by the sight of the women he brought home. Knowing about the existence of the oldest profession did not necessarily prepare one for seeing it at work, up close. Some women were young and sophisticated in appearance and others were cheap, gaudily dressed and uncouth. But all of them had the same look in their eyes that lurked behind the bravado and feigned boredom. She saw the pain, the disgust, the shame and the helplessness in unguarded moments. Their whole lives were sacrificed merely to satisfy the cravings of men day in and day out. Was sex, like death, a great leveller? What were the compulsions that drove these women to seek such a livelihood? Could they ever escape or was it a life sentence?

It was now close to four years of living in hell and Padma could not stand it any longer. She could not bear the depravity for even one more day. She planned her flight. She chose a Friday for that was when she knew he would come home late. On Friday evenings he would go straight to his favourite haunt to unwind and get drunk. Then he would either go to a brothel or bring a woman home. Either way he would not come home till midnight.

She waited an hour after he left for work and set out. She did not want to leave a letter. He did not deserve any courtesy whatsoever. She took all the money she could find around the house. She left through the back door to avoid any neighbors lurking around. She had a very light suitcase and a shoulder bag. As she stepped out she felt a huge weight roll off her shoulders although her heart beat wildly. Like a prey in flight she turned every so often and looked all around her dreading that he might materialize from nowhere. She found an auto-rickshaw and reached the bus station. The wait of 10 minutes for the bus to start was harrowing but once it set off she heaved a huge sigh of relief. It was nearly lunch time when she arrived in Calcutta and it took a further hour for her to reach home.

The familiarity of the house sent a fresh surge of hope in her veins. It looked a bit neglected and the small garden outside was unkempt. Her mother who loved gardening had obviously not taken care of it. A cold hand of fear gripped her heart. Did the unkempt garden mean her mother was not well or was not alive at all?

She raised her hand to the ornate bell but found the door give way when she pushed it. She walked in and closed the door behind her. The room was dark with all the curtains drawn. When her eyes became adjusted to the darkness she found an elderly woman with straggly salt and pepper hair sitting in a chair. She was nodding over a book, almost half asleep. Looks like a new maid to help out thought Padma. As she moved nearer she was taken aback to recognize her mother. Sharada had given up dying her hair that had become more white than black. Her hair was in dire need of a trim. Her plumpness had vanished, she had lost weight and her shoulders had shrunk. With a heart rending cry Padma ran and knelt at her feet, sobbing uncontrollably.

Sharada stiffened and looked down at her daughter. Padma's long black hair was a mess, her skin sallow, her eyes dull with a hunted look. Her collar bones stood out forming great hollows. There were dark circles under her eyes and Sharada spotted some signs of bruises just healing. The mother in her was moved to tears. She put out one hand gingerly to touch Padma's rough hair and with the other drew her closer with an alarmed cry. They clung to each other, each weeping for the other's sorrow and suffering. Padma could only whisper "I am sorry" over and over again while Sharada went "Shshsh. Do not worry. You are home. I thought you were happy and did not want us."

Wiping the tears streaking down her cheeks Padma whispered "How is Appa"? Because she had left in stealth and came back in stealth, she felt it was in keeping with the mood to whisper. Sharada stood up and raised Padma to her feet and led her by the hand to the next room. On the familiar large four poster bed was the frail figure of a man with the sheet drawn up to his chest and one arm resting by the side.

The immensity of the change hit Padma with renewed force. The tall, hefty man who used to walk with an air of authority was a shriveled forlorn figure. Her one thoughtless act born of sexual obsession had wrought havoc on the health of the whole family. Brutally frank with herself, Padma realized that if she had not been blinded by Madhav's physical charm she might have not plunged into the relationship. She had been seduced with consummate skill and she had given in only too readily.

Her father raised one hand and she went forward to clasp it in both of hers. She kissed his hand, tears flowing down her cheeks. Only then did she notice that one hand lay lifeless and that her father had not spoken. His mouth was twisted slightly askew and there was no trace of the old confidence, arrogance or authority. He was just an old paralyzed man. Heart broken she rested her head on his chest, her sobs coming from the pit of her stomach. She wept for her guilt, for her parents' suffering; for her weakness and for their lack of understanding that had pushed her over the edge.

She realized that she was not the only one to be blamed. If her parents had spent more time with her may be she would have turned out differently. But the "may be" and the "could" and "would" made no sense now. She had a mission in life. Her parents had forgiven her and that alone was strength enough. "I am back home now Appa. I will never leave you both. Never. Never ever" she sobbed. And his good hand tightened its grip on hers and she squeezed his hand in reply.

After four years of humiliation she had found a purpose in life. Education was essential and she was still young enough to make a fresh start. She looked up at her mother standing near, her eyes already bright with a glint of happiness. Her father turned his eyes to her mother and the look they exchanged said it all. They could lean on their daughter for love and Padma smiled through her tears. She had taken a long time to find the right path but she had done it. There was no holding her back now.

Julie

COIMBATORE: 1984

Julie's visit to her home, the sight of her father's body in the coffin, his face calm and at peace pushed her own sorrow to the back of her mind. She was still in agony and her abused body still ached for justice but the arrangements for the funeral had to go on. People had to be greeted, spoken to and acknowledged. She also had to deal with her stepmother who made a public spectacle of her grief while keeping a strict eye on the expenditure; a consummate actress and gold digger rolled into one.

After the funeral Julie collected all her possessions knowing that she would not be visiting often if ever at all. She had to say goodbye to her life as a daughter. Now she was truly an orphan with no family to call her own. From now onwards her friends were her family. But then she consoled herself that her friends had always been her family anyway.

When she returned to her hostel room, coming back to the scene of the crime was like a sucker punch taking her unawares and leaving her gasping for air.

Three weeks had gone by after the traumatic night, three weeks of loneliness, fleeting self pity, frequent self-recriminations and constant simmering anger. Anger at her foolishness was coupled with frustration at the arrogance of men who committed such crimes with impunity. It was an impunity built upon the helplessness of women like her. She was even more helpless because she had no details, no memory and absolutely no concrete evidence or witness. She felt she was banging her head against not a brick wall but a rubber wall. So finally, silence had been the only answer, a resounding silence that echoed only inside her head. She needed to get away, far, far away among strangers and immerse herself totally in back breaking work. She needed to work day and night, to fill her mind with thoughts of others, to be so bone weary that the moment she finished with work she could crash into slumber land.

The village was the ideal place for a bruised mind and body to recoup. She enjoyed the simple meals, the *jowar* and *bajra ki roti* and pungent vegetable and dal. The women were shy and giggly but once she gained their confidence they opened their hearts to her. Almost every day Julie heard a horror story. Not fiction but cold, hard, true stories. Heart rending tales told with a voice devoid of all emotion or anger that made it all the more difficult to bear. While her blood boiled they spoke of their past woes with a *duppatta* or sari hiding half their faces; they spoke without anger; without envy, without hate, without bitterness; just a hollow tone of resignation and tiredness. They had seen many people come and go. Men and women in Kholapuri chappals, white Kurtas and toting a shaan bag or politicians exuding strong smells of aftershave lotion and women in handloom saris and shirts; they all came at periodic intervals, spoke to them at length, gave them some money or clothes, took photographs and vanished.

Their suffering continued.

Girl babies were strangled even by mothers themselves. Women were burnt or hacked to death by their own parents or siblings for daring to fall in love and marrying a man from another caste. Girls were branded and whipped or paraded naked. The unending saga of woes was depressing more so because there seemed to be no solution and no hope. Newspaper reporters and television crews came to interview them.

Their suffering continued

So how could they hope for anything from yet another visitor from the city? There were many worlds in this one world, each one revolving separately in its own specific orbit; all with blinkers on so that they could see but only one view, have but only one thought. There were some who got thrown out of the orbit sometime and went wheeling into space, free and wholesome while the others left behind tightened their reins and made the blinkers even bigger, convincing themselves that they were on the right path and the ones that broke away were outcasts. The downtrodden dragged the others even further down and some women themselves were the worst enemies of women.

More than a month after moving into her own hut in the village Julie felt nauseous. She put it down to the heat and the food. When it continued for a few days she became aware that she had not had her periods. Realization and panic set in almost together. An ingrained Catholic streak ruled out abortion. She struggled with her conscience and finally decided she would keep the baby. The thought of abortion though practical was tantamount to murder and she could not go through with it.

She had no one to turn to about the baby but Rajat and her friends. She knew that all her friends would advise her to abort but her mind was already made up. She invited Rajat to visit the village, to see its simplicity, the glorious sunsets, the clear sky, and the lilting songs of women bearing pots of water with the elegance of queens wearing tiaras. He said he was tempted but could take time off only after two months. She harped on her solitude, her empty hut and arms that longed to hold him. He said he knew exactly how she felt because he was a mirror image of her emotionally but wait they must. Finally she beseeched him to come to her aid without which she could well lose her sanity. The desperation in her message brought him scurrying to her side and seeing her hale and hearty, reprimanded her for calling him under false pretences.

Hundreds of tiny star like pale green flowers carpeted the grass under the huge *neem* tree. Rajat, who had been annoyed at being called urgently to the village, was relaxed and had begun to enjoy the mild and mellow sunshine, the chirpings of birds returning to their nests and the distant mooing of cows. The tight knots in his shoulders seemed to open up and clean air made him truly hungry for the first time in months.

Julie nestled against his shoulder loath to begin her story. "What if something terrible happened to me Rajat? Would you still be my friend?"

"Of course not. I will be your husband first."

"Stop quibbling. What if I had been raped?"

Rajat sat up with a jerk unsettling her head and making her tumble on to the grass. "What utter rubbish. Is this why you asked me to come all the way here? To test my love by asking me stupid questions?"

Julie sat up straight, her brown curly hair catching the rays of the setting sun turning it to burnished copper. Her hands were on her lap as she played with the silver ring, the ring that Rajat had slipped on her finger not so many years ago.

"No. Not to test your love. I have full faith and trust in you. I am not the same Julie you met the last time. Something devastating has happened that makes me doubt my own worthiness for you."

Her voice was filled with emotion as she recounted the night of the party, her eagerness to leave the party, her thirst that made her unwittingly drink up the whole glass of coke, her dizziness and blackout; her waking up to an odious reality; her tortuous walk back to her room; the mental and physical agony and the news of the death of her father.

Rajat sat stunned, unable to speak or move. He could not even move an arm to comfort her or hug her. His mind was suffused with the image of her limp form being ravaged by a faceless brute or brutes. Even the imaginary vision of the crime roused his anger to a feverish pitch.

He lunged forward to grasp her by the shoulders, gave her a little shake as he said hoarsely, "Why did you not tell me this earlier? We should have reported this to the police. Don't you remember even a little bit of his face or voice? Think hard Julie, just some hint and we will nail him."

"No Rajat. If I knew I would have complained at once. I do not know anything. But there is something even worse. I am pregnant. And before you say anything I am not going to abort it."

Rajat groaned as he put up a hand to his head. "There is nothing wrong about an abortion. You are a doctor. You should know" he pleaded.

They argued back and forth, although Rajat knew full well that once Julie made up her mind about anything no one could sway her. They walked back in silence as darkness draped the land and little lights flickered in the houses and huts, mimicking the ones in the sky. There was not a breath of air, the very clouds hung still in the sky. As they neared the houses there was a slight breeze as if nature had sighed at her self-imposed silence. Dinner was a quiet affair broken only by the scraping of the metal spoon in the bowl, some dogs howling and a cricket that trilled tirelessly.

As Rajat helped Julie clear the dishes he sighed "Let us work out the practical steps ahead."

Julie smiled her first brilliant smile in a long while, her eyes flashing merrily. She had misplaced her cheerfulness and Rajat had found it for her. Her dimples deepened as looked at him with love in her eyes. "Now you know why I needed you." She came over to give him a tight hug. "Tell me what to do".

"First of all we have to look for an auspicious day".
"To do what?"
"For us to get married".
Julie laughed out loud. "If that is a proposal it is the worst I have ever heard. Because you are not asking me, you are taking my "yes" for granted".
"Do you want me to go down on one knee?" he asked turning her around to face him.

"It is not a joke Rajat. The baby is not yours and God only knows whose it is. Do you think I am crazy to risk our happiness? It may be very heroic of you…."

"This is not heroism" he cut in, hurt and angry. "Proves how little you know me."

"If not heroism it is foolishness. I will always feel obliged to you and guilty as hell and as the years go by the sight of the child will be a constant reminder. The best of relations go wrong most of the time and ours will be built on shaky ground right from the start. It just will not work Rajat."

Rajat's counter arguments, entreaties and cajoling had no effect and they went to bed tired and confused. It took them two days to reach a compromise. Two days of studying various options and discarding each one of them. The night before Rajat was to leave they sought comfort in each other's arms and drowned all their fears and doubts in love. For the first time since the rape she let Rajat kiss her and touch her and she in turn responded warmly. They started with gentle overtures and gradually moved towards more passion until they culminated in a frenzy of pleasure. Their breathing came slowly down to normal and they rested in each other's arms, liquid languor flowing through their veins. They began to speak softly. The skeins of love tempered their thoughts and each understood the reason for the other's view.

Rajat agreed marriage could wait but that did not mean they had to be separate. He would tell his family and if they accepted their decision then Julie could stay with them in Coimbatore. Julie realized that in her delicate condition she did need the love and support of a family and she had no one on her side of the family except her step-mother who was not worth thinking about. She insisted she would get a job in Coimbatore and pay Rajat's parents for her upkeep. If in future, they were still in love and wanted to get married they would consider it. Till then they would be good friends.

"How about friends and lovers?" whispered Rajat, moving his hands gently over her body, stopping tantalizingly to stroke her. She moaned happily. "You mean live in sin?"

"Why not? Sin is in."

They snuggled comfortably, at peace that they had come to some sort of an agreement. Rajat would talk to his parents and let them get used to the idea. Julie would finish her commitments in the village in three months and move to Coimbatore to look for a job.

Sunita was quick to accept Julie but her husband Praful Varma was not too happy. It took him some time to come to terms with it all but Sunita without forcing his hand or pressuring him brought him around. By the time Julie made her way into the Varma household she was in her seventh month. Sunita forbid her to take up a job till the baby was born but Julie was lucky to get a job in a hospital not too far away and insisted on working till the last day. Always practical she planned to utilize the medical benefits and the facilities of the hospital for the child birth.

In mid December one night, Julie was jolted awake from her sleep by a mild spasm low down on her back. Her night dress felt wet. She called Sunita who immediately took charge. "Your water bag has burst. It is a mite too early and could make it dry for the baby. We better get to the hospital soon" she said as she put together the things that were needed. Julie cleaned herself and got into a loose caftan. Praful got up; his grey hair all messed up, looking quite bewildered. He had the car out and ready to go within a few minutes.

In spite of having mulled over this so many times Julie had a touch of panic. It was good to have sensible persons like Sunita and Praful around her. The little life within her had gone from being an "it" to "him or her". She had hated it for manifesting itself inside her, an uninvited guest she was forced to welcome. Now she thought of it as a baby with a face and limbs, little fingers and toes, a personality of its own.

She had to first go through the indignity of an enema and then the mortification of a nurse shaving her private parts talking all the while to her friend standing on the other side peering at her vagina. Did a person become a mannequin on entering a hospital- just a plastic model devoid of all feelings or thought? Were all patients treated like unfeeling objects? She felt a contraction coming on in the middle of it all and had to stop the nurse.

The pain knifed through her at periodic intervals. It started and rapidly grew worse and worse rising to a crescendo making her clutch the bed on both sides. Her eyes staring wide she bit her lips to stop screaming till Sunita told her not to restrain herself. Screaming might actually help. Julie, as a doctor knew all about childbirth but when she had to go through it herself she found she was just another woman in pain.

Julie was taken to the labour room at nine in the morning. It was a large bare room with four rectangular metal tables. She needed help to get on to the table. The metal felt cold through her thin hospital gown. How primitive thought Julie. It just proved that pregnancy and child birth was not considered a worthwhile cause for spending money. It was better than the clinic at the village but one would have thought a big hospital would have a better labour room.

There was a green oil cloth covering the lower half of the table. Julie was made to lie down and then the nurses left. Half an hour later a nurse came to take a peek at her between her legs and went away again. Pain ebbed and flowed but there was not much progress. Julie lost all track of time. She was on her back and soon knew every crack on the ceiling; every cobweb and spindly legged spider in the corners. Doctors, nurses, interns, all who came into the labour room stopped to look between Julie's legs without the least hesitation or embarrassment. She might just as well have been a lifeless toy. At least the women in the villages had more privacy.

Within five hours three women were brought into the labour room, howling and screaming. The wails and the curses ended in the first mewling cry of a baby and she would hear the nurse say "boy" or "girl" and the woman would say "oh" or "aah" accordingly. By seven in the evening there had been six deliveries while Julie still struggled with nothing to show for her effort. She dozed off in between. She was put on an IV drip for a while but the baby within her seemed to be in no hurry to come out and face the world.

It was late at night that the doctor decided to give her anesthesia and take the child out with the help of forceps. Julie floated into blissful, black velvety nothingness. When she regained consciousness she momentarily went blank. Nothing around her made any sense. Then slowly she remembered she was going to have a baby. Her voice came out all slurred over. "Baby. Baby" was all she could say.

"It is a girl. Lakshmi has entered into your house", smiled the dark girl with a mole on her left eyebrow. Julie's heart sank and a totally deep all pervading sadness enveloped her. It was a fleeting, bleak emotion, a bleakness that was so complete that she could feel it permeating every fiber of her being. It was not sadness because she had a girl baby. Perhaps it was something in the subconscious, a deep rooted thought in the dark recesses of the mind that grieved for the inevitable pain that was a woman's lot. There was no cogent reasoning that her daughter would have to go through all the pain she had just been through; or deal with marauding males, liars and cheats; be strong to withstand heartaches, betrayals and abuse; or cope with passive aggression, lecherous glances, harassment in many places in many ways just because an accident of birth had made her a girl. It was just a sense of deep depression without any solid reason that lasted a few intense moments and was gone as swiftly as it came.

Her gaze was riveted on the little baby all swaddled in soft cloth. Julie wished she had been conscious to see the baby as soon as she was born; she wanted to feel the baby emerging from her body, to see the separation of the child from the mother, the severing of the umbilical cord; to hear the first cry and feel the baby against her skin. She wanted to protect her from all harm and give her all the wisdom and strength to enjoy life to the full without giving in to despondency. But she also knew that her baby would depend on her only during her infancy and early years. As she grew up her daughter would make her own decisions, follow her heart and mind, ignore warnings, make her own assessment of people and places, commit mistakes and learn to live. Love had to be experienced firsthand and mistakes had to be made first hand too.

But for now, she is mine, all mine exulted Julie. Tired as she was, she found great joy gazing at the tiny little clenched fists and the pink toes. The baby was fair, with a mass of curly hair. Just like me she thought with great relief. It would have been so much more difficult if the baby had taken after the father whoever he was. What a joy creation was and how perfect? It was a miracle that manifested itself, almost effortlessly, thousands of times, every minute, all over the world, every day. A miracle of life that produced these small perfect babies that were equipped to grow into great thinkers, musicians, writers, doctors and spiritual leaders or become rapists, criminals and charlatans.

Sunita and Praful were ecstatic with the new born and Julie's eyes welled up when she saw the shawl of spontaneous love and care that enveloped her and her baby. Julie could not believe the myriad changes wrought by a newborn. Everything in the house revolved around the baby. The helpless little bundle commanded and controlled every move in the house by day and at night. Smiles bloomed readily on faces just looking at the baby. Rajat made as many visits as he could and was a natural with the little girl. He would carry her, feed her and make her coo and gurgle. It was as if they shared a special relationship.

The first three months were the most difficult as well as the most delectable. The total helplessness of the child made her even more precious. Just holding the infant in her arms was enough to send a surge of love all through her. Bringing her to her breasts and watching her suckle suffused her with an unbelievable happiness born of giving herself totally and unconditionally.

Each week she could see a change, a growth, an awareness that filled her with awe. The eyes had to learn to focus, the hands and feet started pumping; the head grew steadier; folds and creases filled out with firm plumpness and the baby began to recognize her mother's touch and voice very early. Julie just had to talk to her or call her to make her stop crying. It gave Julie a sense of being loved and needed just for herself – something she had never felt so strongly before. She had found love in Rajat and his family but this was love from her own blood, something that had been denied to her all these years. The void she had nursed at the loss of her mother was in a way filled by being a mother herself. The baby's struggle to produce its first sound was followed soon after by the nonstop cooing and gurgling that was so fascinating.

She was a happy baby, a charmer, who smiled at everyone. Her eyes were a darkish brown that gradually became a lighter brown that were always sparkling and full of life. By the time she was three months she already had a huge circle of friends and admirers. The neighbours, their children and Rajat's relatives could not resist playing with her. She spread such an aura of love and happiness that no one paused to think of or question her origin. She was a striking likeness of her mother - but a much more beautiful version said Julie proudly. Rajat filled the place of the father and insisted on teaching the baby to call him "daddy".

Laughter and sweetness followed her wherever she went. They named her Madhuri.

Babli

London: 1985

Babli sat still for a few minutes before going to the kitchen and getting a glass of cold water. Holding the glass in her hands steadied her nerves and sipping the water gave her a sense of normalcy.

Mandakini's call from Delhi had been unexpected and she had managed to fob her off. Obviously it was not just a casual phone call. Manda seemed to be probing – for what?

Babli had been very distraught when Kunal told her he was going to India. She wanted to go with him and had met with a flat refusal. At least this time he had told her about his trip. On earlier occasions when he went on a so called tour she had found out by chance that he was actually visiting India. Why was he lying? Of course his whole life was a lie. He had begun the very first moment of their married life with a lie.

Her first day in London had been a grey day, one of many grey days in a grey life. The city was very much as she had pictured it from viewing English movies. Having read books or watched movies she had a sense of deja vue when she saw Piccadilly, Trafalgar Square, Buckingham Palace and Bakers Street. The row upon row of similar looking houses with white lace curtains, brickwork and little window boxes were charming.

Kunal and Babli had arrived at an unspoken understanding. Each realized that the other had accepted the situation temporarily and the only way to survive was to be pleasant to each other. There was no point moping around or shouting at each other. Babli for all her traditional background was a practical girl. She could not rely on Kunal all the time and she had to be independent.

The very next day after their arrival she said "Can you take me out on the tube please".

"Sure. What is the hurry?"

"I want to be free to go out on my own. I do not want to hang around waiting for you".

Kunal brought her the colour coded guide maps and in no time at all Babli got to know the routes.

She could hop on and off for changing trains to different destinations. The first question Kunal asked when he came home from work was "where did you go today"? And she took great pride in showing him how independent she could be. If he had any doubt that she would be a burden and a clinging vine she proved in a couple of days that she did not need him around at all. She loved to roam around on her own, browse at flea markets and listen to the buskers. It stirred her to hear strains of sweet music float from the belly of the dank underground. She was at times a very appreciative audience of one while most people walked past briskly.

She spent time window shopping, looking at items that were way beyond her reach. More often she would be looking at reflections of people walking behind her and not at the merchandise inside. This way she could stare at the people and yet not be obvious. Coming from a land of vibrant colours she was surprised at the predominantly black, grey and brown colours that the British chose to wear. An occasional splash of red or blue was all that brightened the overall image of grays and browns against the background of a city that was also mostly grey. Adorned by even small earrings and a bindi she felt like a Christmas tree in her bright salwar kameez.

She was thrilled with their house in Wembly, so compact and so comfortable. The kitchen was small with all the conveniences close at hand. Every little thing fascinated her. The pretty patterned paper towels, the oven, the little niche with scissors and gloves and small pans hanging from a row of hooks. At first she was stingy with the paper towels, reluctant to use them and throw them away.

There was one bedroom, a living room and a study with a couch. Kunal took the study and gave her the bedroom. They lived like friends, civil to each other. Kunal ensured that she was well provided for with whatever she wanted and Babli took care of the house and made sure that he had a hot Indian meal when he was at home.

Living in Wembly was a bit like living in a little India. In fact, the white faces were the foreigners in a sea of brown, black or yellow ones. There were many restaurants that served Indian food and plenty of vegetable and fruits shops. Babli immediately took charge of the house. One would have not known that this was her first trip away from an Indian city. Her practical attitude and her organized approach combined with her childlike curiosity and naïveté was a pleasure to watch and intrigued Kunal.

Some days he would say casually, just as he was leaving, "I will not be back for a couple of days. Need to go out". If he expected a show of anger or curiosity he was disappointed. Her silence and quiet acceptance shrouded her displeasure and anger as she replied, "That's ok. Let me know if you are going to stay away longer."

How could she be so cool? He knew that she knew his absences meant he was with the other woman but apart from a studied cold silence for a few hours after his return she refrained from questioning him or quarrelling with him. Wonder when she will react. Looked vulnerable but was really stronger - there was more to her than she revealed. In spite of himself he was stirred by a curiosity to know her better. Kunal tried to be at home on weekends and took her out to the Tower of London, Madame Tassauds or the Kew Gardens.

May be it was her Indian mentality she thought whimsically. Indian women were more accustomed to the idea of a man having two women and running two establishments. Some even had two wives living together in the same house. There was a very famous dancer who lived with both his wives most amicably in the same house and a well known political leader who had two wives in full public knowledge and perhaps more in private. Most Indian TV serials aired the same theme of one man with two wives.

Her calls home were very regular - once a week on Sunday mornings that were Sunday afternoons in India. She usually spoke to her mother at length and briefly with her father. She wanted to know each little detail of their life in India right down to what the neighbours were doing, whom they had visited and what they were wearing when they were speaking to her. She wanted to bring in the breath of India to her cold life in London. She was normal and cheerful most of the time but could not help breaking down and crying now and then which was all put down to homesickness.

It was just after their first wedding anniversary – an anniversary that they both ignored. Babli was setting out their dinner on two trays that they carried to the couch in front of the television. It was easier that way. They did not have to face each other across a table and make small talk. The TV filled the emptiness between them.

"I have got a job at Marks and Spencer's", she said.
"What was the need for that? Don't I earn enough for the both of us?"
"I get bored at home."
"You will soon get bored there too."
"Let's see. Anyway I have accepted and there is nothing you can do about it."
"Have I stopped you from doing anything so far?"

She shook her head. "What do you care anyway? I will be home before you arrive so it does not matter."

"Guess not" he mumbled.

She would rather he shouted at her or fought with her. This compliance, this indifference was what irked her more because it meant they did not mean anything to each other.

He looked at her when she set off for work looking pretty, her pert figure clad in western dresses. Kunal could not help noticing the changes in her appearance and attitude. In fact it had all worked out better than he imagined because there were no tantrums or fights at home, just some caustic comments and occasional coldness.

Contrary to what he had expected it was Patricia, his British mistress who was crotchety.

She kept nagging him to spend more time with her although he was actually giving her more attention after marrying Babli than before. He felt guilty in the presence of both women and tried to make it up to them. It was taking a heavy toll on him.

The two women were as different as chalk and cheese. Patricia was fiercely independent and aggressive in behaviour but inwardly insecure and manipulative. Babli under her gentle demeanor had a strong mind of her own, brutally honest and with a quiet courage.

What irritated Kunal most about Babli was her cheerfulness. How could a woman who had been treated so badly remain pleasant and amiable to the one person who had ruined her whole life? Was this just a ploy to make him feel guilty? Her docility initially made him angry and provoked him to be curt with her. Gradually by the end of the second year the irritation turned to grudging respect. Almost imperceptibly and unthinkingly Kunal caught himself helping Babli at home and doing her shopping for her, surprising himself and her at the same time.

By the third year of their marriage his absences from home came down to twice a week and then to just once a week. He began to look forward to their weekend trips and enjoyed revisiting all the tourist spots he had been to before and looking at everything through Babli's eyes. She made a humdrum boat ride more exciting. She spotted little charming details that he had overlooked altogether. Strangers and fellow companions on bus tours struck up conversations with her and she responded with warmth.

He could not believe that they had been married for three years. Although they had not consummated their marriage they had been living together under one roof as husband and wife in name if not in fact.

As they had both deliberately ignored their earlier anniversaries he decided to celebrate their third year. He bought her an expensive diamond ring - for appearances sake he told himself. Why then did he feel so much pleasure in buying it for her? Why was he so excited when he thought of how he would give it to her? Why was he so nervous and jittery that she might not accept it?

On the morning of their anniversary as they sat down at the breakfast table Babli surprised him by wishing him and giving him a gift. He held it rather awkwardly when she said "Open it. Just now. See if you like it." The smile and eagerness on her face was very touching. So maybe she did not think of their wedding day as a black day after all.

He opened it with some misgiving. What if it was something he did not like and he had to make the right noises? His little cry of pleasure was all the more convincing because it was genuine. Wrapped in white tissue paper was a beautiful Italian leather wallet and leather bound diary. It was obviously an expensive gift and she must have saved up for it from her salary. It was thoughtful of her to have noticed that his wallet was worn out and he needed a new one. His gruff "thank you" fogged by emotion came out sounding rather abrupt and he saw the apprehensive look on her face. He longed to take her in his arms but held back.

"I really needed this and you have chosen just the right size" he smiled and was relieved to see the clouds lift from her face.

"I have something for you too" he said taking out the small gift wrapped square box. She took it with an excited smile and tore open the paper. She looked upon the burgundy velvet box, caressed it lightly and then opened it very gently. Her eyes grew wide and her full lips were slightly parted in surprise. Wonder what it would be like to kiss those lips he thought. Her silence made him panic. Maybe she did not like diamonds. Most girls did but he knew there were some who were averse to diamonds and preferred pearls or rubies. Or may be a ring was the wrong thing to give when they were not really living as husband and wife. It stood for intimacy and love both of which were undeclared or nonexistent.

When she did look up he saw her eyes glistening with unshed tears. "Oh it is so beautiful" she whispered. "Will you put it on for me please?" He stood rooted to the ground for a minute and then hurried to her side in case she mistook his hesitation for reluctance. He took the box from her grasp and lifted the ring out. As she held out her hand he gazed at the smooth fairness and the beautifully shaped fingers with mauve pink nails. He took her hand in his and felt the warmth and softness rest like a little bird in his clasp. He felt her hand tremble a little before steadying itself. Her closeness and her lavender fragrance almost broke his resolution but he quickly controlled himself and taking the ring he slipped it onto her ring finger mentally sighing in gratitude that it was the right size. He held her hand for just a moment admiring the way the ring was set off by her complexion. Then before she could withdraw her hand he quickly brought it up, pressed it to his lips and just as quickly turned away.

Left alone, Babli continued to gaze at her ring and wondered at their complex relationship. She sensed his affection and attraction. Something he would never admit to himself. Not a single day had he forced himself on her. She could sense a struggle within him, something or someone who was pressurizing him to act the way he was. Where had he got the money for such an expensive ring? He had always been generous with his money – far beyond the norm of a doctor's salary.

Suspicion was her constant companion. She was always watching for the slightest trace, a hint, and a suggestion of guilt or an intimation of anything illegal. He did not let slip even a word or look that could be termed suspicious. It was as if he had a clean conscience without a shadow of doubt.

Lulled by his amiable ways, his respect and consideration for her, she wondered if she was being unduly paranoid.

They continued to exchange gifts on birthdays and anniversaries but it was more a matter of form. She wondered if he had regretted the slight show of emotion on that one occasion. He obviously did not want her to read too much into that one episode. And if, momentarily her hopes had been raised that was her fault. There were odd moments of closeness like the time he had fallen ill with flu and she had taken care of him, sitting by his side all night or the day she had a fall and sprained an ankle and needed medical attention. He had held her up and supported her to the car and on to the hospital. He had tried to help her at home and stayed back a couple of days till she was able to hobble around.

They were now in the fifth year of marriage, settled into a companionable existence. They even joked about it at times saying that theirs was a model marriage without any ego trips on either side and the clear cut agreement between them made it a good working relationship. Now and then Babli would toy with the idea of raising the topic of a divorce but put it off as she saw no sense in destroying the happiness of her parents especially when she had no other man in mind.

Babli had got used to Kunal's week long trips. Although she had dealt with Mandakini's probing questions, Babli's doubts came back with renewed force. She spent sleepless nights when he was away and there was something in his demeanour that made her uneasy. He had been away for nearly a week and was scheduled to return the day before. It was possible he had gone directly to be with Patricia but he usually came home first.

She called the hospital asking for Dr. Kunal and was surprised to hear that he had returned from his tour but had extended his leave by four days. If he was in London why had he not come home? Why was his study always locked when he was not at home? She had respected his privacy long enough. Now she had to know. She decided to look into his room at any cost. She called a locksmith urgently. She had lost the key she said and there were important documents that were needed immediately.

He was a small wiry man with a tool kit and took just five minutes to open the study. The moment he left she hurried to the room. She paused a moment before stepping inside. This was a big decision and she knew that he would be very angry. Well, now she would just have to deal with it.

She looked at the desk that had a photograph of a five year old Kunal leaning against his mother. There was such a difference between the serious Kunal now and the little boy with an impish expression in the photo that it brought a smile to her lips.

She spotted a key half hidden under a folder on the table. She hesitated a moment again. They were getting along well and she could see the small changes in him and his attitude towards her. Where was the need to rock the boat? Her hand inched towards the key and taking it, she inserted it into the drawer below.

There was an address book, a note pad, some pens and visiting cards. She took out everything and felt around inside. She was just about to put everything back when she felt a small protrusion at the back. A slight pressure made the false bottom come up. It slid smoothly back revealing more space for papers. It was neatly divided into two segments. The right side held cheque books and deposit slips, tabulated figures, a bunch of lists with names, list of flight timings with some flights highlighted.

The left side had contact details of one British doctor and two Indian doctors. There were small photographs clipped to two sheets of information about the doctors. Another note had the names and profiles of some regional Indian politicians, from UP and Bihar.

Babli's blood ran cold as she read each sheet of paper. Kunal was involved in some way in smuggling of drugs as well as arranging kidney donors from India. The drugs were brought into the UK packed into capsules or in tablet form as part of prescription drugs and were routed through Kunal and a few other doctors. He was also one of the go betweens, the middle man for arranging the supply of kidneys to foreigners.

There were records of his trips to India, names of donors in UP and Bihar. He had probably got very good money for his services. The list of foreign recipients' names and dates recorded their visits to India ostensibly as tourists. Babli could imagine the rest. The "tourist" would contact a specified surgeon and get a new kidney for a price that was enough to line the nests of the doctor and the middle man. The donor collected the remainder of the price but would be short of a kidney for the rest of his life.

Kunal had obviously kept these records to be used against the criminals if he was threatened but in doing so he had placed himself in a very vulnerable position. If they had the faintest inkling of the proof he had accumulated he would be killed. Babli quickly noted down most of the relevant names and numbers on a separate sheet of paper, took it to her room, folded it and pushed it right to the back of the drawer that held all her negligee. She put back all the documents in exactly the same way as it had been and left the key in exactly the same position. All the while her mind was a cauldron of thoughts, bubbling and boiling with all the bits of information she had stumbled upon. One false move and she knew that their lives would be at risk. Kunal was only a cog in the wheel. Many big names would be involved. She quaked at the knowledge of her husband's deceit and criminal activities.

She could think of nothing else the whole day. She barely slept that night and when she did she dreamt of prisons and men chasing her with scalpels. Kunal did not come back the next day or the next. She did not dare complain or inform the police and kept praying he would turn up alive. On the fourth day she was at the end of her tether. She called his hospital.

"May I speak to Dr. Kunal please?"

She was put on hold to listen to some music.

"I am afraid Dr. Kunal is not available."

"Can you tell me when he will be in?"

"He had taken leave for four days. So he should be back tomorrow."

Babli was sure he could not have taken leave. She knew him well enough to realize that he would have come home if he had returned to India. Somebody had informed the hospital that he would not be coming for the next four days. Did that mean that he was being kept against his will?

She had not been able to eat or drink very much for the past three days and forced herself to have some toast and soup. It was almost 10 at night and she was turning on the television when she heard the sound of a car stop at the house and a thud of something being thrown out. She heard the car roar away and waited. She moved very slowly and softly. She stood still near the door, her ears straining for the faintest of sounds.

After few minutes she heard a shuffling noise. Her heart beating wildly she put her ear against the door. She thought she could hear a soft groan. She steeled herself, grabbed the knob and turned it ever so slowly without making any noise. She eased the door gently back, mentally thanking her stars for oiling the door a few days ago.

Opening the door she choked back a scream as she saw Kunal's limp form fall against her legs. He had been propping himself on the door and fell in as she opened it. He had crawled the few yards up to the house. She looked around and fortunately there were no neighbours outside.

She opened the door wide and bent down to see where he was hurt and bleeding.

She hooked her hands under his shoulders, dragged him in with all her might and closed the door. She brought a sheet, managed to pull him on to it and then holding on to the corners of the sheet dragged him into the bedroom. He opened his eyes, his lips moved and she thought she heard her name before his eyes closed again. She got warm water, poured some antibacterial liquid into it and dipped a soft hand towel, wrung out the water and began to clean him gently. She had to change the water at least six times before he was clean. She had to strip him completely and check every inch of him to see where he had been wounded.

He had a cut on his cheek and he had been bleeding profusely from his nose. She recalled hearing that a nose bleed always looked much worse than it was. He had purple bruises all over his torso and hips where he had been kicked or beaten savagely. He had a long slash on one leg as if he had scraped it against a sharp metal and a couple of gashes on his arms and chest but it did not look deep enough for stitches. In fact after cleaning him up he looked much better. He also had a lump on his head as if he had been hit hard with a blunt instrument. It was probably weakness and starvation that made him so faint. He kept opening his eyes and closing them again.

She bandaged him as well as she could and dressed him in a soft shirt and pyjama. She had been his wife for so many years and yet this was the first time she had seen him completely naked. He was a well knit man, not really rippling with muscles but firm and strong. His stomach was as flat as a washboard and she could feel the hardness under the skin. His hands and legs showed evidence of having been worked out. He probably went to a gym regularly from his office. That was something she had not known. There was so much she did not know about him and she had to tread warily. She sensed that both their lives were in danger.

She cleaned the blood stains on the floor and fixed herself a couple of sandwiches as she realized she was starving. She had not had a proper meal in four days. Now that she knew Kunal was alive she felt alive too. She forced some brandy with warm water down his throat that made him open his eyes and mutter incoherently. She made him swallow a pain killer before he fell back limply on the pillow. She watched over him till dawn when he came awake slowly. He struggled to get up and in a few moments he managed to sit up.

"Shall I call for a doctor?"

"No way. That is the one thing we should avoid". His voice was hoarse and he winced in pain as he spoke through cut and swollen lips. One eye was almost completely shut.

"Should I call an Indian doctor - may be one of your friends?"
He shook his head "No. No. I just need to rest."

He closed his eyes and opened them again after a while. "I can look after myself. I am sorry you had to change all my clothes."

"You mean sorry I saw you stark naked?" She could not resist teasing him. "Don't worry. You looked good" she added as he groaned in utter mortification.

"But I think you should still see a doctor – in case there are any internal injuries."

"Of course I have. It is all in my head". He tried to smile and sank back into a stupor again.

She left him alone after that but was glad when he recovered enough to ask for water and food in another couple of hours. She did not ask him anything about what had happened knowing he would tell her when he was ready. He, in turn would be on the brink of telling her something, open his mouth and change his mind. Both of them wanted to come clean but neither knew how to begin.

He slept a drug induced sleep for one whole day and recovered enough to sit up and walk on the third day but not without wincing at each step. He sat at the dining table nursing a cup of coffee in his hands. She got herself another cup and sat down facing him.

She took a deep breath. She was tired of playing games. "I opened your room and found your key on the table."

He looked up startled as she continued, "I opened the drawer. I have no right to ask you and there is no way I can make you listen to me. But I am legally your wife; I have left my family and have been with you for five years now. I have to know everything."

"It is enough that I am in danger. I do not want to risk your life as well."

"After what happened to you last week I am not safe anyway. Whoever dumped you at the door step knows that I am here and I am equally vulnerable".

Kunal sighed and sat quietly for a while marshalling his thoughts. He was impressed with Babli's courage and honesty. Not only had she put in a stellar role as his wife and had had the gumption to open the room; she had also digested the shocking revelations and now faced him resolutely with hints of an unspoken support. She was a truly remarkable woman and deserved to know the whole truth. He took a deep breath and started from the very beginning.

"It was nearly 10 years ago. I finished my MBBS from Calcutta and came here to specialize in surgery, organ transplants. It was a difficult time. I got a small stipend here and some money every month from home. I took a room in one of the cheaper localities.

"It was bitterly cold. The damp walls made it worse. I longed for the warmth of the Indian sun. I do not remember ever having a good meal. I would stave off the gnawing hunger by nibbling at biscuits or suck a small piece of chocolate or toffee for a long time. The money from home and the stipend just about covered my expenses and whatever I could save from that was used up in the first 20 days of the month. The rest of the month I survived on scraps. There is no one poorer than a middle class Indian abroad. A princely sum in rupees shrunk to a few meager pounds and shillings after conversion.

"The only consolation was that I was a good doctor, quick to learn and made some friends. It was December. Money from home came in very late that month and I had caught the flu as well. All alone, I was in bed for a whole day with very high fever swallowing medicines brought from India. When the fever abated slightly I ventured out to get something to eat, not realizing that the lack of food and the fever had made me so very weak.

"A few yards from the house I must have fainted. I do not know for how long and what happened. Next thing I knew I was in a bed that was not my own. A woman, who happened to be passing by, had taken me in. Not many care to bring in people off the streets. If Patricia had not nursed me back to health I doubt if I would have lasted long in the sleet and ice. I was too ill to be moved out of the house where Pat lived with her brother, Jason.

"She was by my side all the time when I had a raging fever for a week. I was grateful for the warmth of a clean house, simple but wholesome food and the easy camaraderie. I learnt that their parents had been killed in a car accident when they were still young and both had grown up with foster parents. Although they were together with one foster family for two years they had to be separated when Jason was sent to live with another couple. Brother and sister were traumatized by the separation and as soon as they were majors they both took up jobs and moved in together.

"I admired their courage and determination in not only surviving a difficult childhood but having also found stability and security in the adult world. I found Patricia attractive and it was almost a very natural development to move from being friends to lovers. Jason worked for a courier firm and was doing very well indeed. He had money to spare for a bit of luxury now and then, a bottle of wine, a slap up dinner in a good restaurant and a small trip to nearby places.

We made a very compatible threesome and the little amount of money that I gave them was enough to cover my costs.

Kunal paused to sip at his coffee and remained lost in thought for a while. Perhaps thinking of his happy days with Patricia thought Babli with a stab of jealousy.

"One day Jason asked me to drop off a parcel at a house in a posh area and promptly paid me handsomely for my services despite my protests. The money did not come from his pocket he said. They were short staffed and they needed reliable people. If I was happy to do some job now and then whenever I was free, I could earn some extra money.

"In the first year I had done just five errands when Jason asked me if I was willing to do it on a regular basis, with occasional trips outside London. I agreed as long as it did not interfere with my duties at the hospital. A year down the line I was comfortably ensconced in a satisfying job at the hospital and a laid back relationship with Patricia. I told Jason I wanted to stop his deliveries as I wanted to put in more time at the hospital and take on extra work load.

"That was when I got a rude shock. I was astounded to learn that Jason was dealing in drugs and all the deliveries had been varieties of drugs. They had photographs of me handing over parcels to various people and some of them were wanted by the police. Jason's boss, a suave British gentleman, "offered" me another alternative. All I had to do was to use my influence and knowledge as a doctor and an Indian to line up kidney donors and doctors who would do the transplant surgery in India. Once I had set up a donor, the patient would travel to India as a tourist, contact the doctor, get the transplant done, recoup in a good tourist spot and return home hale and hearty. There was big money in this and I would get my due. It was not really a crime he said. I would be giving life to people who would die waiting for a transplant and would be doing my duty as a doctor. If I refused, I could either land up in jail or dead."

It was getting quite dark outside. Babli sighed as she got up to pull the curtains and switched on some subdued lights. She took a couple of glasses of milk and cookies and went back to the table. They sat quietly for a few minutes, sipping the milk and munching the cookies. She waited for him to resume his story at his own pace.

Kunal reached out and gently stroked her hand. "That was about the time my father had a heart attack and I had to come to India. My parents insisted on my getting married and I met you." Babli waited just a few moments before pulling her hand away.

"After my return from India, Jason made me meet his boss again and this time I was threatened. Do the job or face death he said - alone or with my bride. I was caught in a bind. I had to deal with my father's health; the threat of death; committing a huge crime and the prospect of marrying an innocent girl under false pretences and putting her life also at risk.

"That was the beginning of long years of lying and cheating. I led two parallel lives. I was a successful doctor in a hospital of repute, healed people; brought joy to families and that was a reward in itself. I made more than enough money for my bread and butter.

"I brought together donors and patients for kidney transplants, and assuaged my conscience that the donor got money that was very much needed and the patient got his health back. The earning from this got me jam and cheese to supplement my bread and butter. And an occasional diamond ring." His lips broke into a self-deprecatory smile while his eyes pleaded for understanding.

"During my last visit to India I met up with a friend in the Ministry of External Affairs at a party hosted by an old college mate. I explored the possibility of coming back to India in a bid to distance myself from London. You see

I had already begun to love you Babli and wanted to keep you safe." Babli looked up into his eyes and quickly lowered them again. Could she believe all that he said?

"But somehow the people in London became suspicious and the beating was part of a threat to keep me quiet, a warning that if I tried anything against them, death was definite".

Babli sat still, numb with fear. "If you leave them they will kill you. And me. We have to go to the police. Maybe they can give us witness protection. If you turn approver you may get off lightly and we can move to a safer place later."

"That only happens in the movies Babli. It is not so simple in real life. Death is almost certain, sooner or later. I want you safe. I do not care what happens to me".

"How can you even think of such a thing?" Babli's voice rang out with clear conviction. "I have sworn by the holy fire to be by your side till the very end. We began on a bad note and we may be husband and wife in name only but these five years do have some meaning. We have become friends and that counts for something, for me definitely and maybe for you as well."

Kunal reached across to take her hand. "I want to make amends Babli. More than that, I have so much to say to you before it is too late. I think we have wasted too much time already. I do not expect to be alive very much longer. Even if I play along with them they know that my heart is not in this. It is a matter of time. I am a weak link in their organization and I have to be eliminated. I can give you a divorce and you can go back home. Although even then they may get rid of you as well just in case you know anything."

"I will not go back to India and I do not want a divorce" she said firmly, "I will fight you tooth and nail in court". Kunal laughed out loud at the expression on her face and the fervor in her voice. He came over to her side, held both her hands and lifted her up. They were standing very close, staring into each other's eyes.

It seemed an eternity to Kunal as held his breath, afraid that the least movement would send her running back behind the invisible curtain that separated them. He gently leaned forward and drew her closer and brought his lips closer to hers. He saw her half close her eyes and encouraged that he was on the right track he kissed his bride for the first time. Her arms came up to stroke his head and moved down his neck. He felt a thrill go through his whole body and as her hands moved across his shoulder he winced in pain as she touched a bruise. She sensed it and lightened her touch. Her lips murmured sorry as she continued to kiss him. They spoke through their kisses as he led her to the bedroom.

Their lovemaking was leisurely and caring. Much later, spent and happy they both lay still, reluctant to move and break the magic they had woven together. Their limbs fitted very comfortably against each other; an extension of each other. Patricia was taller and big boned and her elbows and knees would dig into him. Babli fitted him perfectly, her soft rounded curves touching him with a soothing caress. He had been a complete idiot. And now time was running short. The thought of anything happening to Babli filled him with horror. He had to do something, anything to keep her safe.

He took the week off and spent all the time with Babli. This was their real honeymoon. They had to learn so much about each other after so many years. He wanted to hear about her childhood and her life, every memory, every incident. He heard all about Mandakini's house which played such a huge role in Babli's early years and about the lives of her three best friends.

She told him about their dreams; Padma's elopement and her depraved lover; her disillusionment and escape; she spoke of Julie's well spring of cheerfulness in spite of a very unhappy childhood and the horrifying rape that had put an end to all her dreams of a marriage to the man she loved; and finally she spoke at length of Mandakini, the leader of the gang, who carried deep rooted scars from an ordeal she refused to divulge. Strong, independent and courageous Mandakini would know what to do to save them. Kunal who had met her friends briefly understood how much Babli had relied on them. Although they had not visited each other very frequently they had all kept in touch with each other, with their families and mutual friends. There was a strong bond between them, a tacit understanding that they were all there for each other.

Desperate to save Babli, Kunal decided to visit India one last time. He had to find somebody truly reliable who could help them get out of this mess. His school friend in the Ministry of External Affairs might be able to give them protection and find a way of getting them back to India. He would risk his life if he could ensure Babli's safety. When Kunal said he was going to India for a week, she begged him to stay but he in turn was adamant. This would be his last tour he said. It will all be over soon.

When she could not stop him from going to India she decided to seek Mandakini's help. She would know someone in London, may be a foreign correspondent of her newspaper posted in London, who could help them. She dared not talk to Mandakini on the phone for fear of the phone being tapped.

As soon as Kunal left for the hospital, Babli took out a few sheets of paper and started writing to Mandakini. She poured out her heart and gave her all the details, chapter and verse. She took out the list of names and numbers she had copied from Kunal's blue book and put it along with her letter. Suddenly, she realized that she had not told Kunal about copying down these details. He would be angry but he would understand.

Having written and posted it she felt very much lighter and relieved. The letter would take at least six working days to reach Mandakini. Kunal was planning his India trip only three weeks later. Enough time for Mandakini to come up with a solution.

Mandakini

Delhi: 1986

Mandakini opened her eyes slightly, groaned and quickly closed them again. The throbbing in the head was the only reality in a world that was pitch dark. The hammering inside her skull pulsated with every heart beat. She tried to move and that hurt even more. Her hands and feet were tied up and her shoulders ached. She wondered where she was and reluctantly opened her eyes again. She was disoriented, not knowing if it was day or night. It could be either twilight or just before dawn. She could not say for sure with the curtains drawn. She was in a room but it was not her room. It felt strange to be in a place she could not identify at a time she could not verify.

She closed her eyes and tried to remember where she was. She drifted in and out of consciousness in a strange dreamy way. Her mind was absolutely blank as if a slate had been wiped completely clean. She had lost all track of time. She could hear cars passing by outside and then suddenly just as she heard a door bang shut her memory came surging back.

It had all begun with Babli's letter. It was an express package and she had kept it aside and taken it home with her to read at leisure. She was delayed at work so by the time she sat down with the letter it was past nine at night. She was appalled to learn that Kunal was in deep trouble, involved in a crime of vast dimensions run by ruthless people in high places. Babli made it very clear that whatever Kunal had done earlier he was willing to go to any lengths now to save himself and Babli. But he was completely mired in the criminal network and Babli feared for his life. Mandakini had looked at the neat list of names and numbers written out in Babli's hand and realized that if these people had even the tiniest inkling that she had access to this information, Babli's life and her own would have no value.

Mandakini had thought of going to the police but immediately swept the idea aside knowing it would not help. Considering that the regional politicians involved wielded great clout and being fully aware of the nexus between politicians and police she knew she had to do something on her own.

She began her investigations the very next day. She began investigating the two doctors on Babli's list. One of them, Dr. Agarwal, was based in Delhi and quite well known. He featured in press photographs of social events and charity functions. Further probing revealed that he had acquired two farm houses and lived in a luxury apartment in the city. His life style was way beyond the affordability of doctors. He was on the board of a charitable organization that collected donations from the wealthy corporate leaders as well as political parties. Some of the money was spent on charity work accompanied by much publicity but the lion's share went into a trust. Mandakini suspected that he had an untraceable account where he could siphon off the money. She also found that he made at least two to three trips a month to Lucknow.

Very soon after, she went to Lucknow where she met her old friend, Surinder. He was the regional correspondent, who had done a special story on female feticide recently.

"What are you working on now?" she asked.

"A land scam" said Surinder. "It involves some politicians and I am beginning to feel the heat. Just when I think I am getting closer to something I hit a road block. What are you up to?"

"Officially I have some interviews set up but unofficially I am looking at the organ racket – kidneys in particular."

"I would tread carefully", cautioned Surinder. "I have heard bits and pieces and the network is quite big. There have been two deaths recently. One, a doctor who is said to have committed suicide but I very much doubt it and a sub inspector who was found stabbed to death. Finish your interview and get back. Forget about unofficial work."

"You are holding out on something. Come on. Tell me." insisted Mandakini.

Reluctantly and after much persuasion Surinder said "There is a chap, Chandu Ram, who is a wheeler dealer and fixer. He is a petty criminal really but his brother seems to have been a donor. Unfortunately, he died on the operating table – some complication or negligence and the doctor was Agarwal. It was all hushed up and the death was passed off as an accident. Of course money must have been paid to the family. The police were in on it too as the body was presumably found on the road and the autopsy confirmed it as a hit and run.

"Chandu came to me and has been pestering me to do something. I do not want to get into it. I have a family and kids but I know that there is more to it than meets the eye. Two days ago Chandu's wife and daughter have disappeared. Read kidnapped. But strangely enough he has not filed a complaint nor pressed charges against anyone. If you contact him you might get some lead but you will also get into deep trouble."

"Well. I am in trouble already or rather one of my good friends is. I have to follow this up come what may."

Surinder sighed. ""You always were an idiot. Go to the chai shop opposite St. Fidelis College around 5.30pm and look out for Chandu Ram –a muscular chap with a large mustache. You cannot miss him. But keep me out of it. I would rather play safe. You should too if you had any sense."

Mandakini was at the bus stop near the tea shop by 5pm. She watched people come and go before strolling across to the shop a little before 5.30. She ordered tea and began sipping it slowly. It was nearly quarter to six when she saw Chandu Ram walk up. He chatted up the owner for a while before going to a table right at corner, his back to the shop. She waited a few minutes and then stood up and walked over to his table and sat down facing him and her back to the road and other customers. She caught the owner of the shop look at her furtively and glanced away.

Chandu looked at her and spoke in Hindi. "The seat is taken. Sit somewhere else".

Mandakini let him have a glimpse of the 500 rupee note in her hand as she replied, "This will take only two minutes.

I need a kidney urgently. Just give me the name and I will go away."

"What makes you think I will do what you ask?"

"Because if not you will be in big trouble. I am a journalist and I can make up a news report about you. Everyone believes what is in the papers. Even if it is proved wrong, the damage will be done."

"Who gave you my name?" he was surly and slightly apprehensive.

"Someone in Delhi. How does that matter."

"It does matter. Now get out. I am already in danger if I am seen talking to a stranger."

"Let us meet somewhere else. I promise I will make it worth your while. I may even get your family back."

He looked startled and stared at her. "No one can do that."

"If you can help me, I will try. It may take time but ..." she shrugged her shoulders.

He thought for a moment and then said "Come to the lane behind the College at 8 tonight. And bring 5000 with you. Now just go" he growled.

Mandakini stood up mumbling "I will be there."

The lane was narrow and dark. The rear of the houses opened on to the lane on both sides and only some houses had lights at the back. Mandakini stood in between two back doors her dupatta covering her head and part of her face. She saw a figure entering from the other end and kept her gaze lowered till he came near.

"First give me the money" he murmured.

She hurriedly gave him the envelope as he quickly thrust a folded piece of paper into her hand.

After a moment's hesitation he said, "If you breathe a word about me I will die and so will you. They have no heart. If you can help me get my family back I will give you enough information to nail them. Meet me here one week later – same time."

Mandakini did not wait to see him scurry down the lane. She quickly turned around and walked the other way thrusting the note into her pocket. She did not stop till she reached her room to look at the paper. It had three names – the first and perhaps the most important was that of a doctor in Lucknow; the second was a Panchayat member and the third a businessman – the owner of a multistoried shop. Obviously the doctor would be the one to decide and if approved the Panchayat member would be responsible for identifying the donor. The businessman probably helped with the money laundering

Two days after Mandakini's return to Delhi she had a call at the office.

"Is that Mandakini?" The voice sounded muffled.

"Yes. Who is it?"

"Listen carefully. Stop interfering in our affairs if you want to stay alive. Otherwise you will end up like Chandu – with your throat slit from end to end. In fact your fate could be so much worse; you will beg to be killed."

Even before she could answer she heard a click as the line was disconnected. She called reception to trace the call and learnt it was a Lucknow number. She called Surinder who confirmed Chandu's death.

"Mandakini. Just forget about this case. Let sleeping dogs lie" was his fervent advice.

The very next day Mandakini got a call from the tea shop owner in Lucknow. He spoke rapidly and in a low tone. "I am Chandu's uncle. I have come to Delhi. Calling from a public phone booth. Chandu's left a packet for you. Meet me at the Lodhi Garden Restaurant at 3 today."

The moment she entered the restaurant she recognized Chandu's uncle at one of the tables near the entrance. He had an empty coffee mug in front of him and seemed to be on the verge of leaving. As she approached he stood up and walked away, leaving behind a brown paper envelope on the table. Mandakini sat down casually letting her shawl fall on the table covering the packet. Having ordered tea, she picked up her shawl along with the packet. Five minutes later she hurried out having gulped down her tea as quickly as possible. She went straight home locked the door and sat down to open the envelope.

It contained three photographs. One of Dr Agarwal, his head turned as if looking behind to see if he was being followed. The other was that of a dead or unconscious man on a table, part of his body stained with blood and Dr. Agarwal standing by the side looking down at the body. The third was a photo of the street with a crowd of people surrounding an accident victim's body. Obviously, it was a record of what happened to Chandu's brother.

That was when she thought of seeking help.

Anand, her 42-year old colleague who looked more like 32, was a karate expert of average height. There was not an ounce of fat on him making him look rather deceptively slim in spite of his strong muscular frame. His face carried evidence of his history. His nose slightly bent after being broken in a fight and a small scar near his mouth gave an impression of a permanent sardonic one sided smile. He had worked with Mandakini on a few stories and had helped her out on more than one occasion. Alert and intelligent he was more like an undercover cop than a journalist. But he was a very good journalist too who had quite a few scoops to his credit and a reputation for frank, free and fearless reporting. Political goons, their threats or physical assaults made no dent in his armour.

Anand, excited by the prospect of a good story, went to work right away putting together all the evidence Mandakini gave him. He disappeared for a week and came back with a terrifying picture of intrigue, violence and ruthless efficiency. All the stray bits of information fell into place one by one. Some of the key players were almost untouchable he said. Mandakini was astounded by the simplicity as well as the magnitude of the operation.

The drugs and organ racket stretched all the way from head men in UP and Bihar villages, to regional party chiefs; via doctors and charitable organizations in Bombay and Delhi to doctors and businessmen in London. While the photographs were proof enough to nail Dr. Agarwal, they needed the backing of a more powerful organization like the police, to deal with the investigation and capturing of the whole gang. But that was out of the question. Mandakini wondered if Sanjay would be the right person and if so how to get him involved.

The next morning the phone rang just as Mandakini was about to leave home. "Manda. Meet me at Bahri's in Khan Market by six." Anand's voice was terse and crisp. "Come alone and be discreet. I have some exciting news". He put down the phone before she could answer.

Mandakini arrived at Bahri's well before 6pm and began browsing around. She lost track of time till suddenly she realized that it was past six and Anand still had not come. Half an hour later she began to panic. Any other person could be late but not Anand, who had a fetish for punctuality. When there was no word from him till 7pm she got worried and made her way to the office.

The night shift staff was just coming in to work to look at the day's news before taking on the work of the next edition. Mandakini quietly made her way to Anand's cubicle and sat down at his desk. She went through the papers on the desk not really looking for anything but hoping she would find a hint of where he was or a message.

She went through all his drawers methodically and occasionally smiled as she came across Anand's cryptic notes and messages to himself. He had a habit of putting down phrases and thoughts at random which he could use at the right moment with great effect. Rather disappointed at drawing a blank she was just about to leave when on the spur of the moment she idly opened the Roget's Thesaurus on the table. Stuck on to the very first page was a yellow Post it with "frozen peas" scribbled on it.

Mandakini recalled that quite some time ago when she visited Anand at home he was treating his dislocated shoulder using a packet of frozen peas as a cold pack. But it made no sense now. She tried calling him at home without any response. Fighting a vague feeling of uneasiness she decided to check up on him at home. Half an hour later she was ringing the bell of the landlady's apartment.

A thin grey haired women who did not look too happy to be disturbed, opened the door and was reluctant to hand over the spare keys to a stranger till Mandakini said that it could be a police case if something had happened to Anand. She insisted on the lady accompanying her to the room and opening the door in her presence.

The woman led the way grumpily, annoyed at the possibility of contact with the police. They opened the door and entered a room that seemed to have been hit by a hurricane. Everything had been upturned, opened, scattered or ripped out. An aura of violence, anger and frustration permeated the room. Mandakini who needed a few moments to herself sent the landlady downstairs to call the police while she waited in the room. The moment she was out of sight, Mandakini ran to the fridge, opened the freezer and took out a pack of frozen peas. She hit it against the granite counterpane to loosen the peas, removed the rubber band and opened the packet. She found a small square clear plastic packet with a piece of paper folded neatly inside. She quickly took it out and thrust it into her pocket, put the peas back and closed the freezer. She was back in the room before the woman came up again.

The woman having resigned herself to a sleepless night was more affable.
"How about having a cup of tea while we wait for the Police?"
"That would be wonderful. Thanks" she said as they walked down to the landlady's apartment. Mandakini had planned on coffee with Anand. With all the quick developments she had forgotten all about food. When a plate of biscuits was put on the table she reached out for it gratefully.

With her innate aptitude for gathering information Mandakini set her hostess at ease. After chatting about her family and problems in running apartments on rent Mandakini brought the topic around to the present.
"Did Anand have any problems with visitors?"

"He hardly ever had any visitors. A very private person he was. Kept very much to himself and in fact always warned me not to let in any visitors unless he first cleared them."

"That sounds very much like my friend" she smiled. "I wonder how these people got in."

"Well. I do remember about two days ago Anand brought a couple of friends with him. They were with him for about an hour maybe. It was about 9pm and I was washing up after dinner and had the radio on too. So I did not hear anything but just as I finished my work and switched off the tap and the radio I heard the door slam upstairs and the roar of a motorbike taking off soon after.

"When I saw Anand the next day he seemed a bit preoccupied. He told me again not to let in any visitors while he was away."

"Is there anything else you remember, anything out of the ordinary?"

"Not really" said the women, munching on another biscuit. "Let me see… There was something… Oh Yes. About a week ago Anand complained that the lock on his front door was defective. I tried it and it seemed fine but he insisted on changing it as it got stuck sometimes and paid for the installation of the new lock"

But that had not succeeded in keeping the intruders out thought Mandakini wryly.

The police arrived along with a photographer and questioned Mandakini and the landlady. Mandakini fielded their questions giving factual replies, keeping as close to the truth as possible without giving anything away. She was relieved to get away without being hassled further.

The first thing she did when she reached home at midnight was to take out the piece of paper from her pocket. It was an address in Sundar Nagar, hastily written out in Anand's spidery scrawl. Below the address was a date and time. With a start she realized that the time given was just three hours away. She hurriedly changed into her black pants and black top, tied her hair up and stuffed some money and papers into her pocket. She had a quick meal of sandwiches and milk before setting out.

She reached Sundar Nagar and found the house with about 25 minutes to spare. It was a single storied house with a wide gate and garden. Just opposite the house was a park, the gate locked for the day. Mandakini scaled the park gate with ease and jumped in. She positioned herself behind a tree near the entrance from where she could have a clear view of the house opposite. Within 15 minutes she could feel the cold seeping in through her pants and longed to stand up and stretch. She kept moving slightly now and again. She felt in her pockets and found a toffee that a shopkeeper had given her in lieu of change, unwrapped it and popped it into her mouth. Half an hour later, she saw a car drawing up outside the gate, two men getting out and entering the house. The car then sped off down the road and turned out of sight. She looked at the watch. It was 2.30am.

Mandakini waited for a while and then scaled the gate again to get out of the park. She opened the gate of the house very softly and entered quietly. She knew there were no dogs around, as the house had been silent when the other two men had entered. She ran crouching below the line of the windows and peeked into the living room which was empty. She made her way down the side, nearly stumbling over a stone. There were two windows, with the curtains drawn. It was a fairly light curtain so she could make out two people seated around a table and one standing nearby. She moved to the other window where the curtain was slightly lifted in one corner. She was trying to get a good view when she heard a soft sound behind her and next moment something hard came crashing down on her head.

She had no idea how long she had been unconscious and whether she was still at Sundar Nagar. She moved by trying to roll but found it slow and painful. It all seemed so much easier in the movies or story books. She had paused to rest awhile next to a settee when she heard a footfall near the door. Whoever it was would soon come in. She next heard scratchy noises like someone was trying to break in. She closed her eyes, lying still, pretending to be unconscious and tried not to be tense. Whoever it was did not have the key which meant that he or she was an intruder too.

The door nudged open and someone stepped softly inside closing the door gently. The person moved quietly but quickly to the table and had not spotted her yet. Mandakini knew the person was looking for something for she heard the drawer slide out smoothly with the faintest of whispers. She heard a small grunt of satisfaction, the rustle of papers as something was taken out and put away. Then the soft footfall came around the table, halting abruptly with a muffled exclamation upon spotting her on the floor. As the figure came closer she smelt a very pleasant and familiar fragrance but could not place it very clearly. It was still quite dark and she heard the man curse under his breath as he shone a single ray of light from the pen torch on her face. He hastened to her side and even before he spoke she knew who it was. The very faint fragrance of his masculine after shave confirmed his identity, even with her eyes still closed.

"What the hell are you doing here?" his voice was tinged with concern as well as anger and irritation. The touch of his hand was electric as he got to work on the ropes around her hands. She let herself go limp and kept her eyes closed. He untied her hands and rubbed them to get the circulation going and half annoyed and half amused he shook her by the shoulders a little saying "You do not have to pretend any longer. Open your eyes. What are you doing here?"

"I could ask you the same thing" she said sitting up, hurrying to untie her legs herself. His closeness and the touch of his hands had sent alarm signals through her body. Averse to being close to or being touched by a male, she drew away to put some distance between them.

Sanjay Coelho looked at her oddly, his bushy eyebrows creating a slight frown. He could not understand her attitude, her bristling at the slightest contact with another person. This was not the first time. At their first meeting they had been seated very close together on the mobike and she had used the child as a wedge or a buffer between them. At their second meeting they had collided and he still remembered how pleasant it had been to hold her for a moment before she pushed him away. And now he had just untied her hands and rubbed them. Well, he had to admit he did rub them for longer than necessary, he thought with a smile tugging at the corner of his lips.

The smile and his scrutiny disconcerted her. "So. What are you doing here?" she asked more belligerently.

"Just what you were doing. Snooping around. But I did not bargain for a surprise package all gift wrapped".

"I think we should get out of this place soon before anyone comes back." She stood up, wincing as she felt the pins and needles in her legs. She dusted off her pants and patted her pocket to see if the paper was still there.

"Somehow I don't think they will come back in a hurry" he mumbled as he continued with the search of the room. It was strange that she should run into him at the hospital and again here. What was his connection with the case and how much did he know? She watched him search the place very thoroughly, making sure that everything was put back exactly as it was. It was obvious that he knew what he was looking for and it would be useful if she knew it too. Moreover, she had already heard him take something from the table drawer when she was still tied up, pretending to be unconscious.

She looked at the time realizing with a start that it was nearly five in the morning. She last remembered approaching the house at 2.30 am. If she had been hit on the head by 3.30am she had been unconscious for more an hour. "Why don't you come home for a cup of coffee?" she said in an offhand sort of way, surprised at herself for inviting him.

He looked at her quizzically one eyebrow slightly raised and his eyes alight with laughter. "Do I take it that I have to trade in some information for a cup of coffee with the ice maiden"?

"I don't know what you mean. It was just an offer of coffee and you read more meaning into it than warranted" she said irritated with him for reading her thoughts so well.

"Oh, come on now. We are both fighting on the same side. And I am interested in trading info. So why pretend?"

As they walked out together he said, "Let us take your car. I will come for my bike later."

Mandakini darted a look at him. "How will you get back? It makes more sense for you to follow me on your bike."

"I have my reasons" the laughter was back in his eyes. "And before you say anything … no… I have no intentions of spending the night with you."

She must be getting used to his irritating remarks she thought because instead of snapping back at him she gave him a cold smile. "Even if you did, it would not get you anywhere" she said as she lengthened her stride. Effortlessly he matched her stride for stride. She slid behind the wheel, barely waiting for him to get in and close the door, before stepping on the accelerator causing the car to shoot forward almost throwing him off balance. He steadied himself, turning to stare at her in mock anger. She stifled a giggle and drove smoothly on.

The half hour drive was a silent one. Not a silence born out of awkwardness but a companionable silence that neither wanted to break. It was still quite dark, the city asleep with the restfulness that comes only in the very early morning. The very clouds stood still and then very slowly as if nature was blushing, a faint pink light smudged the sky. The bird song broke the silence and by the time Mandakini parked her car at her apartment, night was on the wane. She was grateful for his silence that reflected his sensitivity to the vibes around him.

As he stepped into her apartment he paused just for a moment at the door, closing it behind him. His eyes surveyed the uncluttered but colorfully vibrant room. There was a touch of ethnic chic but not too much of it and the total effect was a combination of utility and beauty.

"Mmmm. Good." He said as he came in and chose the largish single sofa embellished with a rust and brown throw draped over the back. He sank into it happily not realizing till then that it had been a long day without any sleep. He watched her graceful yet very efficient movements as she hung up her keys and excused herself for a few minutes. She went to the washroom, took a quick look at herself and added a slight touch of colour to her lips. Her cheeks were slightly flushed and there was an added sparkle in her eyes.

She had never felt like this before. Mandakini wondered why she had invited him home. She had never invited anyone on impulse. She would go to any lengths to keep men away. Only Anand and very few select male friends had ever come home. She was deviating from her normal behaviour.

Taking a deep breath to calm herself she went back to the kitchen. She deftly put together a few slices of brown bread, cut a couple of tomatoes and capsicum and slapped a segment of cheese in between.

He got up and went over to help her, very aware of her strong sexuality. She was not a typical classic beauty. Each one of her features by itself was not beautiful but the total effect was stunning. Strands of her long hair escaped from the clip and framed her broad forehead. Her strong eyebrows arched over two very clear and large eyes that looked out candidly at the world around her. Her glance reminded him of the way little children looked around them – with curiosity and frankness and totally without guile. His glance flickered for a second at her smooth long neck and her voluptuous figure. The pant hugged her slim waist and the flat, flaring hips accentuating the results of her fitness regimen.

They carried the coffee and the sandwiches to the glass dining table. Taking a sip of the coffee he closed his eyes for a moment with a sigh of satisfaction and then straightened up. "I think we are after the same people for different reasons. I have been tracking this organization for the past two years and it is almost nearing the end. I will be very frank with you and in return I would really appreciate your help in plugging some of the holes in our case."

He chose his words with care and marshalled his facts most succinctly.

"It all started when my 10-year old nephew who had been born with a kidney problem, was taken off the list of transplant recipients put out by a charitable organization called the Tree of Life. My sister who is very wealthy and married to a businessman approached me to use my influence to get her son back on the list. I met the secretary of Tree of Life, a woman who combined glamour and hard business acumen.

"She regretted that they had a needier case and had to give my nephew's slot to the other person. But she said they could try and get him a transplant if the family could make a large donation to their organization. My sister was only too happy to pay any amount. Fifty percent of the money was to be deposited in the Tree of Life account and the other 50 percent was to be given in cash. Total confidentiality was required. When it was a matter of a child's life, secrecy was a small price to pay.

"Once the transaction was over a donor was found, the transplant organized and it was all accomplished within two weeks".

Sanjay devoured one sandwich hungrily, washing it down with large gulps of coffee. With a sigh of satisfaction he resumed the story.

"This set me thinking and I started looking more closely at the whole operation and little by little I began to unearth a crime on a colossal scale spanning India and the UK. There was a branch of the charity in London with a few British and Indian doctors forming the panel. The doctors kept a look out for the wealthiest patients in need of a kidney. The volunteers of the charity organization acted as scouts in India visiting cities in UP and Bihar collating names of people who would make good donors. Once a match was made the foreigner would visit India as a tourist, get the transplant done, recoup and go back satisfied. The 10 percent of the donation in cash was used to pay the donor and the other 40 percent was used to pay the doctor, the support staff and other expenses without leaving a paper trail. Part of the money also found its way into the pockets of the local politician and the police.

"Although I have worked it all out in theory I do not have a lot of evidence. I have got some today. But I need more."

Mandakini, even while listening to him, had been weighing the pros and cons of divulging her information. She was usually a very cautious person and not willing to take people at face value. She realized that she could not handle this on her own and with Anand missing it was even more urgent to seek help.

She took a deep breath and decided to confide in Sanjay. She told him all about Babli's wedding to Kunal; her traumatic experience; Kunal's involvement in the crime and the fruits of her own investigations. She also told him about

Anand, his room being ransacked and his disappearance. She showed him Babli's letter with all the details of names and numbers that he read with great interest, his eyebrows drawing together in a scowl now and then.

Mandakini got up to replenish their coffee mugs while he leaned back with his eyes closed, sorting out everything in his own mind. She sneaked a glance at him from the kitchen. It was strange that for the first time she had a male presence in the house without feeling fidgety or nervous she thought. She had to admit that there was an undercurrent of attraction to Sanjay and she could feel the vibes when he looked at her but she was not threatened by him in any way. Perhaps the comfort level came because he was so much older than her.

She took the mugs over and sat down again. He opened his eyes and stared straight into hers making her heart turn. To hide her emotion she had to bring the talk back to business before he could say anything personal. "So what do we do now?" she said looking back directly at him. She was not going to let him stare her down.

"Your eyes are the color of wild honey" he whispered with a tinge of amazement as if he had just discovered it. "Like honey drawn from forest flowers" he murmured.

Mandakini felt helpless, unable to look away. She felt she was drowning in the amber of his eyes. She could deal with banter, repartees or arguments. This was something way beyond her depth. She tore her eyes away from his with great difficulty and in a bid to divert his attention she turned around to pick up an album and started flipping the pages searching for photographs of Babli and Kunal.

When she turned back to show him the page he was still looking at her with an amused smile around his lips and eyes. A thoroughly infuriating man decided Mandakini.

He took the album from her and browsed through it without any comment apart from an occasional lifting of one eyebrow when he saw Mandakini as a young girl. He chose a photograph of Babli and Kunal and asked her for one of Anand.

She remembered there was one taken at the office recently but could not find it. Suddenly in the middle of the album was a loose photograph of Anand and Mandakini together. Obviously something had amused them and they were smiling warmly at each other, with Anand's arm over her shoulder. It was a picture of easy camaraderie and affection. As she handed it to him she realized that the photo captured an image of deep affection; depicting a relationship that seemed to be rooted in a strong foundation of friendship.

He sat up abruptly and his face hardened. The laughter in his eyes dimmed. He seemed to be in a hurry to leave.

"My first priority will be to trace Anand. I will get my team to work on it. We should be able to close the net around the leading players in India starting with the doctors and the regional contacts.

"I will meet Kunal and persuade make him to turn approver. We can give Kunal and Babli the maximum security and protection that a key witness deserves. If need be they would be given a new identity and settled somewhere safe once it was all over". His voice was brusque and business like.

Mandakini wondered what she had said to offend him. All the warmth and banter had been wiped out abruptly. The disappointment and confusion must have showed on her face because his attitude softened slightly. He stood up looking down at her. "Please do take care" he said with seemingly genuine concern, and just as she felt the beginning of a warm glow inside, he spoiled it all by adding "I really cannot afford to keep rescuing you. It truly cuts into my time".

"Who asked you to meddle?" she retorted. "I would have escaped on my own and with much less fuss".

"How quickly you rise to the bait." He remarked smugly. "Well, next time I assure you I will leave you to stew in your own juice."

He bent down to gather all his papers. "At least make sure you are at home because the moment we trace Anand I will bring him here. I do not want him to go back to his place again. You too have to be very careful. Here's my unlisted number and do not hesitate to call me anytime of the day or night".

He was standing very close to her and she could almost feel the heat from his body. She wanted to back away but some magnetic force made her immobile. For just a fleeting moment she felt he was going to bend down and kiss her and instant panic at the very thought made her take a step back and stumble. His reflexes were very quick indeed as his hand shot out to hold her. He held her firmly around the waist, steadying her. She could feel his leg and thigh pressed against hers before she struggled free and stood straight, rather flushed, her breath coming faster.

He coolly turned around as if nothing had happened and walked to the door. At the door he turned around and said very seriously "Thank you for trusting me and sharing your information with me. It is vital for the case. I will do my best to keep Babli and Kunal safe. I will call you soon. Bye."

As the door closed behind him, Mandakini kept her eyes riveted on the door. Suddenly the room seemed to have lost some of its colour and vibrancy. Mandakini sighed. She had to put him out of her mind. What she needed was a hot bath followed by a hot drink and a warm bed. It seemed ages since she bathed or slept.

She was in the bathroom ready to turn on the tap when the phone rang. Hope it is not the office, she thought. That would be really tiresome.

The voice at the other end was a hoarse whisper. She had to strain her ears to catch his words. It was Anand. "Warn Coelho. There is a bomb on his bike." There was a click and the line got disconnected.

Stunned, Mandakini looked down at the receiver in her hand for a few seconds. It must be a good 10 minutes since Coelho had left. She quickly put on her clothes again and ran to her car. She drove like a maniac all the way, her heart and mind churning with anxiety. He must have taken a taxi from the stand nearby but she could not see any vehicle ahead of her. He may have reached the place and got on his bike by now. Damn him for his energy and speed. Why couldn't he dawdle?

She was about to turn the corner when she heard the sound of an explosion and as she turned she saw the remnants of the bike burning, some pieces scattered around, some still flying high in the air. She felt nauseous and a strangled cry rose from her throat as tears started coursing down her cheeks.

Julie

COIMBATORE: 1985

It was Madhuri's first birthday. She was just able to take a few steps hanging on to something or someone for support before falling down with a gurgle and a laugh. The palms of her hands and the soles of her feet were a soft delicate pink. Her lashes had now grown longer much to Julie's joy and envy. She was not a fussy eater and loved the mish mash of vegetables and cereals her mother fed her.

Julie had never realized that babies could be so very enchanting. Each and every day was a new discovery. By the third month she had developed a personality of her own. The moment Madhuri was fed and cleaned in the morning she would kick her feet and pump her hands in the air with a zest and energy that could put an athlete training for the Olympics to shame. Julie sat by her side entranced as Madhuri cooed and gurgled. Very soon the little plump feet had enough strength to push. When Rajat held her upright she would start climbing up his stomach and his chest or just keep jumping on his lap.

On every visit, which was at least once a month over a weekend, Rajat asked Julie if he could give his name to the baby and Julie persisted in refusing. He wanted to adopt Madhuri and provide for her. The birth certificate had no father's name which was not really a problem at that moment. Protected within the four walls of the house Madhuri needed nothing but her own sweet temperament to endear herself to the people around her. But soon she would need to go to a play school and then she would need a full name to get enrolled.

The world at large was a very unreasonable and extremely harsh world. A person needed a proper name more than a good character. A name was needed every day, every time, and everywhere. Right from registering oneself in school, to getting admission into any club, or class, or activity; to be admitted to a hospital; to opening an account in a bank or to having a life insurance certificate one needed a full name not just half a name.

Julie marveled at Rajat's persistence and his steadfast love that seemed to grow stronger not weaker with time. He behaved as if Julie and Madhuri were his family and his alone. Could any man love the child born out of a rape as his own? It was too good to be true and yet true it was. The expression on his face, his words, his easy affectionate manner with the baby, his spontaneous protective attitude was all too genuine to doubt.

Julie had to tear herself away from Madhuri to go to work every day. She was such a captivating child with such endearing ways that every moment away from her seemed to be a waste of time. Julie loved to take Madhuri out in a little pram when she was about seven months old. She loved to see her sitting up and watching the colour and movement of the world around her with wide eyed interest. She would take her along the road to a park about 15 minutes from home. One day she was just nearing the park when a young man on a scooter suddenly lost control of the vehicle. He came straight at Julie and Madhuri. For less than a moment Julie stood transfixed and then as her reflexes took over she pulled the pram out of harm's way and managed to jump aside. But not before the side of the scooter brushed against her legs, ripping her salwar and bruising the skin underneath. Shaken by the near escape and the sight of the blood oozing out of the gash, she turned to see the pram nestling against the hedge.

That night for the first time she thought of Rajat's offer. She needed someone to look after Madhuri if something were to happen to her. Life was so uncertain. Anything could happen to anyone, anytime. On his next visit Julie suggested that instead of going through the cumbersome process of adoption Rajat could be the legal guardian if anything were to happen to her, while Julie's maiden name could be retained for Madhuri in fond memory of her father.

"Nothing is going to happen to you. Why are you so obsessed with the thought of death? You are hale and hearty and will live to be a 101. But I am only too happy to be her legal guardian. If you cannot agree to an adoption I will make do being her guardian."

It was middle of December. Julie was just halfway through a report that had to be submitted the next day when the phone rang. She picked it up with a brusque "hello" that changed to a whoop of surprise and happiness.

"Padma!! Where have you been all these years? You never replied to any of our letters. I must see you at once."

Tears and laughter mingled as the friends bridged the lost years in the telling of a story that plumbed the depths of an abyss of sorrow and soared to emerge, courageous and hopeful. Padma voice was strong and firm, ringing with a tone of self confidence and determination. The cord of friendship, as strong as ever, was evident in every word. Padma may have cut herself off from her friends for a while but the link had not weakened.

'I just needed to have this talk with you, Julie. I feel so much better now. But I must see you Jules - Please come to Calcutta soon. I want to see you and talk to you."

Nearly two weeks later Julie travelled to Calcutta taking Madhuri with her knowing that the child's presence would brighten the lives of Padma and her parents and prove to be a good distraction. Tears welled up in Julie's eyes as she held Padma's rough, work worn hands. The two girls hugged each other, each one mourning the loss of childhood innocence and the dreams of joy that had seemed so very easily attainable. Padma had lost a lot of weight emphasizing her curves even more.

That night neither of them slept. They talked, discussed, argued, cried, counselled and encouraged each other. They found humour in pathos, giggled over their escapades and found that now they were together even the hardships ahead seemed more manageable. Hours went by as they sat up, changed positions, leaned back, lay down, sipped water, took a break to go to the toilet, made tea or had a snack. Finally it was the arrival of the milk man at 5.30am that brought them back to the present.

It had been a much needed therapeutic session for both of them leaving them cleansed and relaxed. Both had been through a very nerve-racking time and both drew strength from each other.

It was Valentine's Day when Rajat came to be with Julie and Madhuri.

He handed her a bunch of roses saying "Will you marry me Julie?"

He had asked her so often that now it was almost the first thing he uttered when he saw her, almost as routine as asking "Would you like a glass of water?" but said with a fervour that did not diminish with time.

"No" said Julie with a laugh. Her answer had not changed either.

"So what is the excuse this time?"

"Mmmm. Let me see…I don't know you very well yet."

"What!! After going through years of torture you still do not know me?"

"I do not know the <u>real</u> you. You are too good to be true. There must be something I do not know about you."

"Yes. I guess you do not know me really" he sighed, the smile wiped off his face. "But I am not going to give up. Whenever you get over whatever reservations you have I will be waiting. And we <u>will</u> get married."

Immediately contrite Julie put her arms around him and resting her head on his chest she murmured "I am sorry Rajat. Give me a little bit more time. Please"

Rajat hugged her tight and then looking down he raised her face to his and kissed her at first gently and then with more passion when he felt her responding. She drew back, her eyes shining and her voice slightly thick with emotion.

"It won't be long Rajat." She smiled impishly. "As you can see my body knows what it wants but..." She was about to say more when the phone rang.

It was Sophie's neighbour calling to say that Sophie was very ill and needed to be hospitalized immediately. Within minutes they were on their way.

Julie felt odd to enter the house after a long time. The last time was after her father's death when she had come to collect her few worldly possessions consisting mainly of books, few clothes and some photographs. Sophie had made it very clear that she did not want to have anything to do with Julie especially after the rape and her pregnancy. They had lived in the same town for nearly three years without visiting each other. They had run into each other at some functions or at the market and exchanged words of stilted polite conversation, but that was all.

The house was completely changed. The simple furnishings and art objects had given way to ornate kitschy décor. Without her father the house was not a home and it had lost all its warmth and character. Sophie was in bed, looking pale and haggard. Her breath was laboured and the doctor by her side was just about to give her an injection.

"This will make her breathe easy, but she needs to be under observation. Her heart condition is not too good. The next 48 hours are critical. I want her in the ICU as soon as possible"

Sophie kept her eyes closed not wanting to see the pity and concern in Julie's eyes and hating every moment of being obliged to somebody whom she had treated very badly.

The ambulance arrived 10 minutes later. In that time Julie had packed a bag for the hospital. Following instructions given by Sophie she slipped her hand under the pillow to take out a bunch of cupboard keys. She took out some night clothes and a few creams and lotions. Julie felt awkward to open Sophie's cupboard but there was no way out. It was more awkward for her to open the locker to take out the money and the handbag.

Just then Sophie's daughter, Evelyn, by her first marriage called from Delhi.

"Mummy, how are you?" she asked and without waiting for an answer launched into a defensive outburst. "I am sorry I have not visited you for so long, but then I know you would be fine. I will come as soon as Kevin comes back from his trip next month…"

"Hey, Evelyn… slow down. This is Julie here. I doubt if Sophie can talk right now. She is sedated."

"What has happened and what are you doing there Julie? Did Mummy call you?"

"No. Sophie did not call me but a neighbour did." Julie said wryly. "But I am glad I am here. Don't worry. I will look after her till you can come down."

"Let me know the moment she gets worse and I will come immediately."

"You mean the moment she gets better don't you?"

Caught on the wrong foot Evelyn snapped "Of course I want mummy to get better soon. Why do you twist things around Julie? Any way I will call again". The line went dead.

Rajat and Julie followed the ambulance to the hospital. Sophie opened her eyes as she was about to be wheeled into the ICU. Julie went up to her, gently pressed her hand and bent down to reassure her. "We will be here. Just relax and don't worry about anything. You will be fine".

"When will Evelyn come?" she asked in a weak voice.

"Very soon" Julie said with a smile and kissed her on the forehead before the attendants took her away.

Rajat had to return to Madras and Julie left Madhuri in his parents' care dedicating herself completely to looking after Sophie. There was nothing she could do but stay in the hospital. The first week was rather rough as Sophie's blood pressure and sugar levels kept fluctuating and she had another mild heart attack even while she was in the ICU. But by the end of the week her health had stabilized and she began to respond to the medicines. In another week she was moved to the room.

Julie spent much of her time with Sophie and brought Madhuri over during visiting hours. The child helped her relax and gradually Sophie began to trust and respond to Julie. There was still some awkwardness at times but the hostility was almost all gone and Julie's easy demeanour helped heal the rift between them. Evelyn had still not come to visit her mother although she rang fairly often. When she knew that Sophie was out of danger she postponed her visit to the next month. Sophie was immensely annoyed at her daughter's indifference that was in such sharp contrast to Julie's concern and instinctive response to all her needs. What amazed Sophie even more was Julie's easy and relaxed attitude as if it was only natural that she should be the caregiver.

One night Sophie was kept awake by a bad cough and Julie was constantly at her side, making her sit up, calling the nurse and giving her hot water to sip. It was almost five in the morning when Sophie drifted off into a deep sleep. She woke an hour later to see Julie still sitting in the chair by her side, her head drooping in sleep. Sophie slowly reached out to touch her and the moment Julie opened her eyes the first question she asked was "Did you sleep a bit Sophie? Shall I get you something to drink?"

Sophie beckoned Julie closer and reached out to put her arms around her neck. Drawing her closer she kissed her and whispered, her eyes moist. "Forgive me Julie. I have been so very cruel and unthinking. I was so insecure and felt so very alone and unloved that I was jealous of your easy popularity. Thank you for loving me in spite of all that".

Julie gave her a hug and smiled. "Don't say anything. Just forget the past Sophie. Madhuri and I need you now more than ever and you have to get well. Stop crying and let me see you smile."

In another week, Sophie was discharged from the hospital. Rajat was there for the weekend and helped to drive them home. He seemed rather preoccupied and more silent than usual and Julie wondered whether there was a problem at work or maybe she herself was the problem. She was not inclined to marriage immediately and was apprehensive that he might raise the topic again.

Just a few hours before his departure, Rajat asked her out for a walk. It was not a spur of the moment decision. He had thought about how to break the news to Julie and realized it was much easier to talk while walking.

When his days were overtaken by work, or he had something on his mind Rajat took refuge in long walks alone or with friends. He felt that there was some connection between the feet and the tongue that set people talking while walking. The joggers and the woggers (a combination of a walking and a jogging) were silent. It was the walkers who inevitably talked. Solitary walkers even talked to themselves at times and some even broke into song. If there were more than two or three persons walking together there could be a full-scale discussion on anything and everything from politics to pollution. Which in a way was one and the same thing thought Rajat.

The most cherished part of walking was the talking. There could be nothing more satisfying than the easy chit chat, the comfortable catching up on events, talking of future plans, discussing books and films, laughing over old anecdotes and just plain and simple gossip born of shared experiences.

Some of his best friendships had blossomed during walks. As the feet settle down to an easy stride, barriers came down, guards were lowered and stiff reserve dissolved into camaraderie. Perhaps it was the fresh air, the pleasant shades of green all around, and the extra oxygen going into ones head and heart that stimulated the conversation. Whatever the reason there was no denying the fact that emotions did find expression readily when walking. Rajat remembered that he had argued fiercely, made up after a quarrel, come to decisions, been mollified, comforted a troubled soul and assuaged pain more effectively during a walk.

Besides, when walking one need not look a person in the eye and he did not want to look at Julie when he told her what he had to tell her. And walks in the dark were even more conducive for difficult conversations. Cloaked by the night it was almost akin to being on the other side of a Confession box. Outpourings flowed smoothly screened by the curtain of darkness. And that was exactly what Rajat wanted.

Julie rather reluctantly accepted his invitation for a walk. Knowing Rajat well she dreaded the prospect of a talk with him now. She felt a bit uneasy, fearing he would broach the subject of marriage again. She could not come up with any logical reason for refusing to marry him. It was just that she was not completely healed, not ready to take on a lifelong commitment that made her feel trapped in some way. In her subconscious the rape still rankled. She knew that she loved Rajat as much as before, if not more. Why then did she feel that there were times when his touch was not welcome? She did not know why and hated herself for it but she had to obey the impulses of her mind and body.

They walked silently for a while. All Julie's attempts to tease him or to make polite conversation fell flat. When she could bear it no longer, rather irritated, she took his hand and turned him to face her.

"Out with it Rajat. Tell me what you have to say. I cannot stand this suspense."

"Well. I do not know how to tell you this." He turned away and continued walking, not daring to look into her face. "I am going away – may be for good. I have been asked to go to the US on a three year contract. They are setting up a new company and I will be trained and then have to work and train others. I do not want to go so far away from you and cannot bear the thought of not seeing you and Madhuri for so long but I cannot turn it down either."

"But you will come back. Right?" Julie's world was on a wild tail spin. She had expected closer ties and here he was chucking everything up altogether. She could not imagine a life without Rajat but neither could she think of a life with him.

"Well. I may visit after a year but it is very doubtful. By the second year I have to decide if I am going to stay there forever. They have hinted at a permanent posting if I fit the bill".

"I have to sit down Rajat". Julie's heart plummeted. They walked in silence till they came to a bench near a tree. Julie turned to peer at him to read his expression in the darkening twilight but all she could make out was the silhouette of his profile while he gazed straight ahead. "You are not running away from me are you? Or making me rethink about us? You do not have to go to that extent. I will understand if you want to be free. God knows I have kept you dangling for years and you have stood by me in spite of all that."

"Of course not. What a complete chump you are Julie. It is an offer that has come my way and it is a good one and a rare one. And I know I can do well. Otherwise I would not even consider it. And I will never force you to marry me – I cannot do it even if I tried and you will never agree. But that does not mean I am not going to keep asking you. If we can get married soon, then all three of us can go to the US together." He turned to clasp her hands and this time it was Julie's turn to avoid his eyes and look into space.

"You know my answer Rajat. I am not yet ready. You have to go. A year will pass very quickly and you will come back to us. I am really sorry. I do love you very much. But for some reason I myself do not know why, marriage scares me. The only person I can ever think of marrying is you but not just yet. What if something goes wrong and we have to part ways. I could not bear that. I would rather be lifelong friends."

Rajat could find no words. He just took her in his arms and they sat clinging to each other not wanting to let go and yet afraid to look ahead. Even one year was a long time and so many things could happen. America was a very long way off and he wondered if either of them would change in any way.

It was almost as if she could read his thoughts when she said "But in spite of all my doubts I know that we will both feel the same Rajat. No matter how long it takes, neither one of us is going to change in any way. It will be better not worse. If our love can withstand this long distance relationship then I will know it is for keeps. If not, then we will be happy we are not married. We have to be sure."

She looked up and said very severely "And don't you dare fall in love with any white woman in the meantime, do you hear?"

"Serves you right if I do" he said effectively preventing her from any more retorts by sealing her lips with his.

Babli

London: 1986

B abli sat waiting for the doctor to come back to her desk. She did not have long to wait. Dr. Anna Joyce came out smiling and extended her hand to Babli.

"Congratulations. You are going to have a baby. You are in your fifth week and I suggest you take things easy for the next seven weeks. I have written out a prescription and a list of what you can do and should not do. If you wish to call your husband right now you could use my phone. I always offer a call because sometimes women cannot wait to share the happy news with their loved one".

"No, thank you" said Babli. "My husband is out of town and I will wait to tell him in person". She knew the wait would be agonizing when she desperately wanted to talk to him, but the sight of his face, his expression and his reaction would be an experience in itself. The ride back home was in a bubble of happiness. She had found love after so many years of marriage and now a fruit of that love would be theirs to hold and to cherish. She kept touching herself in wonder and joy. It was so difficult to believe that cushioned inside her was the beginning of a little person with all the individual traits of a human being as well as some specific traits inherited from her and Kunal alone. She already felt so protective. She knew she would do anything possible to nurture this little soul and keep it safe.

Babli's thoughts winged back to the early days of marriage, the nights she spent awake, crying into her pillow, hours and hours of waiting, in vain, for Kunal to come home; the bitterness of imagining him with another woman. What had given her the strength to hang on and not just pack up and leave? It was not just the fear of upsetting her parents; nor was it fear of being on her own. It was not even just the inner strength she discovered in herself. It was her realization that she had been attracted to Kunal not just for his physical attributes but because of the discovery that in spite of all his cheating and lies she could sense an intrinsic goodness in him, a goodness that would surface and triumph. It was this goodness that prevented him from taking her by force, a goodness that made him take her sightseeing on weekends and ensure she was comfortable.

It was this confidence in him that made her stay in the marriage without rancor or bitterness. In a way it had surprised him because he had expected her to rebel and break away very soon. She herself had been surprised that she could live within a loveless marriage. Somehow, she had felt intuitively that he would learn to love her. She remembered that after their first year of marriage, when she was in one of her disconsolate moods she had unburdened herself to Mandakini over the phone. Initially Manda had been very angry and had asked Babli to leave Kunal immediately and come back to India. But when Babli adamantly refused, Mandakini was the first one to offer her full strength and support.

Padma and Julie too had rallied around and had continued to call her once every few months just to ensure that she was well. Every conversation with them steadied her resolve and lifted her spirit. Right through the years the four had been connected by an almost invisible bond that stretched across the world, linking London, Calcutta, Chennai and Delhi. Their little world withstood the tremors of Julie's rape, Padma's harrowing and very sordid betrayal and Mandakini's deep rooted fear of men.

The day Kunal returned from India was a brilliant day after a week of gloomy weather. The moment she set eyes on him she jumped up and ran to hug him – something that she had never done ever before. Well, she had to admit; she had felt like hugging him many times earlier but had restrained herself not knowing how he felt about her.

Surprised and happy Kunal hugged her back tightly, kissing her upturned face and smiling down at her. He looked much younger and happier. The brief separation had brought them even closer. Their new found love, a love that, undiscovered and undetected, had grown little by little over the past years, was now an unshakeable, passionate longing for each other. They both felt they had lost a lot of time already. Now every minute together was precious.

Their hearts were full and they could not speak of anything but love. Half an hour later, as they lay together, their bodies relaxed and at ease against each other, suffused with a deep, languorous contentment, Kunal told her that he had finished his last assignment and would be free soon. He was sure that they would be given full protection and in a matter of three months they would be whisked away to an unknown destination as protected witnesses.

Babli sighed with a silent prayer that it should all go well. She moved closer and nuzzling against his neck she whispered her joyous news. Kunal with a yelp of joy raised himself on one elbow and looked at her in amazement. Just as suddenly a look of concern shadowed his face as he wondered if he should have been gentler with her. Babli shyly smiled as she reassured him that it was fine and there was no reason to exercise so much caution at this stage.

That whole week both stayed at home, relaxed and at peace. Whenever Babli started to talk about their problems Kunal would tell her to forget it. This one week was exclusively theirs to enjoy and he did not want any doubt to cloud their happiness. They ventured out for dinner or lunch. At times they just strolled around rediscovering the joys of parks in London. Babli's favourite was St James Park while Kunal adored the rich variety of Kew Gardens. They spent a whole day at the Kew Gardens leisurely imbibing the glory of nature. Sometimes they just sat together, savouring each other's nearness, listening to ghazals, old Hindi film songs and English pop songs. Some of the romantic and intensely yearning lyrics seemed to have been written specifically for them. They let the music wash over them and surround them, quietly imbibing every cadence and letting the vibrations enter their minds and bodies. At such times all the predicaments of the everyday world receded so far away as to be almost nonexistent.

At the end of the week Kunal resumed his work. Although he was reluctant to leave Babli behind the whole day, it felt good to be back in harness. He had already made up his mind that when he moved to pastures new he would be a general physician and work towards establishing his reputation as a family doctor. He had enjoyed reading A.J.Cronin and the concept of a family doctor tending to a small population of a township appealed to him. He was sick of administering to a crowd of moneyed hypochondriacs for whom a disease was a status symbol and who preferred to take medicines rather than exercise regularly.

Time fled by and he realized he had not had a moment free to even call Babli. He quickly cleared his desk, put away some papers and handed over some files to his assistant when he saw the plain brown envelope. He wondered how he had missed seeing it earlier. He picked it up and opened it with his paper knife. There was a single sheet of note paper folded in half. It was a plain white note paper and the message on it was made of carefully cut out alphabets from the local newspaper. All the words were in capital letters and it was not pasted very carefully, giving the impression of dancing letters. Except that the message was so sinister that dance seemed light years away.

The message was simple and direct. It said "YOU CANNOT ESCAPE. NEITHER CAN BABLI". Kunal immediately called home and started fidgeting when the phone went unanswered for a long time. He felt a gush of panic sweep over him when he heard the phone being lifted and Babli voiced a sleep fogged hello. His relief made his voice sharper. "What took you so long?"

"Sorry Kunal" she said contritely. "I must have dozed off".

"Not to worry. I am sorry I snapped at you. I have been worried sick. Listen. Do not open the door to anyone. I have my key and I will let myself in. Promise me that on no account will you let anyone into the house."

"I promise" said Babli smiling at his love and concern for her.

Kunal arrived home in 45 minutes and immediately began to check the rooms, the doors and the windows. He drew the curtains, locked up the back door as well and went down to check the basement and the attic. Only when he was satisfied that all was well did he come to sit down next to Babli. She looked at him, her eyes clouded with concern. "What is the matter Kunal? Why are you so jittery?"

"Nothing really. I just want to be safe. The next two months are crucial and we have to be cautious. They suspect that something is happening and I think they know Coelho and his team are on to them. They will do anything to stop him and we are soft targets too. But I do not want you getting tensed up. It is not good for you. Just stay indoors and follow my instructions. You need rest anyway for the first few months so just relax" he said, drawing her close and taking her hand in his.

They sat together dreaming about the future and then he helped her with the dinner – a quick meal of stir fry vegetables and noodles. Kunal scooped out generous helpings of ice cream for dessert and they sat together on the couch relishing every moment of it. For a while Kunal forgot all about the threatening letter. It was nearly half past ten and Babli had already got into bed waiting for Kunal to join her when the phone rang. Kunal picked it up with a casual hello.

"Take care of your wife Kunal. Tomorrow may be more difficult than today" said a muffled voice. The line was cut immediately after the message leaving Kunal holding the phone, annoyed, bewildered and just a bit scared.

"Who was that" asked Babli settling herself more comfortably in bed.

"Probably a wrong number" he answered. "The moment he heard my voice he kept the phone down." He switched off the light got into bed and drew her closer to him for his own comfort. He could not bear to think of anything happening to her or to the precious burden she carried within her. Sleep evaded him for a long time. He wondered what to do and how safe it would be to send her to India.

Kunal continued to go to work cautioning Babli over and over again to keep all the doors locked. Everything was fine for the next few weeks and just when he thought the tormentor had stopped, he got another threatening letter.

The threat was always made of alphabets cut out from newspapers or journals. Thereafter, every week there was a threatening letter. And it was not always on the same day of the week. If the idea was to keep Kunal on tenterhooks the ploy was working. The tension of keeping these letters a secret from Babli, being on the alert every single hour of the day, slowly took its toll on Kunal. He became more irritable and restrained Babli from going out anywhere. It was four weeks later when he came home that he saw Babli agitated. This time the letter had been sent to Babli at home.

He had to tell her all about the other letters, at least some of them. It was a great relief to share his worry and his fears and he wished he had told her earlier. He found Babli had a fount of courage and strength that belied her gentle appearance. Especially, when she saw that Kunal needed reassurance she readily suppressed her own fears and put up a brave front that helped him to calm down.

Kunal got in touch with Rana Mukherjee, the person Coelho had designated to help them with their escape and new identity. They were scheduled to leave in another three weeks but Kunal wanted to bring it forward. The problem was that Babli could only travel after her next visit to her obstetrician which was exactly two weeks away. Rana was most helpful and understanding but told him it was advisable not to be too hasty as there could be some serious repercussions. Finally it was agreed that the couple would flee in two weeks time, immediately after Babli's next medical test.

They began to choose the most important or vital possessions they needed so that they could travel light. As they had to have a new life they had to destroy all evidence of the present life. And each day they could feel the threat coming closer. They were provided with around the clock plain clothes men standing guard around their house and Kunal felt a bit easier. He began to go to work as usual and tried to tidy up the papers so that once he was gone, his replacement would not have difficulty following up on his cases. At the same time he had to be very careful and not give anyone an inkling that he was going away. Their disappearance would have to be convincing and sudden.

Four days before their flight Babli went for her check up accompanied by Kunal. It was exciting to see the ultra sound image on the computer, the little embryo, the beginning of life, their own child, a son who already meant the world to them. In India they would not have disclosed the sex of the child but here, in the UK, they could let them know if they so wished. Everything was fine and Babli could travel and begin to do some exercises said the doctor.

As they drove back home they started thinking of names for a boy baby and both laughed over long Indian names and how that could be mutilated and distorted by westerners. They decided to have lunch at one of their favourite spots, a cave like restaurant in a basement that served the most delicious variety of breads and soups. They loitered over the baked potato, fish and chips and sumptuous apple pie and ice cream. They were startled to find that it was past 3pm when they finished. When they came out they were surprised to find that the sun had disappeared behind black clouds and it had been raining for a while. It was like emerging into a different world. The trees on the road side were all rain- washed, the leaves glistening. The headlights of the cars lit up the trees and the rain drops hanging tremulously on the leaves looked like it had been sprinkled with tiny crystals.

They walked hand in hand, pausing to gaze at shop windows and then walked back to the car and drove home. They inserted the CD of the ultra sound and gazed again in wonder and amazement at their son, very cozy and comfortable in his mother's womb.

They relaxed, cuddling in front of the TV before Babli called home for a long leisurely chat. Babli's mother could hear the happiness in her daughter's voice, a lilt that had not been there for years. It was only this last year that her voice and words conveyed unalloyed joy. Whatever it was had been sorted out and Sarita was happy that a baby was on it way. She was sure a child would cement the relationship further. God had listened to her prayers thought Sarita. She decided to make a pilgrimage to Vaishno Devi.

Babli finished her chat with her mother, glowing with the affection that she had lavished on her. Sarita had given a whole lot of instructions on what to eat, what to do and what not to do. Whenever Babli changed the topic and they began to talk about another subject Sarita would suddenly remember something and interrupt, saying "Remember not to kneel down too much. I know you have a habit of doing that. Kneeling will get your baby entangled in his umbilical cord" or "Don't watch horror films. Listen to good music not some of those loud clanging modern noises that is called music"; or "Have six almonds every day – soaked and peeled". Babli kept saying "All right mama; yes mamma" until finally she said with a laugh "Please Mummy. Save some instructions for later on; I will call you again very soon. And I love you very, very much, especially now that I know how you would have felt when you were expecting me."

The next day dawned gloomy and cold. There was hardly any sunlight but nothing could dampen Babli's spirits. She was chirpy, with a song on her lips. Kunal smiled at her infectious cheerfulness. He would be happy only if they had a safe getaway. Till they were in London or anywhere in the UK he felt threatened. He felt even more uneasy that the threatening letters and calls had stopped for a while.

It was Friday. He had to wind up a lot of things by the end of the day so he left for work earlier than usual. He was meeting Rana that afternoon and he would tell him the final details of their plan. The next day, Saturday, was scheduled for the disappearing act and nothing should go wrong. He gave Babli a long hug, made her promise to be extra careful and looked across at the plainclothes man on duty. He caught his eye, nodded his head and drove on.

As soon as Kunal left, Babli sat down to write a detailed letter to Mandakini. She gave her the happy news, the threats, the suspense and the hope of a safe haven. She felt like taking a walk and decided to trudge to the Post Office. The half an hour stroll felt very good. As soon as the letter to Mandakini was posted she felt an immense sense of relief, confident that even if anything went wrong there was someone who knew the truth. Her main worry was that if something happened to her, Kunal would be left alone without anyone to confide in.

It was three in the afternoon when Kunal left the hospital to meet Rana. They had arranged to meet at Paddington tube station. Kunal knew he would reach there slightly earlier but it was better than being late. He did not want to get caught in a traffic jam. His thoughts wandered to Babli, the baby and the future ahead. Today he would know the destination and no matter where it was he would be happy. Sanjay Coelho would keep both the families informed and once the people were caught and convicted, they would be free.

He was nearing Paddington when he saw the crowd and the police cars and vans parked outside. Feeling very apprehensive he parked the car and ran towards the crowd. "It is an accident. A hit and run. Indian chap has been killed. Car seems to have hit him from behind and sped off", said an elderly man in a blue cardigan. Kunal felt sick. He could imagine who the Indian might be. He inched closer and pushed his way to the front. Looking down he saw Rana, in a pool of blood, flat on his back and his hand stretched out as if he had clutched on to someone or something. Not wanting to get involved right away he backed out, staggered to the side of the road and retched. He called Babli. The phone kept ringing. She could not be sleeping in the evening he thought. She never missed her tea at 4pm.

He got back in the car and drove like a mad man towards home. As he neared the house he could sense something was wrong. The security guard outside was not at his post. He entered warily, opening the gate very gently. He circled the house from the left to the right. He had turned the corner and was walking on the right of the house when he saw the body of the guard lying by the side of the path in a rather grotesque position. There were two gunshot wounds, caused by firing at very close range. He was obviously very dead.

Kunal approached the front door and was about to take out his key when he noticed that the door was not locked. He gave it a gentle push and went in. It was all very silent and the living room was undisturbed. He walked in and entered the dining area. As soon as he entered he saw Babli hanging from the fan, a bright orange dupatta wound tightly around her neck.

A hoarse, anguished cry escaped his lips as he ran forward, grabbed a chair and brought her down with great difficulty. He put her down and desperately looked for some signs of life. He continued his efforts to revive her and when he realized it was impossible he sat down, lifted her gently into his arms and held her, sobbing uncontrollably.

He wept for his folly, for his earlier poverty that had made him so vulnerable to a path of crime, for his weakness in seeking shelter behind lies; wept for a little life that had been snuffed out even before it was born; for Babli's loyalty and courage; and for the futility of all things good and great in the face of vicious, and totally heartless greed.

Even as he held Babli in his arms he realized that he should have called the police immediately, perhaps even before cutting her down. But he could not bear to see her hanging and there had been a forlorn hope that she might still be alive. He gazed at her face that had been so beautiful and vivacious but was now distorted in death. A savage fury began to burn in him. Life held no meaning any more except to avenge the death of Babli and that of his unborn son. His mission now would be to destroy the people who had committed this monstrous crime.

If he called the police now he would be held for questioning and perhaps arrested for his past crimes which would now come to light. Under the circumstances and given the murder of the plainclothes man outside the police would know that this could not be a suicide. He had very little time to plan and Kunal decided that the best way was the quick and direct way. He lifted Babli, laid her gently on the bed, settled her head on a pillow and closed her eyes.

He then methodically prepared for what would be his last day. His tears had run dry. There was a cold heavy weight on his heart but his mind was clear. He knew that by eight in the evening most of the gang would assemble at the club. Friday night was usually when the "boss" was in the private room with his inner circle of aides. Plans were finalized for the week ahead, payments were made and accounts settled – with a reward for good work or punishment for mistakes and goof ups which in some cases could be death.

He gathered all the evidence he had, his lists of numbers and names, his diary and his jottings. He added a single sheet of a handwritten statement confessing to his earlier crimes; his intention to turn approver, the subsequent murder of Rana, the security guard and Babli and finally his intentions to kill as many of the gang as possible.

He took his gun from under the clothes in the drawer, checked it thoroughly and loaded it fully. He also took the silencer attachment and some extra bullets although he doubted if he would have the time to reload it. He remembered he had bought a bullet proof vest long ago. He put it on. Although he had no wish to survive, he wanted to live long enough to shoot down as many people as possible. Until and unless he got shot in the head he could fight. And when it was all over and he was still alive he decided he would reserve one last bullet for himself.

Once he was ready he sat for a moment next to Babli. He could scarcely believe that she had been vibrantly alive in the morning. His whole life had changed in a matter of hours. Once he had so much to live for and now there was nothing. He bent down to kiss her first on her cold forehead and then on her lips. He then kissed her womb that sheltered his son.

Now he did not have to worry about being caught or sent to jail. It was really strange that the moment a person was ready to embrace death nothing else mattered. One could do anything one desired because one did not have to face the consequences. It gave an exhilarating feeling of invincibility because ultimately no power on earth can fight death.

Was this how the suicide bombers felt? Did the Jehadis who embraced death so happily, looking forward to being immortalized on earth and welcomed to Paradise, experience this same feeling of elation and lightheadedness? It was so easy to face death when one had nothing to live for, nobody to love. In a way it helped to be an Asian who believed in God and rebirth. If he had been an atheist he wondered if he would have been more scared of death and the leap into the unknown. He was looking forward to joining Babli in the other world. He looked down at her cold face. This was also the last moment with Babli he would ever have. "I will get them Babli. I swear I will get them. Then I will join you my love. We will be together forever" he whispered.

He locked the house and by the time he got into the car it was 7.30 pm. He took a roundabout route, glancing at the rear view mirror every few minutes. Once when he saw a car behind him for nearly five minutes he started weaving in and out of the traffic and making sudden turns to the left or right. But he was just being paranoid for the car had no interest in following him. By the time he reached the Club it was 8.15 pm.

He parked the car and walked towards the club entrance. He still had his membership card. He waved it in front of the guard while walking briskly forward. "Hope Moulana is in. I have an appointment" he said with a grimace hinting that he was not really looking forward to the meeting. The doorman gave a sympathetic smile and waved him on.

He went straight to the cloak room. It was empty. He went into one of the cubicles, took out his gun, fixed the silencer on to it and slipped it into his coat with the nozzle fitting snugly into the inside corner of pocket. He peeped out. The bathroom was still empty. He walked out quickly and made his way towards the Club room.

He walked briskly past, smiling at the black man guarding the door. He walked through the hall full of gaming tables and men and women in various moods – few on a high at having won, some extremely tense waiting for the luck to turn and most totally devastated at their run of bad luck. He walked on, his strides firm and steady, his gaze fixed on the private room ahead. The man at the door of the room recognized him and was about to go in to announce his arrival but Kunal was swifter. His hand grasping the gun in his pocket tilted to point at the man and a soft "plop" was followed by the guard sliding down.

Without pausing or slowing down he opened the door, his eyes quickly taking in the occupants of the room. Seated in the middle of the crescent shaped table was Moulana, a 55 year old second generation Indian. Not many knew his real name or his religion. He was a thin, tall man with an olive complexion, small, mean looking eyes and a close cropped beard. He was meticulously dressed in a cream coloured shirt and suit, a red tie with blue diagonal stripes. He hardly ever smiled and had a fetish about cleanliness. He was the moving spirit behind the drugs and organ racket. Flanking him on either side were his partners, a British ex-cop who took care of the execution, at times literally and a British African doctor.

As soon as he entered, two men came forward to seize him but Moulana gestured them away.

"What brings you here? I thought you would be hanging out with Babli." Moulana said in a rasping voice. He had once been shot near the throat and his vocal cords had been repaired but were never the same. The savage pun angered Kunal even more.

In reply Kunal tilted the hand in his pocket again and began shooting rapidly moving his body around to take in as many people as possible. His first two bullets hit Moulana, one in the chest and another in the stomach sprouting bright red carnations on his cream coloured suit. He took the gun out very quickly and managed to hit the cop when he felt a bullet smack into his left side. He staggered but managed to remain on his feet still shooting with his gun now in the open. He was happy to see three more people go down when he leapt to his right and went behind a sofa. He could see two men behind the bar and waited for a movement when he heard the door open. Hidden behind the sofa Kunal could not see who it was but the moment he heard the voice he knew.

The man walked in saying "I strung her up boss…. What the hell?"

Kunal stood up, an open target for the men behind the bar. But he did not care. Here was the man who had "strung up" Babli and he was the man who had initiated him in the world of crime. He had been his friend and at one time he had cherished the thought of marrying his sister.

Jason saw him and snarled "Serves you right for ditching my sister. She …" Before he could finish Kunal shot at Jason, the man who had befriended him, led him into the murky world of lying and cheating. Kunal had once looked upon him as a brother, the brother of his lover. As Jason body jerked backwards Kunal took a hail of bullets from the two men behind the bar. One bullet hit him on the thigh and another glanced off his shoulder grazing his neck. Kunal crouched and rapidly reloaded his gun, turned around and shot at the bar. He was losing a lot of blood but he had to be sure that he would die. He did not want to be rescued and revived. Realizing that he could faint any moment he raised the gun to his head and pulled the trigger.

Mandakini

DELHI: 1986

Thinking back Mandakini knew that the moment she saw Sanjay's bike blown to smithereens, was the catalyst that healed her body and mind. In that moment, without realizing it, she had been cured of the horror of all her childhood nightmares. She had fought to keep love and friendship with men as far away from her life as possible but now nothing mattered any more. She had built a fortress around her that she thought was impregnable. After meeting Sanjay, she had been blind to the fact that a little chink in her armour had set in, growing wider and deeper, a small crack that would one day bring the fortress walls crumbling down. All she knew was that now she wanted to see Sanjay alive.

She had reconciled herself, quite happily to a life of single blessedness. There was no room for a man in her world. She was convinced she was just one among the legion of spinsters in every country, race or creed and a very contented one at that. Why then did the world come crashing down when she saw the bomb go off? Why had Sanjay become so vital to her life, so crucial that life without him did not seem worth living?

She stood immobile, weeping uncontrollably till she felt someone standing right behind her and she turned to see Sanjay, safe and alive. He looked down at her, his eyes taking in her pale, horror stricken and tear-stained face, and the sudden light in her eyes when she saw him alive. For a while the world stood still. They could not see anything or anyone except each other. Both were aware of how much they needed each other.

As they looked into each other's eyes they entered a different space, a seamless existence of their own. It was a long moment. His hand sought hers and grasped it firmly. With the other hand he gently wiped her tears and drew her closer. They were only aware of drowning in each other's eyes; of their nearness to each other as they almost melted into one; aware of a silent, timeless life that would extend far into the universe. Eyes still locked his head came down slowly closer towards her upturned face and his lips were just touching hers very lightly when the siren of police cars broke the spell, making them pull apart abruptly.

Mandakini withdrew her hand quickly, took a step back and turned away from him, wiping the tears off her cheeks. The deep harmony of the moment splintered and she felt her nerves jangled harshly. It was like having a bucket of ice cold water thrown to awaken them from a beautiful dream. Both of them came up gasping for air, completely shaken.

She made a tremendous effort to keep her voice steady. "What happened? Who was on the bike?"

"I was just lucky I guess." He cleared his throat, trying to shake off the intoxication of her nearness. He spoke in halting sentences, as if he was having trouble breathing the rarefied air.

"If I had taken the bike ...I would have been history by now. I took a taxi back and got down a few blocks away...... suspicious that there may be someone around the house. Saw a young chap trying to start the bike."

His voice steadied as he turned to look at her. "Some of these thieves can open any car or start a bike with very little effort. If I had known about the bomb I would have stopped him immediately but as it turned out I waited a few minutes just to be sure there was none of the gang around the house. The very moment the young lad succeeded in starting the bike it exploded and went up in flames. But what are you doing here?" *Did that moment really happen or was it a dream?*

"Anand called me. I do not where he is or how he knew. He just asked me to warn you about the bomb. He asked me to stop you. But you were gone already." *And I thought I had lost you forever.*

"Well. I am glad that Anand is safe." *And I am glad I saw what was in your eyes before you pulled the blinds down. Why are you fighting it? Why are you afraid of love?* "Will you wait for me? I will deal with the police and then come back with you." *I hope I can kiss you properly then. How stupid of you not to know how you feel.* The laughter was back in his voice as he said "You see I cannot keep away from you."

She watched him walk away, his legs, arms and shoulders moving with an easy grace. She could already recognize his walk and the way he held his head as if she had known him for years. She could spot him immediately in a crowd. She remembered her mother telling her that if you really loved someone you could spot the person in the thickest of crowds. Even from a long distance it was as if there was an invisible cord that connected them, a cord that though imperceptible and intangible carried an electrifying sensation that engulfed them both in a circuit of its own.

His every little gesture was so endearing, so unique. Was this what love was all about?

Unexpectedly he turned around to look at her and she felt a thrill run through her body as their gaze met. He waved as he turned away. She waited in the shadows. The last thing she wanted at the moment was to be associated with the police. She knew that Sanjay would strut out some convincing story about why his bike was parked there at this time of night but she would have a tough time explaining her presence. She walked back to her car that was parked quite some distance away and got in.

A good 20 minutes later Sanjay came along and slid in beside her. "I am bone tired. I need to sleep at least for a couple of hours before I can think straight. May be I can sleep at your place."

"You cannot. I do not have a spare bedroom."

"Who said anything about a spare bedroom" he asked with an air of innocence.

When they arrived at Mandakini's flat, they were surprised to find Anand there already having let himself in with the spare key that was hidden under a potted plant. They were shocked by his appearance. He had been beaten up quite badly with a small cut above the left eye. The shirt had some blood stains and one arm looked swollen. "Sorry Mandy. I used your bathroom and have had a wash. I have ruined your towel I am afraid. I will buy you a new one."

"Stop blabbering you idiot and tell us what happened" she cut in. She took out a bottle of red wine from the fridge and poured some into three glasses. "I do not know about you guys but I need something a wee bit stronger than coffee." She gulped it down closing her eyes for a moment as the warmth went coursing down her throat and body.

Sanjay looked at them, so very comfortable with each other. How had Anand known about the spare key? He knew his way around the apartment as if he had been there many times before, almost as if he had lived there. A hot flush of jealousy suffused his heart. Mandakini herself betrayed no sign of awkwardness. She touched him without being self conscious, was attending to his wounds, gently applying an ointment, covering it up with gauze and tapes.

Anand was relaxed, stretched out on the couch and talking while Mandakini finished ministering to his injuries and smiled up at her, giving her hand a little squeeze. Sanjay's flash of jealousy was now tinged with anger and irritation.

She who had withdrawn from his slightest touch and even proximity seemed to have no problem washing and touching Anand's bare torso, a torso that was one of the fittest and well knitted ones he had ever seen. So much for her innocent image.

He realized that Anand was talking about his fight with the goons who had attacked him at home and searched his apartment. One against three had been difficult especially as one of them had hit him on the head and made him unconscious. He had woken up in a room with one window that overlooked an open area. After nearly an hour two men had arrived, one rather short and bald dressed in worn out blue jeans and a black t shirt. He had rings on almost every tubby finger and was all out to please the other man who seemed to be his boss. The "boss" was dressed in a dark blue suit with a grey and red striped tie. His salt and pepper hair was slicked down with a lot of brilliantine cream. He had sharp features and a thin mouth with a thin moustache.

Anand was tied up and the "boss" kept asking questions and when Anand did not respond the bald man beat him up. With every unanswered question the beating got worse. They kept it up till he faked unconsciousness. It was then that he heard them talking about the bomb on the bike.

Anand waited till the door opened again to let in a single man carrying a tray with some food and a glass of water. He knew they were playing the good cop, bad cop routine. He had to act before they came in together. He began to moan terribly and when the man came slightly closer Anand jackknifed himself off the floor to overpower him and ran out locking the door behind him.

Sanjay sat quietly watching Mandakini. She gave Anand a hug out of sheer relief. "I am so glad you escaped" she said fetching him another glass of wine. Sanjay stood up. He had seen enough and could not stand any more of this display of affection. His voice was cold and devoid of all emotion. "Well. I guess I will be on my way. The two of you can take it easy and please stay away from the case from now onwards. I do not want either of you doing anything at all."

"You mean do not interfere. That's gratitude for you. We get nearly killed investigating the case and not a word of thanks from you". *He is getting up on his high horse again.*

"You are free to think what you like. Just do not expect me to be effusive." This was followed by a stiff "Good night" and the closing of the door behind him.

"What got into him? Is there anything between you two?" Anand's eyebrow rose half an inch.

Mandakini felt a blush creeping up her face. "What utter rot. It is the exact opposite. We keep rubbing each other the wrong way".

"Which I think is suspect too" the mischief in Anand's smile brought an answering smile on Mandakini's face. She sank into the sofa. "It is good to have you around Anand. You gave me some very bad moments. I thought you were gone forever!' *I want to run after Sanjay, call him back. What did I say to upset him? Why did he have to act so rude?*

"Not that easy to get rid of me. I must have something to eat. I am starving". Mandakini headed for the kitchen, her mind still full of Sanjay and her heart full of confusion.

Within two days she had a call from Sanjay. After a brief awkward pause he asked "How are you?"
"Fine. How about you?" said Mandakini happy to hear his voice but not knowing what to say.
"We have tracked down Kunal here. He is visiting India. I have spoken to him and everything has been arranged. They will be given protection but it would take a while to set it all up. In three to four weeks they should be free somewhere."

"Thank you so much. I ..."

"There is still a lot to be done" he cut in. "I will be in touch with you."

Mandakini kept holding the phone a moment longer. Had she imagined the moment of bliss when he had almost kissed her? Or was it just a passing fancy for him – a feeling of release after hours of tension?

A week later Mandakini spoke to a very happy and ecstatic Babli who could talk of nothing else but the baby she was carrying and the hope of a new life. Like the rain after a long drought, the love of Kunal had touched her parched soul. Flowers of hope and joy bloomed instantly and in profusion, a joy that she reveled in every minute.

Babli spoke highly of Sanjay about whom she had heard from Kunal. She spoke of his efficiency, his diplomatic skills, and his ability to plan and execute a delicate operation most meticulously and above all his humane approach in a moment fraught with mental and physical agony. Mandakini took deep pride in her fulsome praise of Sanjay, as if he were a part of her. Even as she savoured the pleasure she chided herself for being foolish enough to presume that he was so close to her. He was a stranger, a charismatic and helpful stranger but a stranger for all purposes. After all he was a MAN, and like all men he would also probably take pleasure where he found it and move on. He had given no sign of being enchanted by her. On the contrary they had always exchanged banter or harsh words. She resolutely pushed him out of her mind but was annoyed when he kept appearing in her head every now and then.

For two weeks there was neither a call from Sanjay nor any communication whatsoever. Mandakini's anger and frustration grew in intensity by the day. She resisted the temptation to call him and many a time she would pick up the phone and stand holding it next to her heart for a few minutes before slamming it down again.

When she had lost all hopes of ever seeing him again he came home. The door bell rang one Saturday morning. She opened it to find him framed by the dark brown wooden door; his hair unkempt as if he had ploughed his hands through it in frustration, his face pale and his eyes a mixture of grief and despondency. She stood still, turned to stone, surprised and alarmed by his sudden arrival and his dishevelled appearance, so much so that she forgot to invite him in.

He kept staring at her for a couple of minutes and then stepped forward. She stepped aside hastily mumbling "come in". He went straight to the sofa and sat down waving her to sit too. When she sat a little distance away from him he moved nearer.

"I am sorry that I have brought bad news. You have to be strong and listen to me calmly", he said, his troubled eyes never leaving her face.

She felt a wave of panic. If Sanjay had to give all this build up it must be really bad news. She clasped her hands together and looked straight back at him.

"All our plans for Kunal and Babli are useless. They killed Babli and Kunal has avenged her death by killing a whole lot of them and killing himself too."

"What!! What do you mean they killed Babli? I thought they were given protection."

"They were given protection but the security guard was murdered too".

"It cannot be true. Tell me it is not true." Her eyes were pleading with him. He shook his head sadly and as the grim reality seeped in, her mouth opened in a silent cry. Her hands went up and burying her face in her hands she gave vent to her grief, her shoulders shaking as she wept uncontrollably.

He let her cry for a while before leaning forward to comfort her when she lashed out at him. "Don't touch me. I should never have trusted you. You people just want to solve a case at any cost. Did you know Babli was pregnant?"

Sanjay held her by the shoulders. "Calm down Manda. You are getting hysterical. You know I was not responsible. We did our best."

Visions of the effervescent Babli and the happiness in Babli's voice during her last conversation were devastating and tore her apart. Great rasping sobs came right from her stomach as she pummeled his chest with her hands, all the while accusing him and his team of negligence and crass cruelty.

"Your best was not good enough was it? What if this had been your friend or family? Would this be your best? How dare you. I hate you … I hate you…"

Sanjay let her rant and rave and then gently pulled her closer to him. She struggled and pushed him back but his strong hands held her securely. She slowly leaned against his chest, her heart rending sobs vibrating through his body. He let her cry making no effort to say anything knowing that once the hysteria ended she would be able to think straight. His hand gently stroked her head and gradually her sobs subsided. He could feel her body quivering as she caught her breath on the remnants of her tears. A great wave of weariness overtook him as the days of sleepless nights and tension took its toll. He was devastated that he had failed to save two or rather three precious lives as he had learnt just now, lives that had mattered most to her and wondered if he really was to blame.

He looked down at her as she stirred gently, slowly raising her head. His eyes pleaded with hers to forgive him, misery written large on his face. The sight of his wretchedness wrenched at her heart. Suddenly overcome with the emotions she had been fighting against for so long, she let her heart take over completely. She raised herself, her arm traveling up over his shoulder, her face uplifted, bringing her lips very close to his. Their eyes searched each other for what seemed to be a very long time before he bent his head just that little bit nearer.

Mandakini for the very first time in her life knew the ecstasy of a lover's kiss and Sanjay who had kissed many women many times before discovered that this was a very different experience, a once in a lifetime occurrence that he would preserve and cherish. He tasted the salt of her tears as their lips and tongues explored each other. As she melted into his arms, all her doubts melted away as well. Much later as they reluctantly broke free, he still held her close. "Do you think that is the longest kiss on record?" he murmured.

"I don't know about that but it surely must be the longest first kiss for a 31 year old woman", her eyes sparkled.

"You have to make up for a lot of lost time I see" he replied as he promptly tried to kiss her again.

Mandakini turned her face away and leaning against him comfortably she took his hand in hers. "Let us not say or do anything more. I have a lot to tell you and a lot to work out within myself. I need time... loads of it."

He kissed the top of her head and tightened his grip on her shoulder. "Take all the time in the world. I do not want to think or speak of the future. Time has no meaning for us. Every moment is a year, every year a moment. We do not have to plan our moves. Let us not demand anything of each other, let us not expect anything. Let us catch this thermal of joy and float on it as long as we can."

Mandakini smiled in surprise and joy. "That is exactly what I would like. To be free, to experience this emotional high without giving it a name, without trying to nail it down or explain it to myself or to others. This moment is far too precious to be analyzed and labeled and docketed." A cloud passed over her face a she sighed "I do so wish Babli were alive".

"I am sorry."

"I am sorry too. I flew off the handle. I should not have said some of the things I did. Especially after all that you have done. I cannot bear to think of Babli's last moments." Silent grief overpowered her again.

"Everything would have been fine had it not been for Jason's interference. He wanted to punish Kunal for ditching his sister. Jason was ordered to kill Kunal but he hanged Babli first just to torture him before killing him. He did not realize that Kunal would have no wish to live without Babli and would go to any lengths to avenge her death. We have managed to clean up the operation here in India and Kunal has done more than what was needed in London. He has left complete details for the police that would help them put the facts together and mop up those that Kunal did not kill.

But I still feel responsible. I am truly sorry. This is something that will haunt me for the rest of my life."

"Please…don't say that. You are not guilty and should never say so. Think of all the lives you have saved. The thousands of people who would have fallen prey to this gang of callous men."

"I would need you to give a statement on some angles of the case and may be testify in court. I will avoid it if I can. Now I really have to finish what I started and tear myself away." His lips sought hers with more passion. One hand crushed her to him while the other strayed down from her neck, over her back to settle comfortably further below. A tremor passed through Mandakini as she responded with equal ardor, her body aflame with longing. With great difficulty she pushed him gently away.

He untangled himself, stood up and pulled her to her feet. He walked to the door, his arm around her waist.
They looked at each other, the strong desire electrifying the air around them.
He took both her hands firmly in his "See you soon".
She smiled at him, her eyes reflecting the laughter in his eyes. "See you very soon."

Padmaja

CALCUTTA: 1988

The house was very quiet. Padmaja arranged the sheets, bent down to kiss her father on the forehead and then straightened up, looking at his peaceful face, relaxed in slumber. He was a very different man now, far removed from the skeletal, depressed figure she had seen when she returned home four years ago. He had regained some of his lost weight, recovered partial use of his limbs that had been affected by the stroke and was able to speak a little although at times it was only Padmaja who could understand him well. The pallor of his complexion had been somewhat replaced by a healthier glow and more important; he was mentally stronger and more positive. He looked forward to each day and went to bed hoping for an even better tomorrow.

It was only 10 at night and her mother was also fast asleep. Another sea change thought Padma. Here was a woman who had frittered away the better part of her life as a social butterfly, constantly visiting beauty salons and spending hours on dying her hair, doing her nails, shopping for utterly unnecessary things and least bothered about what her family was doing.

On her return Padmaja had found Sharada a bedraggled woman, her hair unwashed and untrimmed, mostly white with some bits of black. The once plump, fair woman had become a thin, wrinkled one with no interest in life or herself. It took months of coaxing and threats before her mother, agreed to visit the parlour again with Padma, this time for a short hair cut and styling. She now had a shining cap of silver, cut short. She was still thin and wrinkled with pouches under her eyes. But the eyes themselves had regained some of their lustre. She stopped going to the club and worked as an administrative officer in an NGO that helped women who were sexually harassed and those who suffered domestic violence. She went to work five days a week and found that she had a talent for managing money and budgets.

Padma switched off the lights in the living room and made her way into her study. Her table was covered with law books, some open at pages marked with a pencil stroke; others closed but with little yellow tongues of Post It sticking out from various places. Tomorrow was an important day when she had to give her final summing up speech before the Judge.

She was not nervous and she had prepared what she had to say. She felt she needed to put in some more fire and brimstone to catch the attention of the public. She had the facts, the logic and cold reasoning which was what mattered but in cases of sexual harassment or rape she felt one had to appeal to the mind and heart as well.

Well...She did not have to look far for inspiration she thought. She only had to look at her own past. She sighed as she sank into the leather couch. She had been forced to fight every step of the way for the past many years. There were times when she had taken two steps forward only to fall back one.

It had been wonderful to come back home but very painful to see the depths to which her parents had fallen. She had to have the courage to pick herself up and also help her parents fight their way back to health and happiness. From the very first day she had to steel herself against her neighbors' curiosity, their innuendos, and their veiled and at times direct questions. She had decided to meet her problems head on and she looked people directly in the eye when replying to their prying remarks. Almost 99 percent of the people, she found, did not have the guts to meet her eyes, inevitably looking away or changing the subject.

Some, however, were persistent, deriving great pleasure from prodding a healing wound.

"So where did you get married?" full of unarticulated doubt.

"I am not really married. We just exchanged garlands in a temple" said with a candid stare with a hint of a smile.

"Aiyai yo! You have been a mistress all this time." Horror or sympathy or perhaps even envy?

"Fortunately, yes. Otherwise I would not have been able to just run away so easily" which was very logical indeed.

"You have set a bad example for the younger children" someone would say in a very disapproving tone.

"Not really", said Padma. "I think they can learn better from my experience now. You should really point me out to them and tell them not to follow in my footsteps" dripping with sarcasm and impish humour.

"But look what suffering your parents have been through" a tinge of gloating at another person's suffering.

"I think we have all suffered - in different ways. Suffering teaches one to cherish happiness where one finds it and we have found happiness again. No one can take that away from us" Padma said very emphatically, winding up and firmly putting a full stop to the nosy parker.

That was just one encounter. Multiply that by a million times in five years thought Padma and that was what she had been through. But no one could go on eternally. After a while the voices stopped, the stares turned away. People get bored with scandals very easily and look for fresh blood. Today's headlines would be tomorrow's tail piece. Other people's misery and tribulations were delectable only when very fresh. As one scandal grew stale another one would crop up. There was always grist for the mill.

But that applied only to the gossiping women. The lecherous men, however, could go on much longer, even forever. There was no stopping them. Time and age made no difference to them. They maligned with their tongues as well as with their eyes.

Opting to resume her education was an easy decision. Implementing it, however, was fraught with problems.

Padma had finished two years of college before dropping out and opting for cookery classes, embroidery and fabric painting. Now in order to graduate as a private student she had to join a tutorial class at a coaching institute nearby. The 15 minute walk to the institute was initially very awkward as she was very conscious of the glances and attempts at eve teasing. Groups of boys would suddenly burst into some

Hindi film song as she walked by or talk loudly in double entendres among themselves. After a week or two she just ignored it all and walked faster.

She was older than the other students in her class. There was an innate voluptuousness and sexuality about her walk and her posture that drew attention. The boys in her class called her ma'am and found many excuses to talk to her and she treated them with indulgent humour, as she would deal with younger brothers. But the teachers were a pain. She could feel their eyes roving all over her body. She wore salwar kameez suits that covered her completely and the day she wore saris, she made sure that the pallu was firmly pinned up and the blouse was not too revealing. Her blood boiled when men undressed her with their eyes and she felt helpless because she could not say or do anything. She could not reprimand them for they had not touched her or spoken to her. What action could she take against people ogling or staring at her? It was only the victim who was always acutely aware of the harassment. There was no proof and no sympathy. The humiliation had to swallowed, ignored, suffered or accepted. Any outburst against covert sexual harassment would be swept aside as a figment of the imagination or worse still deemed to be a result of provocative behaviour or attire. The victim would be seen as the original sinner.

One oily, fat faced teacher from Lucknow would call her up to his desk and while she was standing by, he would begin talking to some other person; making her cool her heels next to his table while his eyes flicked over her now and again. Tired of standing she would turn back only to be called again.

Once she was asked to stay back after class to do some extra work. She was just finishing her assignment when the teacher came up to stand by her side. She ignored him and continued with her work when she was startled by something hard brushing against her arm. She let out a scream and turned to find that he had rubbed himself on her arm. Disgusted to see a little wet patch on the sleeve of her blouse she jumped up, gathered her books and ran out. She went to the Administrative Office to find it deserted. She went home, seething with anger and frustration, not daring to tell her mother for fear of upsetting her.

The next day she made a formal complaint with the head of the coaching Institute, a balding, mild mannered man. He listened to her patiently, sympathized with her and then said "I realize your plight but I am sorry, we really cannot do anything."

Seeing Padma's furious expression he hastened to add "We are very short of teachers and with the examinations looming ahead we cannot afford to sack anyone. Besides the tutor is very well connected and has brought in some very much needed funds for the institute. I suggest you do not stay alone in the class and find safety in numbers."

Angry, defeated and unable to confide in anyone she was forced to attend the remaining three weeks of classes loathing every minute of the time when his lecherous eyes wandered in her direction. Amazingly enough, the anger within her fed her ambition. She had never been able to concentrate on her studies earlier but now there was a perennial fountain of energy within her driving her to stretch herself. She chose History as her major and graduated with honours. By then she had decided to study Law that would help her fight for women too weak to defend themselves.

Law School at the university meant a longer distance to commute, by tram or bus. This was her first exposure to regular travelling in public transport after a pampered existence as the daughter of a wealthy parent. Now with her father's career cut short and no regular income she wanted to be careful with the money in hand. Her mother protested that they still had a fairly healthy bank balance. Padma, however, looked on this austerity as a way of being independent as well as an atonement for all the suffering she had caused her parents.

She discovered afresh that the moment a woman stepped out of her home she was a prey and a "fair" game for male predators. Age, colour or marital status was no deterrent. Men made use of an overcrowded bus for rubbing themselves against women standing near them. The lurching of the bus from one side to another was another golden opportunity that was almost never wasted. Women sitting near the aisle had to be prepared for standing men passengers to rub themselves against their shoulders and arms.

Padma found the body language of women was always that of the hunted. Even when seated on a bus they cringed to one corner, legs close together while men tended to sit comfortably, occupying more space by spreading their legs wide open. Of course, that was a generalization but one that was more true in the observance than in the breach. What was it that gave the men the authority and confidence to violate the modesty of a woman with such impunity? And what made woman so powerless and voiceless that they cringed from striking out and tended to accept the invasion of their privacy so meekly? Educated or illiterate, when it came to making a fuss most women tried to ignore the lecherous advances of men and pretended they had not seen it, as if it did not exist. In fact, in some cases it was the illiterate or rural women who fought back. The urban women just suffered the indignity not wanting to start a fight.

Padma herself did not want to create a scene and when she experienced instances of "eve teasing" she swallowed the humiliation telling herself that it was so much less of a suffering compared to what she had been through already. The gossip grapevine was aware that she had run away and returned after having lived with a man for four years. This gave plenty of scope for frequent snide remarks that flicked the raw wound every time. It took a long while for her to brush off these taunts and harden herself to the world's callousness. She built a wall around herself that protected her from all the jibes and meanness. The saving grace was that there were some good souls who accepted her and admired her for what she was doing and who formed a small group of understanding friends.

The years at Law College fled by and she was always at the top of the class. She stunned her teachers with her sharp mind that helped her grasp and retain what was taught and the ability to argue her stand most convincingly and persuasively on any issue. She was amazed and amused at herself, thinking back to her school days. What an utter idiot she had been. Gifted with an intelligent mind she had wanted nothing but domestic bliss. She had always hovered around the middle rank and had not been the least interested in studies. She had managed to pass with a little above average mark without studying. Most of what she wrote in her exams was what she had retained from hearing in class. If she had bothered to put in some hard work she was sure she could have topped.

She joined a very well known senior advocate, Rasgotra, as an assistant to undergo rigorous training. That was when she really understood the meaning of the word "rigorous". He kept her nose to the grindstone, making her prepare the ground for some very interesting cases, encouraging her to look beyond the run of the mill arguments and was forever pushing her towards excellence. The two years of training were a long stretch of unremitting and relentless work and there were times when she almost broke down under the burden of high expectations. She was amazed at the reserve of strength that seemed to well up within her. There was a feverish energy and a fire within her that had been kindled by life's adversities. This helped her gain her employer's confidence and she was entrusted to help in even some high profile cases.

The one she was handling presently was about sexual harassment. An 18 year old school girl, Koel Chopra, had committed suicide following sexual harassment by her teacher, Prakash Malhotra, a big boned middle aged man with a paunch. He had taken a special interest in Koel; insisted on meeting her parents to express his admiration for her hard work and dedication and sought their permission to coach her after class so that she could realize her full potential. Coming from a middle class background and with limited finances they were only too happy that the teacher was kind enough to take on the extra responsibility without any extra fee.

Koel, genuinely keen to excel in her studies, was thrilled with the arrangement and would frequently talk of Mr. Malhotra who made her classes so very interesting. Gradually she began to refer to him as Uncle Malhotra "because that is what he wants me to call him" she said.

Nearly six months later she began showing reluctance to stay back for the coaching classes and would think of excuses for avoiding it. She complained of headaches or stomach aches or work for some other subject that had to be finished. Malhotra complained to the parents that her attention was wandering because she had fallen into some bad company in school and asked the parents to be strict with her and ensure that the classes were not missed.

Koel at that time was just a little over 18 years old. Scolded by her parents and pressurized to make use of the "extra" classes provided by the "kind" Mr. Malhotra, Koel meekly stayed back for her classes but became more and more quiet and preoccupied and was not her usual cheerful self. She refused to go out with her friends preferring to stay and study at home or read books. Sometimes at night her mother would find her crying but no amount of coaxing would make her talk about what was troubling her.

One day she came home with a bruise on her arm and when her mother questioned her about it she broke down and told her that the Uncle in the coaching class had grabbed her very tightly by the arm and made it turn black and blue. She then sobbed out the full saga of the way he had molested her. He had threatened her with a knife and warned her that if she breathed a word of it to anyone he would drag her name in the mud and bring ruin to her parents.

The incredulous and incensed parents complained to the Principal who immediately called Malhotra to his office for an explanation. Malhotra, totally unruffled and smiling, countered the accusations. The girl was getting to be very forward he said. She was losing interest in her studies and he had in fact complained to the parents about it. Why would he complain if he was misbehaving with her? Her head was full of silly notions picked up from films and he had to frequently fend her off and try to make her more attentive to the studies on hand. With no proof either way the Principal regretted that nothing could be done but cautioned both the parties to behave themselves and observe the decorum and propriety that was expected of them.

Two days later Koel was found hanging from the fan strangled by her own dupatta. The parents immediately filed a case with the police accusing the teacher for driving the girl to suicide and seeking justice for their daughter. Although friends and neighbours sympathized with them the parents could not afford a good lawyer to argue their case. They were advised that it was worse to fight such a case and lose as the reputation of their daughter would be tarnished forever. It was better to settle out of court and get some compensation. Their determination to avenge their daughter's honour made them resist the pressure. Just when they were struggling to get a good lawyer, Rasgotra, of his own accord, offered his services free of charge.

The trial had gone on for months. Many false allegations were made against Koel, and her parents. It was alleged that the cause of suicide was not the torture by the teacher but the vitiated atmosphere at home. Unfortunately there was no concrete proof that could help nail the culprit. Rasgotra managed to salvage the situation somewhat by finding another girl to confess that she also had been subjected to harassment by Malhotra.

After some adjournments due to the delaying tactics of the opposing lawyer the case was finally coming to a close. Public opinion was building up against Malhotra but he still seemed confident that he would get off lightly. There was one school of thought that blamed the Chopras for seeking publicity and money by defaming a man of standing in the community. Koel was spoken of as a girl who used her youth to get out of turn opportunities and benefits.

Three days before the hearing, Rasgotra was diagnosed with a heart problem and had to be taken to the cardiac unit for observation and it was up to Padma to make the closing statement the next day.

Faced with a big challenge she had been a bundle of nervous energy but as she sat in the silence of the night Padma felt a sudden deep calm descend upon her, calm so all pervading that it seemed to envelope her, a peaceful blanket of confidence and complete surrender to the moment ahead. She collected the papers on her desk, put them in order and separated the ones she needed for the morrow. It was nearly midnight and in another 15 minutes she had changed into her night dress, brushed her teeth and got into bed. She lay awake for a few minutes before closing her eyes in meditation and was fast asleep within a few minutes.

Padma awoke early the next morning carrying forward the calm confidence of the previous night. She knew her mother would fret so she spent a few minutes setting her at ease before leaving for the court.

After the initial formalities the rustle in the courtroom subsided gradually. There were quite a few reporters at the back who had been cautioned to maintain decorum right through the proceedings. The parents of the girl sat looking very tense, their faces drawn having been through three years of protracted fight for justice. If it did not end now they knew that it would be difficult for them to keep on fighting much longer with their funds and strength running low.

Malhotra on the other hand was still apparently unworried. He smiled and waved to some of his friends in the crowd.

The Judge was a small, diminutive man with a reputation for strict discipline and integrity. He did not suffer fools gladly and was averse to wasting time on non essential arguments. Even seasoned lawyers quaked in their shoes when he reprimanded them or pulled them up. His voice was always soft and well modulated and the angrier and more annoyed he got his voice became softer, each word enunciated with more pressure. He would hiss his knife edged remarks and demolish the lawyers, the accused, the defendant and the public whoever incurred his wrath.

Padma believed in doing her research very thoroughly and she always paid a lot of attention to the character and the personality of the person confronting her. She had found that Judge Swaminathan was a fairly conservative Hindu. He had a son who was settled in the US and married to an African American. The Judge had not approved of it and had ignored the existence of his daughter in law for a few years before reluctantly accepting the inevitable.

He made up for this "flaw" in his family by arranging the marriage of his daughter, a brilliant student and a talented musician, to a boy from a very traditional and wealthy south Indian family. The marriage was doomed from the start as the girl was traumatized by her husband and in-laws who prevented her from singing. Carnatic music was her passion and her very breath of life. Life without music was not worth living. Being a fighter and a woman of substance she refused to cow down to the diktat and after a year of suffering she walked out of the marriage, went back to her parents and sued for divorce.

Heartbroken by his daughter's fate and guilty that he had made a wrong choice for her, the judge did his best to ensure that the divorce was as painless as possible and encouraged her to return to music. As a very talented disciple of one of the leading musicians of the day she soon gained a reputation for her finesse and innovative singing. In a way Padma felt she could not have asked for a better judge. He would understand the humiliation and trauma of a beleaguered girl caught in the manipulative webs of men in authority.

Padmaja stood up to speak, looking very attractive in her black blouse and white sari with black block prints, the stiff white collar setting off her slim dusky neck; the black lawyer's cloak was draped regally over her shoulders. Her long black hair was coiled smoothly in a low *jooda,* her height and curvaceous figure lending her a statuesque dignity.

She began to speak, her voice steady and calm, outlining all the facts of the case. For the first 15 minutes she set out a cold, very factual and totally dispassionate report of the case. The very detachment and objective analysis focused the attention on the events emphasizing the gravity of the crime. The narrative devoid of all passion let the bald facts speak volumes.

Then gradually her voice acquiring more force and fire, she ended her argument on a note of high emotion.

"Your Honour. I seek justice for a young girl who is no more. Justice against a crime that is not only unjust and unimaginable but also unseen, unheard and unfelt by all except the victim herself.

"She was just eighteen when her torture began. She was a trusting girl with absolutely no knowledge or experience of the evils of the world today. Imagine her distress, her panic and her helplessness when she had to fend off lecherous glances and groping hands from a person who held the status of a teacher, a guru.

"He tortured her not just once or for one day but many times over, day after day. It was a full year of intimidation, bullying and coercion of a sexual nature that stopped just short of full scale rape of the body. He raped her mind, her emotions, her innocence and her trust – a crime as despicable if not more, than rape of the body; a crime that needs to be punished most severely.

"One would presume that all right thinking adults would immediately rush to take up the cause of the innocent. One presumed wrong. Especially in areas of education, sexual harassment is a "forgotten secret" with the authorities continuing to be in a denial mode; a total refusal to admit the existence of such obnoxious behavior and a complete rejection of all ethical responsibility.

"What can a young girl do in such a situation? Understanding sexual harassment or making others understand is extremely difficult because it involves a range of behaviour that is often almost impossible for the victim to describe to themselves let alone to others. The experience most often causes trauma and guilt making the victim wonder why she has been the target and the fear of loss of face if it were known by everyone. A harasser who targets people in public flagrantly, can be brought to book somehow but the private harasser poses as a respectable person in the presence of others and when alone with the victim he changes his demeanour completely. He is a wolf in sheep's clothing making it well nigh impossible for the victim to convince others of the truth. This is all the more reason why it needs to be punished so as to send a strong message to all other similar criminals.

"This is not the case of a man misusing his power with promises of a better job; excellent recommendations and credentials or a prize project in exchange for physical gratification. This is far, far worse. This is a person who had the status of a father, a person who was looked upon as a counselor to guide a youth in the right direction; he was a mentor who held more sway even than one's own parents; a friend, philosopher and guide. Instead of guiding, protecting, teaching, training and encouraging he plagued her with his deeds of sexual harassment. Initially, he made his physical contact seem accidental, brushing against her, sitting or standing very close pretending to study a book or some problem. Gradually his hands started wandering and then the so called confidante became a bully, a pest and a blackmailer who threatened the young girl with not only bodily harm and educational disaster but vowed to ruin her parents and her brother and sister.

"A year of living in constant fear, fear of exposure, fear of recriminations, and fear of public shame for the family and for herself haunted her day and night. She could not eat properly, she did not sleep well and she could not confide in anyone. She became a victim of deep depression, anxiety, panic and nightmares. She lived through circumstances under which even the toughest of the tough would crumble down. She withstood all the humiliation for weeks on end until the last straw, the final blow that really broke her down completely which was the threat that he would subject her friend to the same ordeal if she did not comply with his demands.

"How traumatic must it have been to drive a young girl of 18 to suicide? What had convinced her that facing up to the crime and dealing with it in public was so much worse than suffering in silence, so much worse, that death was a better option?

"Eighteen is an age when thoughts of death and mortality are unthinkable. Sweet eighteen was what it should have been - not terrifying or scary eighteen. Instead of planning an outing with her friends, instead of thinking of a vacation she thought of how to commit suicide. Imagine the last 24 hours, Your Honour. Imagine her sitting down to dinner with the knowledge that it would be her last meal, that she would be leaving her family without a goodbye. Did she hug her mother more tightly that night and did she cry before she tied the dupatta and climbed the chair? We will never know.

"But we do know that the person who drove her to that extreme step is now sitting with us, smiling at times and confident that his clout with people in high places will give him his freedom. It is up to us to prove him wrong. It is up to us to inform similar criminals that contacts with people in high places do not pay, that the judiciary can never be bought and that integrity does exist.

"Perhaps there is no law as yet severe enough to deal with sexual harassment but surely there is one that punishes abetment to suicide. And that is what I appeal for. I want the accused to be awarded the punishment of the most severe degree for pushing a young girl on the threshold of life into an abyss of depression and shame leading to her death. I want justice not only for Koel but for all the millions of children all over India and the world who are dumb victims to harassment, who flinch, shrink and quail to utter a single word of complaint.

"I appeal for a sentence that would confound, appall and astound future perpetrators of such crimes. I appeal for a sentence that would bring some solace to the hearts of the grieving parents for their wounds can never be healed. I appeal and demand justice for a girl who was betrayed by the very people she trusted and for all the girls of future generations to come who hopefully will not have to go through the same painful process to live a normal life fulfilling their very simple desires and ambitions. I hope that you will judge not only as a luminary of the legal system but also as a father, a mentor and a responsible citizen; ensuring that justice is done. I hope I will not be disappointed."

Padmaja walked slowly back to her seat emotionally and mentally drained. She took a sip of water and looked up at the Judge. He was looking at her with an enigmatic expression and before she could fathom what it meant he looked down at his noting and announced an adjournment for the following day.

The next day the court room was packed to capacity. It was one of the first cases of this kind where a senior person of some status in society was fighting to salvage his reputation against a silent cry from the grave of an 18-year old girl from a middle class family. Newspaper reporters were waiting to file their reports as soon as the judgment was pronounced.

Everyone rose to their feet as the Judge entered and sat down again. The Judge took out his spectacles from his case, cleaned them and put them on before arranging all his papers before him. He took a sip of water, cleared his throat and began to talk about the salient points of the case. He spoke of the responsibility of teachers, their commitment and debt to society. He emphasized that any crime committed by an ordinary citizen would be multiplied manifold if committed by a teacher and should be punished more severely. He also spoke of the duty of the parents to monitor their child's activities in school and not leave everything to the teacher.

He further elaborated that sexual harassment and molestation was not confined only to girls but boys as well. All children irrespective of class or creed needed the full protection of the legal system, the police force and most importantly, the family. If the parents had kept a closer watch on their daughter she might have revealed her traumatic experience at a much earlier stage when it could have been contained. He spoke of the bad influence of some films and the corrosion of morals and ethical conduct in each new generation.

When he paused to give his judgment there was a hushed silence in the court. He had given no indication which way he would decide for he had chastised both parties at different stages of his speech.

Padma felt herself distanced from all the proceedings. She had made up her mind that if she was not happy with the judgment she would appeal again and fight till the smug villain got at least some punishment. She suddenly realized the Judge was speaking again and looked up.

"Having considered all the angles of the case I have arrived at my decision. I want this case to be a guiding landmark to all the future generations of parents, teachers and students so that no more young lives are snuffed out and no more children are harassed and tortured with impunity. I find the accused, Malhotra, guilty of abetment to the suicide of Koel Chopra, due to sexual harassment. The maximum sentence for abetment to suicide under Sec 305 is 10 years to which I am adding a compensation of Rs. 10 lakhs to be paid by Mr.

Malhotra to Mr. Chopra for all the mental cruelty they have suffered over the past few years. This is taking into account the fact that this heinous crime was committed by a person in the status of a leader and a mentor. Anything less than this I believe would be a mockery of justice."

Pandemonium broke loose in the court as the reporters rushed out and the public stood up and cheered. Koel's parents were weeping tears of happiness and Padma hugged them. She herself was choked with emotion. She was happier still to see Mr. Malhotra seated at his table, staring down glumly at his hands. His counsel said something to him to which he merely glared in reply.

Padma fought her way through the crowd and coming out of Court she was besieged by the Press. She smilingly replied to their questions. Yes. It felt good to be on the winning side. Yes, she had been convinced that they would win because she was fighting for a just cause. No. she had no personal stakes in the case – only the pleasure of seeing the guilty convicted. No. She had no immediate plans for the future. She would continue to work for Mr. Rasgotra.

She went home very happy with her place in the world. Her mother had already heard about it and was waiting with a plate of *aarati* and a sweet which she popped into Padma's mouth. She moved the plate with the red *aarati* water three times to the left and three times to the right, then up and down. She then took it out and threw the red water just outside the gates.

It felt good to be successful. She was truly happy to have handled it on her own and was confident this would be the first of many more successes. The phone began to ring and she kept getting calls from her friends and colleagues congratulating her. Rasgotra called her from the hospital to tell her how proud he was and hinted that if she kept on like this he may have to make room for a partner. This call gave her the maximum pleasure next only to her father's reaction when she told him about the judgment. His eyes smiled while his lips twisted themselves into what looked like a grimace but which she knew was a grin. One hand gripped her firmly and he struggled to get his words out "I am very proud of you". Then she saw a tear drop roll down from the corner of his eyes.

The phone rang again. Another well wisher she thought with a smile and said a cheery hello. The voice at the other end made her nearly drop her phone. "Hello Kali maa... You have not lost your fire. I am always thinking of you. May I come and pick you up?"

Padma gripped the phone tightly and said through clenched teeth "Don't you dare call me again you wretch. I can put you in jail too" and slammed down the phone. For the next five minutes she sat by the phone, trembling. Even after all these years the very sound of the voice set off alarm bells and fear. For all her bravado she knew it was not easy to put him behind bars and as long as he was free he would be a menace. She, who had fought against sexual harassment, had to learn to fight it herself. Suddenly her success had lost some of its shine.

Julie

COIMBATORE: 1990

Julie gazed wonderstruck at the computer screen in front of her. It was nothing short of magic, a rather intimidating magic till Rajat tutored her to unravel the mystery. She had seen computers in some offices and in the hospital too. But so far she had not handled a computer herself. It had been a dream to own a computer and Rajat with his unerring instinct had fulfilled her desires.

She stole a sidelong glance at Rajat who was concentrating on setting up a programme for her. How he had changed! His wore his hair slightly longer letting it curl at the ends. His slight frame had filled out with hard muscles that spoke of a gym culture, his biceps filling the sleeves of his T shirt and the shoulders stretching the fabric. He had a slight American accent that was not put on but acquired naturally over the four years of talking and listening to Americans.

There had been a brief moment of awkwardness when they first met. They stood looking at each other and then hugged, briefly and hurriedly. Madhuri effortlessly bridged their discomfiture turning their ineptness and embarrassment to a semblance of their old camaraderie. Once the ice was broken the warmth seeped through.

Four years of the past, strung together on letters at periodic intervals, stilted phone calls that distorted sounds; occasional parcels of cards, books and music for Julie and Madhuri had culminated in a confused, poignant and emotional present. Gifts had been unpacked, something for everyone in the family. Exclamations of joy, surprise and wonder followed each parcel that was unwrapped. Rajat's parents could not have enough of their son. They kept touching him, gazing at him and talking to him every waking moment. He had promised to visit every year but that had never happened. He had come back now; almost a stranger and they had to get to know each other all over again.

At times it would be as if he had never left and nothing had changed. Then a chance word, a sudden reaction, a different opinion, or a spontaneous gesture would delineate a new personality, someone they had not known before. He was still their son but a stranger in some ways, a stranger that they had to discover and accept.

Rajat's mother plied him with food and tasty snacks and sweets almost every hour till he began to groan at the sight of food. Madhuri's excited hyper activity centered on Rajat and could barely be controlled. In no time at all Julie found that five days had gone by and she still had not had a moment alone with him. Chances of that happening in the near future were dim as he was planning a trip to Mettupalayam to meet a friend and go on to Ooty for a couple of days.

"Rajat, why don't you take Julie along? She really needs a break" Sunita piped up.

Julie's protests were drowned in Praful's hearty endorsement. "Yes. Julie has not had a single day off in months. She has been on night shifts at the hospital and day duties at home. Leave Madhuri to us and take her with you Rajat".

Rajat laughed out loud looking fondly at his parents. "You are both incorrigible and very bad actors too. I was just getting around to asking Julie myself before the two of you piled on. What say you Julie?" He looked directly at her.

Julie suddenly felt like a girl being asked out on her first date. A slow blush crept up her cheeks and she could feel the warmth in her face. "Sure …that would be nice…" she mumbled as she got up and escaped to the kitchen, joy and apprehension jostling in her heart.

She reminded herself that he was her childhood friend, who had shared her school experiences and had stood by her when most needed. And yet there was something new between them now. They had been lovers too, sharing very intimate moments and the very memory of those days sent a warmth coursing all over her body. But what if he had fallen out of love and wanted to break the news to her? Surely he could tell her that in Coimbatore itself instead of going all the way to Ooty.

He insisted on taking a bus, wanting to see the country side and the people. "Like an American who wants to see the real India?" teased Julie her dimples deepening.

The bus terminus was teeming with people and the dank odour of sweat rose up with the heat waves. They left the noisy crowd and the welter of sing song voices behind them as they entered the waiting room. As she turned to Rajat with a smile he got up in haste "Let me get you a drink" and even before she could refuse he was gone. How long could he avoid her or postpone their talk thought Julie. These omens were not very encouraging.

Soon they were sipping tall cool glasses of fresh lime with miniature icebergs that kept bobbing up and down. They were the first to get on to the bus and watched other passengers board before setting off in a cloud of dust. Sitting side by side she could feel his nearness, their arms touching now and then. They talked of inanities till there was a welcome halt midway to their destination where they refreshed themselves with cucumbers slit down the middle and filled with black salt and spice, juicy melon slices and translucent *"nongu"* with the water trapped inside. They both talked of mutual friends and Rajat spoke of his varied experiences in America.

As the journey became more tedious Julie slipped into drowsiness and found her head slipping on to Rajat's shoulder. She pulled back with a jerk only to tilt sideways again until she succumbed completely to a deep slumber induced by the swaying of the bus. Rajat's arm came protectively around her. Much later when she woke up from sleep she kept her eyes closed, savouring the smell of his shirt and his closeness. These rare unguarded moments were precious for Rajat was wary of demonstrating his love and care. She wondered if Rajat was also pretending not to be aware that she was awake.

After a day's halt in Mettupalayam, which was spent in the company of Rajat's friend, they set off for Ootacamund.

The hills caressed by the clouds somehow seemed closer to God and the people of the hills, wrapped in honesty and simplicity were closer to divinity thought Julie. This retreat in the hills was a welcome refuge from the noisy and aggressive world; away from the fumes of rattle-trap trucks and clouds of dust raised by speeding cars; away from a world of pretence and pomp to one of pine-covered splendour that was also a panacea.

The magic of the hills cast a spell over the visitors from the plain, injecting instant cheerfulness. Breathing in the cool and crisp air, surrounded by the heart stopping beauty of nature on all sides, it was easier to smile at strangers while chirpy greetings rose unbidden to the lips.

Fresh faced school children, their cheeks stained pink; urchins with their joie de vivre shining through the grime of poverty, gamboled on the slopes with inborn nimbleness. Men and women, their direct gaze full of candour and curiosity (far removed from the cold, calculating look of their city-bred brethren) were childlike in their friendliness.

Life on the hills could also be hard for nothing comes easily thought Julie. Nature reigned supreme and man had to learn to respect, love and understand her ways if he wanted to enjoy her bounty. This was a lesson etched on the weather beaten faces of the hill folk. Nature's generosity and cruelty both had to be accepted with a calmness that brooked no protest and a wisdom that needed no explanation. That same philosophy extended itself to life anywhere. Julie felt a deep contentment descend upon her. Nothing really mattered in the end but the love of people close to you and your own ability to help others. All incidents in life had to be dealt with and once overcome one had to move on.

As they approached the hotel Rajat turned to her. "Should we share a room or take two?" It was a serious question that was uttered in the most matter of fact, easy and comfortable way.

Julie answered equally comfortably not displaying the bubble of hope within her. "Let us share one". There was no coyness, no flirting, and no underlying shades of pretence at politeness. It was as if it was the most natural thing in the world to be together, as if it was ordained and they had known their destiny.

Their friendship with its roots in school had branched out in all directions and now enveloped them in a huge canopy of trust and faith. Like a banyan tree, the tendrils from the branches had taken root too, stabilizing and upholding their relationship even more securely. Both knew that neither one of them would take undue advantage of the situation; both were aware that there was a dire need to work out, to formalize, or conclude a bond that had ruled their lives and both knew that it could not be put off any longer. Nor could they fool themselves and the world that this could go on forever.

When they entered the room they did not fall into each other's arms. There was no embarrassment, no clumsiness, no discomfiture or shame. They were two good friends out on holiday, intent on having a good time.

He let Julie have her first choice of which side of the bed she wished to take and put away their clothes in the cupboard. They went on hikes, coming back dead tired and falling asleep. They watched movies holding hands; they enjoyed the breakfast of eggs, bread, juice, cornflakes and coffee; read books, explored little wayside inns for hot simple meals and visited all the tourist spots, argued at length over politics, films and music, discussed his life in the US but never once did they ever talk of themselves.

At the end of three days Julie moved closer to him in bed and leaned against his shoulder. She realized that Rajat wanted her to make the first move. He had chased her and proposed to her so many times over the years that he was now letting her take the lead. He put his arms around her to draw her even closer. She snuggled against his neck whispering "I have come home". Her tears of happiness rolled down her cheeks. This was not a time for kisses or passion. It was a quiet, firm step taken in full faith and trust and he pressed his lips to the top of her head. They sat for a long time enjoying the complete bliss of the moment, a moment of great happiness that filled every pore of their being, a happiness that did not need to ask a question or need an answer. "Will you marry me" seemed a tame as well as an unnecessary question after so many years of unconditional love. Their gestures said "I am yours forever and you are mine – till we draw our last breath."

They continued to move and live in this cloud of bliss, doing all the ordinary everyday things of eating, brushing their teeth, bathing and going out, meeting his friend, almost as if they had been married for 20 years. They were like an old married couple whose love had stood the test of time. On the last night before their return home they came together with a passion that was as blissful and as spontaneous as their calm. Again there was no question asked or permission given. They knew instinctively that it was the right time and the right place. It was the beginning of their life together. Their family and friends would need answers for all the questions. When and where would the marriage take place? Will he take Julie and the baby with him? Or would they settle in India? They had no need or time for questions or answers. They knew it all instinctively.

Padmaja

CALCUTTA: 1990

Padmaja stood at the window of her fourth floor office on Park Street looking out at the afternoon traffic, the trams, toy like and the motley Lilliputian crowd of pedestrians moving back and forth. She watched a woman pulling at the hand of a little boy, dragging his feet; two teenaged girls in front of a shop window, peering in, nudging and laughing, and small groups of men and women rushing to or from work trying to fit in a quick bite or a coffee date at lunch time.

She had taken a risk setting up practice on her own but it was a well calculated risk that should work. She had not done too badly. A rather small and modest office but in a prime location, four cases on hand and two possible clients with interesting briefs was more than what she had expected.

Rasgotra had been reluctant to let her go but understood why she wanted to break away.

The best part of it all was that she had managed to get rid of Madhav once and for all. His calls and letters to her office became such a nuisance that she had to seek the assistance of the police. She never knew what they did but the harassment stopped and she had not heard from him again.

Her house had a makeover and was transformed from the aging, high maintenance residence to a more modern, smart, functional as well as artistic abode. Her father recovered enough to walk with the help of a walker although one hand still had restricted movements. He recovered his speech with a slight slur making Padma tease him for his French accent. Her mother's makeover was even more dramatic. Her hair, cut short, was completely white without the slightest trace of black. She had donated most of her silk sarees and was comfortable in cool cotton salwar and kameez or simple cotton saris. She wore the minimum of jewellery, simple and attractive. Her face always had a clean scrubbed look with a touch of lipstick and kaajal. The layers of foundation and powder had given way to fresh glowing skin with the fine wrinkles and crow's feet adding more charm to her face and personality.

Padma too had changed. Her health restored, her dull scruffy hair regained its lustrous sheen, her complexion cleared to its original dusky radiance. She began a regimen of exercise and yoga to garner strength and stamina. While she repaired herself externally in a fairly short time she was still raw inside. It took more than a year to push back memories and scars. Very gradually she talked herself into making the journey from a hurt, insulted and thoroughly degraded young woman to a practical, forward looking, professional.

She accepted her own foolishness in running away with Madhav as part of her life's experience. There was no room for bitterness, no point in blaming herself or others, no need to resign oneself to despondency. She was happy, content with her life as it was.

She knew that in the course of time if Mr. Right came along she would recognize him and she would not make the same mistake again. Sex was a part of life, not life itself. She was not looking out for Mr. Right and would be glad to be single for the rest of her life. But what she could not live without were children. They added spice and fun to everything. That was driven home to her quite forcefully in the few days she had spent with Julie's daughter, Madhuri.

She felt a sudden urgent need to talk to Mandakini. Ever since Babli's death, the three of them had come to cling together even more for support. The void created by the absence of Babli could never be filled and the ache would never go. But the need to hear each other's voices, to talk and to meet was more vital than ever before. Their contact with each other made Babli come alive again.

The first time they had got together after Babli's death was replete with tears, reminiscence and laughter. Once the catharsis was over, the three friends decided to keep Babli alive and living with happy thoughts. She had proved to them that she was the strongest of them all. Protected and pampered she had stoically and very wisely lived through years of a loveless marriage in a foreign land and won over her husband with patience and understanding. She had revelled in her brief hours of joy and been courageous in the face of danger.

As Padma dialed Mandakini's number she wished she could talk to Babli instead. She would understand the craving she had to adopt a child better than Manda would. After the usual pleasantries Mandakini felt that Padma was trying to tell her something.

"Padma. What is it? Spill the beans. I know you did not call me to enquire about my health."
"Well. I want to adopt a baby".

"Why? Don't you have enough problems already?

"I have had problems enough. But now I want some joy in my life."

"You know that is not easy Padma. It would be a long drawn out process. You know all the legal hassles better than I do."

"Yes I do. I have all the time in the world to go through it all. I know there will be one stumbling block after another. Just like the heads of Ravan. Solve one problem and another will sprout in its place."

"And you are a single woman – that is a handicap" Mandakini loved to play the Devil's advocate. "Society and friends applaud the married adoptive couple, but single motherhood would be linked to a variety of social ills for the child."

"But single women have the same needs as a married one to love and care for a child of their own."

"Suppose you get married later. The fate of the child will depend on your husband accepting the child and loving the baby as much as you do."

"Manda stop it. Why don't you just say it is all a bad idea?"

"Hey hey.. Padma. You know I want the best for you. I was just making you face reality. If you really want to adopt a baby go ahead. We are all with you. But just remember that you are a busy professional and there will be times when you want solitude and your own space, and there will be no partner to share the burden. You will be a single parent."

"I have all of you to help me out" laughed Padma. "I want to adopt four girl babies."

"You are crazy. That would be impossible and it is utter madness. Why don't you adopt a boy first and a girl later? That way you will rear a boy who will know the true worth of a girl; who will respect and love women and treat them as they ought to - treat them as equals – not put them on a pedestal and then beat them or treat them as menials or doormats."

"Well. I still want a large family. Maybe two boys and two girls."

"You are completely mad. Did you know that?"

"Only as mad as any of you! As crazy as Julie birthing a baby born of rape instead of aborting it and marrying Rajat, who is crazy enough to still hang around for her. And you who cling to your past and cannot see beyond your nose when the handsome hunk right in front of you has his heart in his eyes when he looks at you."

"Hey. I thought we were discussing your adoption theory not my love life. And I do have to run. I will come and see your babies when they arrive". Panic reaction again thought Padma. Manda had a long way to go still.

Then she smiled. She would start with the first girl child and name her Babli. She took down the telephone directory and starting noting down numbers of agencies.

The intercom buzzed stridently. She wondered if she should ignore it but she knew that if she did not answer someone would come in person. She obviously had a visitor and she was not in the mood for it now. She picked up the phone with a crisp hello all set to say she was busy.

"Sorry ma'am. I know you did not want to be disturbed but the woman here is really desperate. She looks exhausted and she will not take no for an answer. She has to meet you now before it is too late she says."

"Well send her in." sighed Padma. She trusted her secretary's instincts completely.

Few minutes later her visitor was ushered into the room. She hesitated at the door for a moment before entering as if a blind determination had guided her steps so far but now on the very threshold of action her mind questioned the logic of her motivation.

Sensing her dilemma Padma got up from her desk and stepped briskly towards the woman, stretched out her hand, clasping it warmly with an encouraging smile. Her visitor smiled weakly back at her.

"I am Anuga. I am sorry I came without an appointment." Her voice was low and slightly rasping as if she needed to clear her throat. She seemed taller than she actually was because of her painfully thin frame. She had a pink and grey scarf covering her head that screamed "I have been singed by cancer". But there was an exquisite air of elegance about the ravaged body and face, an elegance born of innate breeding. The subdued beauty of the sari, the string of pearls and the way she carried herself spoke of an aristocratic past. Like a beautiful, faded painting one could see the stunning beauty of the past behind the patina of pain and age on her face.

Padma guided her visitor to the comfortable sofa in the corner rather than to her desk.

She knew intuitively that this was not just a legal consultation but a confession, something that involved the heart and mind, an emotional as well as a legal problem. An expanse of polished wood between them would terrify her and freeze her words.

Padma put a cushion behind her client's back, made her comfortable, got a glass of water and seated herself at the other end of the settee, turning herself slightly to face her.

"I really do not know where to start".

"Tell me what you want me to do first and that will lead to the why and when. Do not be afraid. Whatever you tell me is strictly confidential". Padma smiled reassuringly.

"I want you to be the legal guardian for my daughter. She is 14".

"I am a stranger. Surely you have someone in your family, a very close friend…"

"I have thought about it and come to a decision- the right one for me. Only you can take my place. Please do not refuse. I could not bear it". Anuga's studied calm threatened to give way very soon.

Padma quickly broke in. "Come, come. Don't get agitated now. Where are you going? And why does it have to be me? If you can convince me I can consider but otherwise I think you would do well to approach someone whom you know better".

Anuga remained silent for a while, looking down at her hands clasped together. Then she looked up, directly at Padma then shifting her eyes she gazed out of the window on the other side, her eyes clouding over as if she was looking at a scene many years ago. She took a deep breath and began to speak, her rasping voice low and even, almost as if she was talking to herself or thinking aloud.

"It was 1970. I was 22, passionate about painting, the pampered daughter of a very cultured, very wealthy family. My father's ancestors were linked to royalty and the landed gentry. I met him at a grand Diwali party. He was 23 and very handsome, very charming. He swept me off my feet and I was beautiful too – or so they said."

A smile lit up her wan face. "We made a dashing pair and even though my parents were not too pleased I was obsessed. We both were. He was so sensitive, so loving. But he came from an ordinary family. He was an orphan and was being brought up by his father's brothers. After four years of a torrid relationship we decided we had to get married. My parents reluctantly agreed to our marriage… only because…. because I had become pregnant.

"We were very happy, almost delirious. We could not have enough of each other. My daughter was born and he was the most doting father you could ever see. The only shadow in our lives was that he had no proper job. He was easily bored with routine, hated authority and fought with his bosses. He resigned or was fired from every job in a matter of few months. It was never his fault. There was always someone else to blame. My parents could not bear to see me struggle and helped out with money and gifts. They bought a fridge, fitted air conditioners when it was too hot, and always brought something for the house or for us every time they visited.

"He accepted everything but was not happy. We began to fight ... well maybe not fight but argue about my parents "generosity" undermining his manhood. Sometimes we said harsh words to each other in the heat of the moment and they hung in the air like a poisonous vapour. Then he got a touring job and was away quite often, at times even over the weekend. But the moment he returned he was full of tender loving care. It was nearly two years of blowing hot and cold before I found out that he had a string of other women, mostly prostitutes. When I confronted him he denied it at first but then began to weep and grovel."

Anuga took a few sips of water. She wiped her tremulous lips, started to speak but her voice failed her. She kept swallowing hard and finally closed her eyes for a few minutes. Padma reached out to take her hand in hers with a light reassuring pressure.

Composing herself Anuga resumed "It was terrible to see a man grovel and beg at my feet for forgiveness. He said he had been sodomized and abused repeatedly when he was eighteen by one of his uncles and his friends. He realized the power he wielded over others just by carrying out their sexual fantasies. Sex was a tool, a very easy tool for which he got paid with money or gifts. As he grew older he began to take perverse pleasure out of it too and favoured both men and women. But after every act he would feel worthless and filthy. He hated himself but could not break away.

"It was only when he met me he said that he realized what true love was like. He thought he had found his escape route and for a few years he had been very happy. But my family's superiority and his own inferiority complex drove him back to the only way he knew that made him feel powerful.

"I tried to understand and accepted him back but he would disappear again. This went on until I got tired of his pleading for another chance after every act of debauchery. I was terrified. I sought a divorce that came through very smoothly without any publicity largely due to my father's influence but I have been suffering every single day within myself. It has been years since I held a paint brush in my hand. For the past many years cancer has been my constant companion".

"I fully sympathize with you Anuga. But I am single myself and I, too, have been very foolish in the past. I really do not know if I am the right person to look after a teenager. It would be better to look for a family where there are one or two children younger or older than her."

"No it has to be you. Otherwise I can never rest in peace."

"I am very sorry indeed Anuga. But I still do not see where I come in. In India and elsewhere almost every other woman has a tragic tale. Why me?"

"Because the name of my husband was Madhav. I do not know what you went through with him but I am sure that if you have left him it must have been pretty bad."

Padma sat still and upright, shocked and unable to believe her ears. So Madhav had been properly married and divorced before he "married" her in the temple.

"You see. At times I feel guilty. Madhav was a good man and if my parents and I had given him more respect, or taken him for counseling it may have helped. I think the divorce was what turned his guilt and shame into hatred for women. But what could I do? I put my daughter in a boarding school immediately and did not give him any visiting rights. That broke him completely."

"I am not sure Anuga. I need to think it all over" said Padma slowly and haltingly. "What about your family? They are the ones who have the right to care for her."

Anuga leaned forward and clasped her hands saying urgently "But I do not have the time.

The doctors have given me anything between two to six months at the utmost. I want to bring the two of you together and spend some time seeing you both bonding together. Please say yes. You know how to handle Madhav. After school Aparna can join college and stay in the hostel. By the time she graduates she will be old enough and strong enough to look after herself and even then she will have you for as long as you are alive to guide her and protect her. She will be with you only during holidays so it will not really take up too much of your time. If only I had another few years to see her fully grown up...." Anuga's voice trailed off as she closed her eyes and lifted her hands to her face.

Padma sat still, trying to come to terms with the sudden entry of two more people into her life. She could not turn Anuga away. She now had an idea of the cause of Madhav's depravities and the cause of the need for him to subjugate and humiliate women. Not that it made him any better.

She touched Anuga lightly on her shoulder making her look up. "Let me meet Aparna and let us see if we get on together. She has had a difficult childhood and it will not help her in any way to be foisted on a total stranger. If we can get along and she is also willing I will agree."

Sunshine burst forth on Anuga's face. With new found vigour and strength she hugged Padma thanking her over and over again, tears brimming over in her eyes.

Mandakini

COIMBATORE: 1991

47 Raja Street had been spruced up. A fresh lick of paint had worked wonders. Everything was as it had been but would not be for very much longer. A deal was being finalized and soon the property would change hands. Not only change hands but change in many ways. The two acre "forest" with its myriad trees and bushes, the verdant home of hundreds of birds, squirrels and insects, their green haven of joy was to be razed to the ground very shortly and in its place would sprout hundreds of small pigeon hole flats in which would live little families who scurried through their lives like hamsters in a cage.

Like a person diagnosed with a fatal disease, a canker that chewed up the insides leaving the outside untouched, the house betrayed no signs of the impending doom. The last few days were to be lived to the full, gloriously, magnificently, exploding in a colourful display of fireworks, music and laughter. No. 47 would go down as it had lived for the past 200 odd years, in a blaze of glory.

As a farewell or rather as a celebratory gesture Julie's wedding was to be held in the house and Mandakini was in charge of the decorations. The house had never looked so resplendent, decked out with small golden lights and decorations all over. The entrance outside had a huge green banana stalk on either side, its thick stem, smooth and shiny, with bunches of raw bananas hanging in clusters. Dark green shiny mango leaves were strung across the top of every doorway.

Right through the verandahs, through the little dark passage that was no longer dark; all over the huge hall and all the four massive pillars, it was all a riot of colour. Streams and streams of different coloured floral arrangements, accentuated by single flowers of every hue adorned the walls, pillars and doors. Large lotuses, their petals half open around the pink bud-like centre looked down from the cornices. Pink and red rose garlands were juxtaposed with the fragrant jasmine and champa. Purple "December" and orange *kanakbharams* set off the yellow and maroon marigolds. Right under the skylight was a little square *"mandap"* with four thick banana stems at each corner with white, green, yellow and red garlands hanging in scallops on all four sides. The top and the sides of the mandap were open so that everyone could see the bride and groom as they took their oaths.

Huge traditional *"Kolams"* in exquisitely elaborate designs adorned the street outside as well as the verandahs and all around the mandap. It had all been made the night before by a group of three women. The rice had been soaked and ground fine with water. The women had taken a piece of soft cloth, dipped in the rice flour paste. Their thumb exerted just the right amount of pressure for the white liquid to flow evenly down their fingers that moved in swift assured strokes, curving and weaving delightful designs. Rust red *"semman"* made from powdered bricks etched out a vibrant outline, the embellishment making it stand out quite dramatically.

Even the rooms upstairs were brightly lit and festooned with paper streamers, silken sashes, gold and silver ribbons, all brought together in a tasteful arrangement. The ghosts, if not exorcised by all the gaiety and colour were a hidden, benevolent presence.

The whole theme of the day was red, white and gold – Rajat was clad in an intricately embroidered cream coloured kurta and churidar, the designs picked out in fine gold. A flowing scarf of a rich maroon with streaks of cream and gold was draped elegantly across his shoulders.

Julie was a vision in a heavily embroidered, self embossed cream dress that flared bell like down just above her slim ankles. Her trim waist was further accentuated by the thick gold woven sash. The bodice clinging to her full figure was picked out by very tiny and delicate gold and maroon work that was repeated on one side of her dress. The cascade of curly hair was artfully arranged to fall free with just one swath of hair pinned up and held in place by a pearl and ruby clasp. The pearl and ruby drops in her ears matched the delicate pearl and ruby necklace and the bracelet on her slim wrist. Julie's face glowed with a unique radiance, a sheen that came not from tubes and bottles but was ignited by the happiness and love in her heart.

Seven year old Madhuri by contrast was dressed in a rich silk skirt that came up to her ankles, the colour of old burgundy with gold tendrils all over and a gold embroidered blouse. Gold and red bangles tinkled merrily on her wrists in tune with the silver anklets that jingled as she walked or rather ran.

The most select crowd of relatives and close friends numbered over a hundred. Soft taped music suffused the air, music that represented all faiths and cultures. Hindu chants, Sufi music, ghazals, catchy film songs followed one another right through the function falling silent only when the oaths were taken.

It was neither a church wedding nor a Hindu wedding. The registrar who solemnized the wedding gave a short speech on love, marriage, commitment and loyalty before rings were exchanged. Julie and Rajat both had written their own individual vows that they read in a clear, firm voice looking steadily into each other's eyes. The simplicity, the fervour and deep faith and trust they expressed in each other brought tears to many eyes. Halfway through her oath Julie had a big lump in her throat, and could not speak. She struggled for a while trying to overcome her emotions before concluding the vow, her voice drenched with love.

Friends of the bride and groom toasted and roasted them with speeches that made the hall resound with laughter. A huge wedding cake was cut; Rajat and Julie made short speeches, witty as well as moving. Champagne flowed freely and the bride and groom led the dance that was quickly joined by almost everyone.

Padmaja looked stunning in a bright green sari and held a jolly ten month old baby that she had adopted recently. She had named the baby girl Babli. Plump and brown the baby merrily cooed and gurgled, looking goggle eyed at all the colour and movement around her and clapping her plump little hands gaily in tune with the music being played.

Mandakini in a dramatic black and silver sari stood next to Julie while Sanjay towered over the crowd on the opposite side. Every few minutes Mandakini's eyes would sweep across the crowd and meet Sanjay's. It was as if they had to look at each other every few minutes; touch each other with their eyes, and the moment the glances merged they could feel a little current running down the invisible cord between them. It was their life line. They had to look at each other, to reconnect, to reaffirm and relish the precious link that was tangible only to them. Marriage was not for them, not now, maybe never. They did not need a piece of paper to prove to the world that they were married. They knew that they were as good as married already and the formality might take place when the time was ripe. But for now they were both bound by bonds of love that were far stronger than bonds of steel or little pieces of legal paper.

Mandakini's lips twitched as she thought of the day a month ago when she had been to Chail in Himachal to interview a writer. She was walking back to her room when she had run into Sanjay- a surprise that brought an instant radiance to her face for the entire world to see. With a day to spare they decided to walk to Tapovan. She had heard a lot about the yogi who lived in Tapovan, a place of great serenity made even more tranquil by the powerful cosmic vibrations of the yogi's meditation.

They set out with visions of a picturesque walk culminating in a shrine of sublimity presided over by a radiant ascetic. They walked up some sloping tarred roads for nearly an hour, chatting, arguing and laughing, interspersed with short periods of silence, soaking in the beauty of nature around them and the deep satisfaction in each other's presence.

They trudged a few miles of a steep climb over a rocky path leading to a stretch of a narrow pebbly trail in the midst of trees. They had to hold hands to support each other, a hold that neither of them relinquished on reaching the summit. When Mandakini made a feeble attempt to withdraw her hand he tightened his grip ever so slightly to dissuade her. She was dissuaded very easily.

Mother Nature performed a stunning symphony that carried them along. The walk was the overture, a melody in itself. The breeze sounded more like the waves on a sea shore – not the usual rustling of leaves but a roar that ebbed and flowed like the tide.

Stray sounds floated up from the valley below, a gentle reminder of civilization. The Tapovan loomed suddenly, atop a flat clearing with magnificent views all around. The summit itself was a huge disappointment. The shrine was a half built, wooden structure on a platform of bricks with a shiva linga and various small deities around it. There was no aura to speak about and the ascetic had taken the day off. The only energy they could feel was the one between them.

On the way back the symphony resumed with darkening skies and large slow drops of rain gradually gathering pace and striking the flat rocks, the mud tracks and the trees, rhythmically, in varying cadences. They were nearing their destination when the wind whipped around with mad fury tossing the shaggy manes of the trees like a woman possessed. They quickened their steps and literally ran the last 100 yards approaching the barrack style rooms of their lodging. Mandakini's room was on the other side of the building but there was no time to run there. Sanjay opened his room quickly, pulled her in and switched on the light when a blast of wind opened the door again. Sanjay quickly shut it and pushed the bolts in place.

As she heard the sounds of the door being locked Mandakini waited for her panic to surface, for the horrendous memory of another locked room to wipe out all other thoughts. But to her elation she experienced only a tingling excitement.

They looked at each other for a long moment. Sanjay was just about to say something when the lights went out plunging everything into velvety darkness. They both knew that the mains to the whole area had been switched off to prevent damage to the wires that weaved across the hills like a giant web. There would be no electricity till the storm abated.

They felt their way to the bed, Mandakini taking off her damp cardigan and shoes before sitting down gingerly on one end. It was a moonless night and the inky blackness was so dense that she could not see even her hand in front of her face.

She heard the sound of Sanjay's shoes being dropped on the floor and the rustle of clothes. Safely cocooned in the room they heard the rising crescendo of the wind wailing and whipping through the hill side. The driving rain beat a staccato beat on the roof overhead which was magnified manifold hitting against the asbestos sheets. The din filled the room and seemed to rebound off the walls.

With no ray of light outside or inside the room, the space all around was an impenetrable black. Streaks of lightening lit up the room for a split second followed by ear splitting claps of thunder. Mandakini felt small and insignificant, totally overwhelmed by the might of nature.

Having run the gamut of scales, the storm tapered off only to soar again in a dramatic display of sound and fury that reverberated around them in a dramatic performance. Just as suddenly the orchestra ceased, swallowed up in a complete and overpowering silence. Not a leaf stirred. The world and time stood still in the totally silent and pitch black room.

Wrapped in the deafening silence they realized that this was the first time they had ever listened to silence. It was a silence that was not punctuated by the distant noise of traffic; the chirp of a cricket; the whirring of a fan or the air conditioner; a silence that was not broken by a child whimpering, dog barking or the disjointed crackle of a TV or radio or any one of the myriad man made sounds. Never ever had they heard the silence of nature, becalmed after fury, a vibrant silence that was not merely a cessation of sound but a silence full of promise, an unspoken assertion of supreme bliss. It was not a frightening silence but a warm comforting one, a silence to be savoured and cherished in the memory forever and a day.

Sanjay reached across to touch her hand.

"Hear the silence?" he whispered.

"Yes."

"Don't talk. Pretend we are blind and dumb. Let our fingers do the talking" She could barely hear his whispers.

She felt him move closer and his fingers moved gently from her face, down her throat and on to the buttons of her shirt. He unbuttoned it all the way down and pulled it off her shoulders. His hand traveled to her back, unhooking her bra.

He heard her sharp intake of breath and felt her fingers unbuttoning her jeans followed by the rasping sound of the denim being peeled off her legs. They had only kissed once long ago when he had broken the news of Babli's death. Even then they had not spoken of love. Yet she felt as eager, as relaxed and as comfortable as a lover of long standing. There was no nervousness, no apprehension, only a languorous joy.

Her hands went out to feel him and stopped short in surprise when she realized that he was already naked. She gasped as he drew her closer and they sensed the joy, the sense of liberation and the unique feel of bare skin against bare skin, the gentle motions that rubbed every inch of bare skin against the other. Their senses heightened by the pitch black darkness, their fingers and lips were sensitive to every little nerve and muscle. Her fingers memorized the scar on his shoulder, his hairline, the little bump near the ear, perhaps an old injury. His fingers delighted in the little raised mole on her thigh and the dimple at the end of the spine.

Unhurried, at ease and in silence they moved together in a long seamless, timeless ocean until suddenly seized by the growing passion that could not be restrained any longer they rode the crest of the wave, their mind and body exploding in excruciating ecstasy that left them gasping, shivering, panting and glowing.

"Mandakini. What's the matter? Are you all right?" Padma's voice brought her back to the present with a thud. Mandakini jolted back from the deliciously memorable past, looked a bit confused and at a loss for words. Thank god no one could read her thoughts!

"Sorry Padma. I think I was just feeling a bit weird. I am fine now," she said trying to cover up, conscious of Sanjay's eyes on her from across the room. *I bet he knows what I have been thinking about.*

"Some of your fraternity is here. You had better talk to them" said Padma urgently.

A small group of media persons were waiting in the verandah. They thought it was a welcome relief from the usual stories of murder, rape, scams, kidnappings and political bickering. This was one of the most heartwarming events that the media had come across in a long time, an event that needed to be publicized as the triumph of basic good values; a salute to the reservoir of faith and trust and the importance of a secular attitude.

The inspiring story of a young Catholic girl who had been raped, who had struggled to accept her pregnancy, fought social hostility to bear the child, supported not only by the unwavering loyalty of her beloved but even more astonishingly, with the full consent and cooperation of his Hindu family, was seen as a profile in courage. For the young man to adopt his beloved's child and marry her in the presence of her seven year old daughter was not only poignant but newsworthy as well. The fact that Julie's lover had waited years to claim his true love, culminating in a wedding in an old heritage house was enough to capture media attention. No 47 Raja Street was as much a star and as photogenic as the radiant bridal couple.

The press was eager to know more about Julie, an unwed mother at 29, who had spurned marriage with the man she loved and opted for matrimony now at the age of 35 to the same man she had rejected earlier.

They were also curious about the man who had managed to persuade Julie to make a commitment. Marriage was a gamble. Very few marriages were really happy. And even then one had to work very hard to keep it happy and make it succeed. And yet this man had waited to marry a girl with a past, full of problems without any apprehension of the future.

The reporter from the local newspaper, the correspondent of a magazine and two photographers were waiting at the entrance. Mandakini went to get Julie and Rajat's permission and on her way back was stopped by Sanjay.

"Will you show me around the house after all this is over"?

"I will if you promise to keep your hands off me."

"Your eyes are saying something different to what your lips are."

"Well read my lips and not my eyes" she retorted running away.

Epilogue

DELHI: 2002

Julie could feel the baby kicking inside her.

"He is a budding athlete – cannot seem to keep still."

"Mom. Did I kick as much?" Madhuri at 18 was a beauty with brains. She kept her hands on Julie's abdomen waiting for the next kick, calling out to her sister.

"You were dancing, my love, not kicking" laughed Julie giving her a quick hug.

"Come Akansha, quick. He is going to move again".

Akansha, 10, was slim and dark like Rajat, an epitome of peace and calm; more mature at a younger age and very unlike the older and mercurial Madhuri. She looked up from her lap top, smiled indulgently at Madhuri's exuberance and continued with her typing. "Later sis. Let me finish this".

"He will be asleep by then. Manju you come. We have to let our brother know we are near him".

Manjari, Julie's third daughter aged seven had been resigned to being the baby of the family until now and the sudden prospect of being an older sister excited her no end. She ran up eagerly to Madhuri and put her hands on Julie.

"Julie. Madhuri. I need to go out. Take care of the twins will you"? Mandakini came in to pick up her car keys and bent to give her five- year old twins a kiss. "Be good and help Auntie Julie ok?"

Krish and Karishma had Sanjay's eyes and mouth and Mandakini's nose and hair. Their eyes were always alight with mischief and impishness. Their world revolved around their father and only Sanjay could control their hyper activity. But they had to touch or hug Mandakini every so often. When they were hurt or ill only Mandakini could comfort them.

Christmas was already in the air. Mandakini and Sanjay's farm house in Mehrouli was always the annual meeting ground for the friends every December. Rajat and Julie with their three children and Padma with her two adopted children had been coming to Delhi every year for the past four years. Now Julie was expecting her fourth baby at 46! Her gynecologist had certified it was safe for mother and child after she had run through the battery of tests.

It was past 10 at night on Christmas Eve. The twins had crashed out, tired after running berserk in the evening. Madhuri, Akansha and Manjari had been given the job of packing up the remaining unwrapped presents and labeling them. Padma's adopted son was in bed fast asleep. Only Babli, aged ten and a half was still half awake, her head nestled on Padma's lap.

The electric fire in the hearth radiated gentle warmth and looked like a real log fire, making a crackling sound every now and then. Mandakini got up to fill all the glasses and settled back leaning against Sanjay. They had been married for six years now, a simple registered marriage and a lunch for just the two of them. No invitations, no guests and no fuss. Marriage for Mandakini and Sanjay was a very private event that concerned only them, not even the family. The next day they had a family get together. The twins had followed very soon after. Sanjay had quit his job and was involved in training core groups for Internal Intelligence and discovering ways to use high technology for criminal investigation.

Rajat and Julie were now American citizens while Padma's fame as a legal luminary and a determined crusader of justice for the downtrodden was matched only by her untiring efforts for the welfare of women.

There was a peaceful silence, broken only by the soft crackling sound of the fire, till Padma looked up and said "I have been through the nominations for Babli's Trust this year. The clear winner is Aparna, Anuga's daughter. She has done tremendous work with women in a village in Uttar Pradesh."

Her two friends nodded not in the least bit surprised. "I have been tracking news about her in the media. In fact, I have been afraid that she could have been attacked or injured. She truly deserves the 'Woman of Substance' award." said Mandakini.

The chorus of voices in agreement was interrupted by the jingle of an invisible cell phone. The general hunt for the instrument finally led to its discovery under a cushion. It was Madhuri's phone and she came scurrying in apologetically as Julie called out. As she ran off giggling, Padma, stroking Babli's head gently, looked at Mandakini.

"At her age we hardly ever used the phone. We had to be content with inland letters."

"I still have some of the letters. It is hilarious to read them now. I think life was so much more peaceful. I hate junk mail these days —hoards of mail are forwarded asking us to forward them to 18 different people. All full of sentimental mush and trite words of wisdom." Julie never did have much patience.

"Some things have not changed much. Rape, molestation and sexual harassment of women are still widespread. If anything it has increased." Padma gently shifted Babli's head on to a cushion. She pushed back her long plait. At 47 she still had a good head of hair with a few thick strands of grey that she refused to dye.

Julie helped herself to a few almonds and walnuts from the centre table. "I feel so sad when I look at little girls. They all look so happy and I wonder how their lives will turn out. What demons they may have to fight, what sorrows or heartbreaks they have to endure. We cannot protect them at all."

Rajat leaned over to kiss Julie on her cheek. "They would not want us to. Everyone has to commit his or her own mistakes and learn from them".

"We have to adjust to the present not the other way around." said Sanjay. "They are too busy living in the present. All we can do is to take advantage of the time that they are with us, give them a good sense of values, teach them survival skills and give them our full support and love at all times." At 50, Sanjay looked more like he was in his mid forties.

Mandakini settled herself more comfortably against Sanjay saying "Enough of all this serious talk. How about all of us visiting Rajat and Julie next Christmas? I don't want to play the host again next year to this wearisome, rowdy group."

As her friends' voices rang out in protest, Sanjay and Rajat looked at each other, with a small happy smile. The friends would never grow old. All three still argued with each other as enthusiastically as when they were children. And always will.

****